# DREAM BREAKERS

*Recent Titles by Elizabeth Gill from Severn House*

DREAM BREAKERS
THE FOXGLOVE TREE
THE HOMECOMING
HOME TO THE HIGH FELLS
THE PREACHER'S SON
THE SECRET
SILVER STREET
SWAN ISLAND
SWEET WELLS
WHEN DAY IS DONE
WHERE CURLEWS CRY

# DREAM BREAKERS

## Elizabeth Gill

This first world edition published 2009
in Great Britain and in the USA by
SEVERN HOUSE PUBLISHERS LTD of
9–15 High Street, Sutton, Surrey, England, SM1 1DF
Trade paperback edition published
in Great Britain and the USA 2009 by
SEVERN HOUSE PUBLISHERS LTD

British Library Cataloguing in Publication Data

Gill, Elizabeth, 1950–
  Dream Breakers
  1. Children of coal miners - England, North East - Fiction
  2. Soccer players - England, North East - Fiction
  3. England, North East - Social conditions - 20th century -
  Fiction 4. Love stories
  I. Title
  823.9'14[F]

ISBN-13: 978-0-7278-6777-3     (cased)

Except where actual historical events and characters are being
described for the storyline of this novel, all situations in this
publication are fictitious and any resemblance to living persons
is purely coincidental.

*All Severn House titles are printed on acid-free paper.*

Typeset by Palimpsest Book Production Ltd.,
Grangemouth, Stirlingshire, Scotland.
Printed and bound in Great Britain by
MPG Books Ltd., Bodmin, Cornwall.

*For Jill, Jennifer and Simon, who look after
my summers*

# One

It was Saturday and already noon. Jenna Duncan was standing in the queue in McConachie's fish shop, taking in the reek of chip fat and wishing Mr McConachie could hurry things up. Her mam would be cross if she was late but what could she do? She only got an hour for her dinner and was using up precious time standing there.

Finally, her turn came but the fish that had already been fried had been taken by Mrs Emerson in front who had a big family so Jenna had to wait again because the fish that were in the fryer were not ready. They were better just fried her mam always said but she had been a good quarter of an hour now and her mam would complain when she got back even though there was nothing she could do.

The fish were finally ready. Mr McConachie, who was so skinny that Jenna was convinced he never ate any of his fish and chips which she thought you wouldn't when you fried them day in and day out, wrapped up the fish carefully in case they should break, put the chips into bags and laid it all neatly together before expertly dabbing a moistened finger to separate the sheets of ready torn-up newspaper then wrapped it diamond-shaped from the corner, folded in both sides and ended up with a neat parcel. He did the same thing a second time. Nobody who bought fish and chips at McConachie's ever got home with a cold dinner.

Jenna paid and thanked him. They were good fish and chips, which they should have been, the town being by the sea and the cod sold fresh not far away. She put them into her mother's shopping bag and then she ran around the corner and across the street and down the side and into the unmade back lane.

Ruari Gallacher, her boyfriend, was there. He loved fish and chips and would beg chips from her. She always ended up stopping and unwrapping one of the parcels and he knew that she had had salt and vinegar put on them in the shop and he would eat the biggest and fattest of her chips before she complained.

Ruari spent his life in the back lane with a football when he was not at work, kicking a ball off the back gate or dribbling it endlessly up and down, banging the ball off the walls and outside buildings. He worked as an apprentice electrician in one of the Sunderland shipyards and played football for the apprentices' works team but even so he practised every minute he got.

Ruari was good with a football, that was what everybody said. Jenna couldn't see it really. All the lads were good. There wasn't much else to do when they weren't at work. They took it seriously. Football was a serious business here in the north-east where there was nothing for working-class lads to do other than the pits or the shipyards and a lot of the pits were worked up. The chance of becoming a professional footballer was the big dream, either that or to start a group and become famous like the Beatles or the Rolling Stones and Ruari had no interest in such things.

He dribbled the football all the way down the road but when he turned around he saw her as she had known he would and he abandoned the football and raced up the back lane so that she unwrapped the chips and gave him a whole bag. Ruari's eyes widened.

'Are these all for me?'

'I thought it would be easier buying another bag and then you wouldn't eat mine,' she said though her mam would question her about the money.

Ruari grinned in appreciation. He was a nice-looking lad, she thought warmly, feeling proud. He had lovely black hair and cool blue eyes like the sea in July and he was taller than she was but it was not that she liked best, she liked that he liked her, that it was unsaid.

He started in on the chips as though he hadn't eaten in a week, licking the salt off greasy fingers until she was too hungry herself to wait any longer. That and the fact that her parcel was fast getting cold propelled her away from him at top speed.

She heard his 'Ta, Jenna,' following her on the cool wind.

She didn't have far to go, they lived next door to one another. She ran up the back yard and in by the door, past the pantry and took a step down into the kitchen. She didn't think how cold it was outside until she got inside and her mam said,

'Wherever have you been? You could've been to Seahouses for those, the time you took.'

Her mam always said something like that, as though Seahouses wasn't way up the coast and took ages to get to. She knew because they went there for a fortnight in the summer and the fish and chips were even better than McConachie's.

'And where's my change?'

Jenna handed the change, watched her mother scrutinize it and then her mother shot her a straight look as she put the parcel into the oven to warm it back up.

'Have you been buying chips for that lad again? I've told you . . .'

Finally her father said, 'It was a bag of chips, Vera, let it go,' because he had heard it all before as well and no doubt he was tired of it. 'I just want my dinner in peace.'

He had to get back to work in a few minutes so because Jenna had been late with them he would have to shovel them down and dash back. She felt slightly guilty about that.

Her mother sat down and shut up and ate because as she said Jenna's dad was head of the household and he worked at the Store, in the grocery department. When they had finished eating he sat back in his chair and smoked his dinner-time Capstan and then he said,

'I've been promoted. I've been made head of the department.'

Nothing, Jenna thought, could have pleased her mother more.

'You should have told me when you came in,' her mother said.

'I wanted Jenna to hear it too.'

'Oh, Wilf,' she said, 'now we can move.'

'Move?' Jenna said and her parents looked at one another. Obviously this had been discussed when she was not there.

'It's been on the cards for a while,' her dad said, 'and I promised your mother that we would have a better house if it happened.'

'There's a lovely house for rent in Wesley Road,' her mother said and her eyes shone.

Jenna couldn't believe it. She didn't like to say that she didn't want to leave Back Church Street, that she couldn't leave Ruari. Wesley Road was in the posh end of town.

'Shall I see if we can go and have a look at it?' her mam offered.

'Aye, why don't you?' her dad said.

Jenna had to rush to get back to the drapery department of the Store where she worked in one of the big main streets, Durham Road. It was just beyond her dad's workplace, both were part of the Co-operative Society and he had got her the job there. She wished very much that she could work in a boutique but her mother wouldn't hear of it. She would have to travel into Newcastle or Sunderland for that, there would be buses to pay for and her dinner

*Elizabeth Gill*

and her mother liked her to go home for dinner. Jenna comforted herself by thinking that at least she saw all the new clothes which came into the department and her mother let her buy pretty things. She had just this week bought a short flowery dress and new long white boots to go with it and had her fringe cut and the ends of her long blonde hair. She thought she looked really good.

All I need now, she thought, is somewhere to go, somewhere to wear it and she wished for the umpteenth time that Ruari had some money. She wanted to go out, she wanted to go dancing. She wanted excitement.

More than anything she would have liked a trip to London, to Carnaby Street, to the famous boutiques there. She dreamed of buying clothes at Biba and being very fashionable, she knew that she had the figure for it, not as skinny as Twiggy and not as glamorous of course but she was tall and slender and fitted into fashionable clothes.

The town was busy. The big local football team, Dunelm North End, were playing Arsenal that day so the streets were full of fans from both sides and the pubs were open. There was singing in the streets and there were a lot of policemen about just in case there should be any trouble.

By mid-afternoon when the kick-off began the streets would be empty of men and boys, and the women would come out to do their shopping in peace and even in the drapery department of the Co-op you would be able to hear the roar of the crowd, especially when the home team won. The sound of the cheers when one of their strikers scored echoed through the little alleyways and across the long wide beaches and even further over to the dockyards, the sound would travel for miles, Jenna thought.

Jenna wasn't interested in football but like everybody else in the place she was glad when the team scored and wanted them to win, as much out of pride as anything else. Today, however, she listened in vain for the roar of the local crowd and she had the feeling men would be drowning their sorrows after the match and there would be fighting and somebody's shop window would get broken and several people would end up spending the night in jail.

Her dad resented that he had to work on Saturday afternoons and usually when the team played at home he would finish at six and be in the pub with everybody else soon afterwards but he would have to come straight home tonight, she knew, because her mother would have arranged for them to view the house and he had promised her they would look at it and her dad did not go back on his promises. He said it was just to keep the peace.

Ruari and his friends would be at the match, they never missed especially since it was almost the end of the season but later on she and Ruari would get together and go for a walk on the beach or maybe to the pictures if they had enough money. Saturday nights were sacred that way.

When she finished at tea time her mam dragged them to Wesley Road. It was several streets away, through the centre of the town, past Church Street where the parish church was, just in front of where they lived and through Chapel Street where the Wesleyan chapel was and then further up where the Bethel Chapel was and past the main streets where both Jenna and her father worked and where the schools were and the library and the station and the car-sale showrooms and the garages and small business premises and warehouses.

Jenna hated it straight away. The house looked so posh, too big for its boots, with a little front garden and at the back there was another garden, a piece of grass surrounded by flower beds and there were trees and hedges and it was quiet as though the whole of the people there had died.

The man who owned it was to show them around. It had a dining room, something they didn't have now and her dad probably wouldn't like, he was keen on having his tea by the kitchen fire with the telly on and his chair turned sideways to it though her mam thought everybody should put their chairs right to the table and make conversation.

The kitchen here was tiny, just somewhere to cook and wash up, and there was a big front room beyond the dining room, a lounge her mother called it, so that was two rooms they would never use. There was also a bathroom upstairs. The bathroom they had at their house was on the end of the kitchen and had been built as an afterthought because the houses in their street had had outside lavatories a few years back. Here was a huge spider in the bath so Jenna ran out again and left her mother admiring the fittings.

It seemed daft to Jenna to pay so much more money so that they could have more space when they didn't use what they had already and she wasn't convinced she would like going upstairs at night on her own when it was so much bigger – there were three bedrooms and though they never had anybody to stay her mother had been so enthusiastic about having another bedroom and had gone in and looked admiringly about it and Jenna knew that she was deciding what colour she would have it and how the furnishings would be and it just all seemed so silly somehow, and the house was a long way from the sea.

The bedroom that she would have looked out over the little back garden and the road behind so she was no better off because that was what her bedroom did now and she spent so little time there, she wasn't like a lot of girls who spent their lives upstairs, having secrets and making plans with their best friends and talking about boys.

Ruari had always been her best friend. She knew the girls at school had thought it odd that she went home to spend her evenings with a boy when they were younger but she didn't really think about it, it had just always been so. Ruari was the most important thing in her life and now she felt, stupidly because it wasn't far away, as though she was leaving him.

She was convinced you couldn't lie in bed there on summer nights when it never got dark in June and listen to the tiny waves barely breaking on the warm sand and imagine the flowers in the sand dunes, green, yellow and white. She listened hard when she was left in the bedroom alone but all she could hear was the distant sound of traffic and the shouts of some children playing in the road.

She didn't want to be away from the beach, it seemed ungrateful somehow, as though you had forsaken it, the foghorn which went off when the weather was bad and the lights which flashed from the lighthouse and sometimes you saw seals in the water when you were on the beach, they were so friendly, like big dogs. And people walked their whippets and Labradors and spaniels and threw sticks and children built sandcastles with moats. She couldn't leave all that and most important of all she couldn't leave Ruari.

And then she saw her mother's face and it was shiny with pleasure so she couldn't say anything. She tried to make the right noises and all the way as they walked back home her mother talked about how she would redecorate and where each piece of furniture would go and how nice it would be to live in such a place and she thought, this was her mother's dream and it was such a small dream that she couldn't bear to be the one to break it.

Her dad saw how she felt. When they got back to the house he squeezed her hand and he said, 'Do it for your mam, there's a good lass,' and she knew that he didn't want to go either.

'And you needn't think that boy's coming to visit neither,' her mother said as they went into the house. 'Him and his mucky boots.'

'They're football boots, Mam,' Jenna objected, 'and they aren't mucky either.'

She knew that his mam had saved hard to buy Ruari football boots for his birthday and he treasured them. Ruari would have given up anything for them and looked after them really well. They were never mucky, he would have been horrified to hear her mam saying that.

An hour later Ruari came to the yard gate for her. He didn't often come up the yard, he knew that her mam didn't like him. Jenna thought it was one of the reasons her mam wanted to move. She thought Ruari was common and his family of course. He kissed her briefly and they walked away hand in hand from the house.

Ruari couldn't afford fashionable clothes and Jenna thought it was a shame because he had a really nice figure, a good shape. She thought he was beautiful and though she wouldn't have told him for the world she thought he had the perfect bottom which didn't show to advantage because he couldn't afford tight hipsters with T-shirts and boots like other lads wore on Saturday nights in town. Or nice suits, she loved a nice suit.

She wished they could go to town and she could wear her new dress. Ruari liked her clothes, probably, she thought, because most of her dresses were very short and showed off her long slender legs. He liked it when she wore boots. Her legs, Jenna thought, were her best feature but the rest of her wasn't bad either. She thought her nose was a bit big and maybe her thighs were a trifle heavy but other than that she was happy when she looked into her mirror and saw her blonde blue-eyed looks. She was striking, she knew. Lads gazed at her in the street and she enjoyed it.

'Do you want to go to the pictures?' he enquired and she sensed he was about to tell her what was on so she said quickly,

'No, I want to talk to you.'

He pulled a face.

Nobody said anything else until they got to the beach. What she loved best about their beach was that there was hardly anybody on it, even on a fine night like this, just the odd person walking a dog down by the shore. The tide was out, the rocks showed and the sand was warm because it had been a fine day.

The beach was black with coal where earlier that week there had been a big tide, flat strangely shaped pieces of it like broken roof slates glinted in the evening sunlight, like jet against the sand which was almost white in the spring evening. A cool wind came off the sea, lifting the sand in swirls and through a sky which was almost blue, small flakes of blossom from the trees in the gardens of the better houses drifted like pearls.

The spring tides had left other debris, small mountains of glistening brown seaweed in frills like some of the net curtains which hung in the windows of the pit houses which were too close together for any natural privacy. Mother-of-pearl hills of scallop-edged shells and blue-and-white mussel shells opened like butterflies to the pale cream sunshine which fell upon the beach of the pit town.

The wheels of the three pitheads which graced the blue sky like giants along the edge of the seashore dominated the area. Behind them, like poor relations, crouched the pit rows.

Jenna and Ruari took their shoes off and walked at the water's edge where the waves were moving back and forth and were warmed by the sand and Jenna thought there was nothing better than this though she loved a storm in October when you could feel the sea spray on your face from well up the top of the beach. She loved its noise and movement, something you couldn't control.

'We're moving,' she said, 'not far,' she added hastily, in case he should think she meant another town or even another area, 'to Wesley Road. My dad got promoted and we've been to look at the house tonight and my mam is ever so pleased.'

Ruari didn't say anything. He never went into her house but she very often went into his so in a way she would be losing his house as well as hers because it wouldn't be the same. You couldn't drop in casually the way that she did almost every day and see his mam for a few minutes.

'It's not far,' she said.

'No,' Ruari agreed but neither of them meant it, it was in a lot of respects a whole world away. 'It'll be nice,' he said, 'for your mam.'

And Jenna thought, yes, although he didn't say it, her mam had never fitted into Back Church Street the way that she and her dad had, and her mam would be pleased about that, proud of it.

She kissed him, long and slowly on the mouth. He tasted wonderful. How could a boy taste that sweet? And his kisses were perfect. It had been one of the things she had liked best about him from when they were very young. Ruari's kisses were to die for. She lingered and then he began to get the wrong idea and slide his hands up her legs when she still had something to say so she stopped and said,

'I'm not like my mam. I don't want to leave Back Church Street and I don't want to leave you, ever.'

He smiled, she felt his lips curve under hers.

'You're not going anywhere,' he said.

'I shall never go anywhere really, you know, not without you.'

'I'm not going no place,' he said.

'Are you sure?'

'Aye, I'm quite certain,' he said and then he kissed her and this time she didn't stop him when he slid his hands up her thighs.

Together down on the dunes in the spiky grass there she had him all to herself and in the late evening when the darkness came down and hid them they could have each other and be close and there was never any problem about it. There was never any risk because he took care of it, like he took care of everything, Jenna thought. She looked up at the stars and was glad that he was hers and that he could make her feel like nobody else ever did or ever would or ever could.

She didn't have to stifle her cries of pleasure here with nobody but the birds to notice. This was their place, the little town and the pitheads and the sea, the sounds of their childhood were just the same as now and somehow their relationship was like that, it was unsmirched, untouched, unspoiled. She loved him.

It frightened her in a way, how much she loved him, and then he would hold her and she would stop being frightened because she knew that he was hers and always would be. She just wished they had more time together.

She had the awful feeling that when she moved away she would see him less, she knew it was so, it would have to be planned, it could not be two or three casual meetings a day, waving to him in the back lane, knowing he was there, that he was sleeping just a few yards away, they would have to make sure that they saw one another and what with her job and his job and his football and her mother not wanting her to see him and Wesley Road being at the other side of the town she panicked.

It wouldn't be the same. It would never be the same any more. She wanted never to let him go, she held him closer and closer until there wasn't closer to be for fear that she should let go of him and they would never see one another again.

She wished that they could get married even though they were so young but Ruari's mother needed his wage at the moment, his stepfather drank.

Jenna could only dream of them having a tiny house together somewhere not far off, it didn't have to be anything much, just so that they could be together all the time, somewhere very close to where they had been born and lived. She wanted never to leave this place and never to leave him.

# Two

On a weekday evening several weeks later Sorrel Maddison heard the knocking on the door of his office and recognized the rapping as Harry Philips, the manager of the club. Being chairman of Dunelm North End Football Club was the pinnacle of Sorrel's career. He had done many things in his life but always he had had this goal – he laughed at the pun – this in his mind, this had been what he had intended and now he was here in this great big office and everybody did what he wanted and everybody listened to what he said.

The new stadium had been built not far from the sea and on the site of an old pit and not that far from the old site so that people could not complain about the football being outside the town or inconvenient to get to.

Somehow they wanted to feel as though the place was completely theirs. The move had been his idea and he had wanted it in the very heart of the town because to him the two were indivisible. The new stadium seated fifty thousand people and there was enough room for it to be expanded further and eventually he would get it there, he knew he would.

During the World Cup the year before, two group games and a quarter-final had been played there and he was very proud that his new stadium was chosen for this. There was also very good flood-lighting so that matches could be played at night and in bad weather because football being an almost all year round game and this being the north the weather was at best unpredictable.

He had been very fond of the old stadium which had been used by the local people for over ninety years so they had taken a bit of shifting when the idea was proposed but there was no way they could hang on to the old one, things had to move on and he was the man to move them. He thought of the team and the ground and everything about it as being his, completely belonging to him as nothing else in his life.

Harry was a little afraid of him, Sorrel knew. Most people were. It made things easier, it meant he didn't have to explain himself, it meant that what he said went, everywhere.

'Harry. Come in.'

He was genial because Harry hesitated in the doorway. He shuffled in.

'I wanted to talk to you, about Ruari Gallacher,' Harry said.

'Who's that?'

'Stan Robson's lad, his own father died down the pit years ago and Stan drinks. His mam's a nice woman and Ruari works at Dixon's. He's good, Mr Maddison, really good. Other clubs are sending scouts to watch him. Any day now somebody's going to offer for him and he could be what we're looking for.'

'You think he's special?'

'I don't think he's brilliant yet and I doubt he ever will be but I think he'll make a useful player, I think he could score a few goals, make enough decent passes to make other players score goals. It's good to have local lads who play well and don't cost much.'

Harry had played for Sunderland in his young day but had had so many injuries so often that he had had to come out of it but he knew the game, he knew what made a good footballer. He had been with North End for two years now and Sorrel trusted him. He looked for new talent and sent scouts all over the place, so to find it in his own backyard was very sweet.

'Offer him a deal. And offer Stan a bit of something, Harry, to cement it. If you think he's special then he must be.'

'Aye, I will.'

'But don't go mad. There's no need.'

'They've got nothing so I don't think I'll have to do too much to get him and besides, I'm mates with Stan. It could be cheap and quite lucrative in time.'

'Good.'

Harry looked relieved. He went out and Sorrel sat back in the chair behind his desk and thought how much he disliked Harry. How could such a man manage a football team with success? And yet he did.

The players responded, they worked for him. Sorrel had no idea why. He had seen other managers screaming at their players from the stands, chewing gum and scowling. Harry did none of that. He didn't curse or blame them unless things were really bad, nor, as far as Sorrel could judge, did he do much to encourage them, yet somehow it worked.

Sorrel thought it was the training. They trained in the afternoons and had brand-new facilities for doing so, not just the pitch like so many clubs. The rest of the time they could do what they liked and they were punctual and ready, keen because they knew where they were, they knew how to please and they wanted to please Harry.

Ruari Gallacher would be an asset to the team, Sorrel was sure of it.

Sorrel went home to the twelfth-century manor house he had bought when he had begun to make real money from the betting shops he had started up. He had just sat down on the sofa with a whisky and soda and the local newspaper when his eighteen-year-old son, Paul, came in. Paul had just finished school. He didn't know what he wanted to do next and to Sorrel's frustration didn't want to go to university. He was scowling.

'I heard you're going to sign up Gallacher.'

How in the hell had he heard that, Sorrel wondered, but then a number of people would know since Harry Philips had been at the Dixon's shipyard games lately so there were bound to be rumours.

'So?'

'So he's not that good.'

Sorrel looked at him. This was interesting. Paul had never yet cared about football. Sorrel had taken him to innumerable games when he was little and he had been bored. Paul hated sport. Sorrel could not believe he had fathered a son who didn't like the national game.

'Harry says he'll do well. Have you ever known Harry to be wrong?'

Paul hesitated. He didn't usually argue so this must matter to him a great deal.

'What is it?' Sorrel said.

'What do you mean?'

Sorrel took another swig of his drink and put down his *Evening Chronicle*, folding it carefully as he did so.

'There's something else to this, you couldn't tell a decent foot-baller from a fried egg.'

'I don't want him here. There are other clubs.'

'He's a local lad, which is good for us, and Harry reckons he could make a striker. What the hell's going on with you? Spit it out, for God's sake.'

'He's getting in my way with Jenna Duncan.'

Sorrel stared at him.

'What?'

Paul moved uncomfortably.

'Jenna Duncan,' he said again. 'She's a local girl, I like her.'

'Yes, well, I didn't think she was Miss World,' Sorrel said.

Paul didn't say anything. Sorrel could have kicked himself for the sarcasm, it wasn't often they had a conversation and then only when Paul wanted something, he thought with regret.

'You want me to turn down the prospect of a good footballer because of some lass? Are you a complete idiot?'

'There are half a dozen lads around here just as good if not better than he is, I don't know why everybody goes on about him,' Paul said.

Sorrel stared so hard even he noticed he was doing it. His son was jealous because some lad from a back street was screwing whatever her name was. How ridiculous.

'Ruari Gallacher is poor, uneducated, works in a shipyard to support his mother because her bloody stupid husband is a drunk and he has nothing going for him other than a good right foot. How in the hell could he compete with you? Take her somewhere nice to eat, buy her champagne. How difficult can it be? And if Gallacher is as good as Harry thinks he is we would be daft not to make sure of him.

'Never confuse sentiment and business. Money makes the world go round, at least our world. And business is money. And women for the most part like successful men. Yes?'

He looked hopefully at Paul, who still said nothing.

'Pour me another drink,' Sorrel said and watched his son mix the whisky and soda, not too much soda, he didn't like the whisky drowned, it was expensive malt, he bought it specially, his family knew that and when he had accepted the glass he said, 'Who is she?'

'Her father works in the grocery department of the Store.'

'So she's poor as well and no doubt has no education and lives in a back street too.'

'I don't see that it matters, you came from a back street or so you're always telling me.'

'You're right, it doesn't matter and therefore you're Santa Claus, yes?'

Paul smiled.

'Why don't you ask her out and then if you like her you can invite her to dinner? That way we'll get a look at her,' Sorrel said.

Paul's young face lit like he was still a child and Sorrel could not help being pleased that he had got this right.

'Thanks, Dad,' he said.

Really, Sorrel thought as he sipped at his second whisky and soda, the world was a very simple place.

# Three

Paul Maddison had a car, that was the first thing Jenna noticed about him, other than the fact that he was the richest lad in the area. His car was not an old banger like a lot of the lads' cars, it was an MGB, green, and he had the hood down.

When he stopped to speak to her in the street she noticed the other girls noticing her and being envious. She could not help thinking that Ruari did not have a car, not even an old banger. When she went out with him they couldn't go anywhere much, he couldn't afford to take her anywhere. The furthest they ever went was the local cinema. She didn't really mind but it was nice to see how the other girls craned their necks when Paul stopped his car and said, 'Hi, Jenna,' like he was American or something.

'Hi, Paul. Nice car.' He was good-looking too, fair-haired and tanned.

'My dad bought it for me.'

Well, she didn't think he had gone out and got it for himself. He had just left school, by all accounts.

'Actually, I think he bought it for himself but he never has time to use it. I wondered,' he said, that balmy summer evening, 'if you would like to go for a drink with me. I know a lovely little pub in Bamburgh.'

Bamburgh was miles away, one of the most beautiful of the seaside towns, with the best beach in the area and a castle right beside it. She could imagine going on the beach and putting her feet in the water and then sitting outside a nice pub with a lad like this who wore expensive clothes and could afford to buy her a drink. And she could have worn her new dress, she thought with regret.

'I can't,' she said.

'Why not?'

'Because I'm going with Ruari Gallacher.' Jenna felt awful saying it in a way. She loved Ruari but to somebody like Paul Maddison, Ruari was nobody and she was ashamed at how that made her feel, like she was nobody either. 'We – we're going out tonight, he's taking me somewhere nice.'

It was a lie and she was sorry that she had said it but somehow she felt she had to. He had been distracted with the football of late as never before and she was starting to hate it. They saw one another in passing every day but she did not have him to herself, it was almost as though he was so used to her that he didn't need to take her out or spend time.

Paul smiled at her. 'I didn't know,' he said and drove off.

Jenna went into the back lane. She had just finished work and she wanted to see Ruari but she had the feeling he was playing a football match that night. She was right, he was just coming out of the house with a bag over his arm which no doubt had his kit in it.

'I really, really want to go out,' she said. 'I've hardly seen you in weeks, you've done nothing but play football, you've been out every night practising.'

Sometimes he would give up matches for her if he had enough time to make sure it wasn't putting anybody out but this time he couldn't, she could see. It had been happening more and more often, the football always came first. She was lucky if she came second. She understood how he felt about the game but she was starting to resent how he was treating her.

'I'm going early for practice,' he said.

'Can't you not just this once? I've had an awful day. Somebody nicked something and Miss Hammond got upset and we had the police and it isn't nice, you know.' Miss Hammond was the manageress of the department. It was Jenna's ambition to have Miss Hammond's job but it didn't seem likely to happen since Miss Hammond was about thirty and not very pretty. Nobody would ever want to marry her, she would be manageress of the department forever.

'I'm sorry, Jenna. Mr Hutchinson is hoping there'll be scouts.'

Jenna raised her eyes. 'He's been saying that every game for months.'

'It's nearly the end of the season, it won't last much longer,' he said.

Suddenly Jenna could not stand the idea of going home. Her parents would be sitting over the television and the smell of shepherd's pie would be filling the house.

'Oh, please, Ruari, we don't have to do anything, just go for a walk on the beach.'

'I cannot, you know I cannot.'

Jenna tried to be sensible but they had been going on like this for so long.

'It's never going to happen, you know,' she said. 'There are thousands of lads who want to be top footballers.'

Ruari looked down. 'I'm good,' he said.

He wasn't given to saying such things but she thought, yes, he believed in himself, perhaps he always had done.

'I know but you can't build your life hoping for something like that. You've been going on like this for years, ever since you were a little kid. You aren't going to help your mam like this.'

She had hit the nail on the head, she thought as he looked up.

'I won't do it being an electrician at Dixon's either,' he said.

'It's a good steady job,' she said. 'What's wrong with that? Nobody expects you to do any more. What about us?'

He hesitated. 'I will make it up to you.'

'You're always doing that, always making up to people for what they haven't had. You can't help that. I want to have you to myself. I want us to have a little house, just you and me, to get away from my mam and her big ideas. We could manage. I've got a job and you've got a job and . . . I know we aren't very old but, Ruari, I love you. It isn't going to change. Please, just this once, just this one time. I won't ever ask you for anything else.' She was almost crying. 'I don't want to be by myself tonight.'

'Come to the game,' he said, missing the point completely.

The tears began to slip down her face and she could not bear that he should see them, could not stand the humiliation of him letting her cry and not doing anything. She could see by the way he was standing that he wouldn't compromise.

'I should have known better,' she said and then she ran down the back lane.

He shouted after her but he didn't go after her. She thought he might, for a few moments she waited when she got to the beach but the time slipped past and he didn't come for her.

She stayed down there. It was the perfect spring evening or was it early summer, she could never remember when one started and the other stopped. The weather didn't necessarily make any difference. It could be cold in July and warm in October.

The fields were yellow with cowslips away from the town, she had seen them when she and her mam went into Newcastle shopping. We could have gone for a walk, she thought, the hedges are white with may, the forests are full of bluebells, there's cow parsley in great big swathes beside the river and in the fields rabbits are running around and the lambs playing and you can hear pheasants calling in the fields and here I am all alone on an evening like this when I should be with somebody.

She walked slowly back up the beach. It still wasn't late and she really didn't want to go home. She was beginning to think that her life would go on forever like this, smiling over the counter, being nice to the public, bringing her wage home for her mam and dad when she could have thought of a hundred other things to do with it. Oh, she didn't want to be ungrateful but she wanted a home of her own, a little house with Ruari. Was it so much to ask?

She went slowly up the steps which led to the main road and began to walk home. As she did so a car stopped just in front. It was Paul Maddison.

'Hello again. I thought you were going somewhere,' he said.

'I'm not going anywhere,' she said, trying to ignore him.

He stopped the car and got out.

'The sea's so calm,' he said, 'it's more like July, isn't it?'

It was, she thought regretfully, it was so beautiful.

'The trouble is it's never like this in July,' he said.

That was true. You hoped the summers would be lovely but up here in the north half the time and more you spent watching the rain run down the windows. The local joke was summer's different, the rain's warmer.

'Do you go away in July?' she said.

'Sometimes sooner. Dad's finished with the football season then and—'

'Oh, the bloody football season,' she said.

'Don't you care for the game?'

'No, I don't.'

'To be perfectly honest neither do I,' he confessed.

She laughed, she looked at him to see whether he was stringing her a line but he seemed genuine.

'But your dad owns the club,' she said.

'It's his dream, not mine.'

'What's your dream?'

'Oh, it's very modest,' he said. 'I just want a nice house and a decent job so that I can marry and have a couple of children.'

Jenna looked harder at him. Was he just saying it? She didn't think he was, how funny, no lad wanted that, it was what lasses wanted.

'I want to be able to come home at night and have a nice dinner and chat about daft things and kiss my kids goodnight. My dad never did that, you see, he was too busy making money and being important. I suppose he started from so far down that he wanted to succeed so badly. I don't have that need, I suppose I'm lucky, he did all that so I don't have to do it somehow. Does this make any sense?'

'Oh yes,' Jenna said, 'it makes perfect sense to me. Ruari's like your dad, he has everything to prove to himself and his mam.'

'What are you going to do now?' Paul said.

'Go home, I suppose. What are you going to do?'

'The same. I'd rather go for a drink. I suppose you don't fancy it? Just one?'

'I shouldn't,' she said regretfully. 'I don't drink.'

'Oh, come on. You know me and it's just a drink. It would be nice to have somebody to go with.' As though he was lonely, which he couldn't be, him being so popular and his family being the most important people in the area.

'I'll bring you back in an hour.'

She gave in. And she was glad. It was lovely to sit in the sports car and have the wind make a mess of her hair and to see the coast road whizzing past, the sand dunes and the little villages, and the sea was so bright, glittering like sapphire and people looked as they went past and the speed and the car and the fact that she was with a lad who could afford such luxuries made her feel as though she was having fun.

They went to Bamburgh which was one of her favourite places and had one of the best castles she had ever seen, right on the seashore at the top of the beach, it stood there so proud, she loved it. They left the car on the dunes. A gentle warm breeze was making its way through the spiky grass where people had trekked sand and on the beach boys were playing football and people were walking dogs and little kids were running up and down the shoreline. The shadows were lengthening but the evening would go on and on as it did at this time of the year.

The light was incredible here, bright, not like it was during the day, a whole new white light and just for the next two or three weeks it would be like that nearly all night so that even if you woke up at three in the morning it was not properly dark and there was something very comforting about it.

You made up for it in the winter of course, when it barely got light for weeks and weeks, but she liked that too, fires and sitting inside and listening to the wind and the waves and when you went to bed you had a hot-water bottle.

They paddled, the water had been over the sand and was warm and he was so easy to be with, his trouser legs rolled up to his knees like the old men and she carrying her shoes in her hand. He laced his fingers through hers and he looked so good, the evening sun turning his hair almost cream and when she commented on his tan he said it was because he had been to Spain with his family in February and then to Greece later, what a luxury – she thought it sounded so glamorous and she was envious.

He told her how warm it had been in Spain and of the hotel where they had stayed with a big kidney-shaped swimming pool and how he had drunk cold white wine in the evenings. She thought to be in Spain and to drink white wine and perhaps to wear a long dress and sit in the garden in the late evening and talk with his family must be wonderful. She would never have anything like that, she knew it. Her life was dull.

There were bubbles among the foam at the water's edge but it had been a hot day, there had been four hot days in a row and here in the north-east that didn't happen very often which was why she felt even worse that Ruari was playing football that evening.

The sun went down in spectacular fashion like a big fiery football and after it had done so they went to the pub and there he ordered a bottle of champagne. Jenna could not believe it. They sat out in the garden which overlooked the beach and the champagne came in a silver ice bucket. It was Veuve Clicquot, he said, the label was orange and it tasted delectable, like nothing she had ever tasted before. It was the most wonderful evening of her life.

When the champagne was finally finished it was very late indeed and there were stars. They left the hood down on the car and they sang songs to the night air. There were few other cars on the road. Finally he stopped and with the sound of the sea all around he took her into his arms and kissed her. He tasted of champagne.

They got out of the car and ran down in the darkness on to the beach. It was a blue sky and the stars were so many that Jenna was amazed at them, thousands and thousands of stars. She ran into the waves and there he caught hold of her and kissed her again, lifted her off her bare feet, ran his fingers over her bare legs, picked her up and carried her so that she squealed, thinking he was going to throw her into the sea but he didn't. He carried her back up the sand and into the grass. The grass was cool now but not cold and his mouth was warm and his body was warmer and she was so very happy, happier than she had ever been in her life.

She didn't stop him. It seemed inevitable that she should give herself to him, she wanted to, was glad and it was not that he was arrogant or difficult or filled with triumph. He was a bit clumsy, a bit apologetic and it was only then that she realized he was not Ruari. Ruari was not clumsy or apologetic but Ruari had no need to be because they knew one another's bodies so well.

She had somehow expected him to be Ruari though it was not so much of a shock when he was not. She was even sorry for him that he was not Ruari, that she did not love him. She liked him enough to give him the night, that was how it felt, that it was such a wonderful time that she would not ruin it by refusing.

He told her that he loved her, she did not doubt it. She was aware all the time that she did not love him but it didn't matter. She cared enough about him to be there with him, to enjoy being close, to like that he wanted to be with her. There was nothing taken for granted. The stars had already provided what they could, so she did not need him to give her that. The champagne had done the rest.

If it was not the best sex she had ever had she thought it was not his fault. He did not know much about it, he did not know what to do and his very innocence was her undoing. She did not want to disappoint or upset him when he had given her such a wonderful evening, such a good time. Any girl would have been pleased to have been with him. He faltered, when it was over, he said, 'Jenna . . . was it all right?' and she said it was, she said it was very good, she could not say anything else because he was downcast somehow and not like she had thought rich boys were.

He kissed her. They got dressed, they made their way out of the now cold sand dunes, where the wind had got up and the sea was like black oil and the sand was lifting in little mean drifts against the breeze. The skies had blotted out the stars.

He put the hood up on the car. He put the heater on but Jenna shivered and all the way home she was cold. He covered the distance so fast that she was afraid, the roads snaking and the little car flinging itself across them. She was glad when they finally reached her house, she giving him terse directions. He brought the car to an abrupt halt outside her front door. He said her name but she got out and ran.

Inside she could hear her mother shouting her name because she never came in the front way and had had to hammer on the door so that her mother would unlock it but all she said was, 'Thanks, Mam, I'm going to bed,' and she ran upstairs and when she got into her bed she found that she was shivering.

She could not stop crying. What had she done? Whatever had she been thinking about? She contained her sobs. She could not indulge herself here. The walls were thin, her parents would notice. She could hear their footsteps as they climbed the stairs to bed. They had waited up for her.

Somehow that made things worse and normally she would have been called upon to explain herself. She had no doubt there would be questions in the morning. She tried to breathe quietly and not to cry. It didn't matter. It wouldn't matter. It would be all right. She had done nothing wrong. She and Ruari were not engaged or married or anything like that. She could do what she liked. It was her life. She turned over and slept for a while but she kept waking up because the night was so long, the hours crawled and seemed to go on forever.

It was only when the morning came that she welcomed the light. Another day. She would do better. Everything would be all right. She went off to work early, not only because she couldn't sleep but she knew that her mother 'wanted to have words' with her, as she called it. She would have to face the music tonight no doubt.

# Four

Stan Robson, Ruari's stepfather, had known the manager, Harry Philips, since they were little lads. Stan grinned at him when Harry turned up at the Black Lion on Church Street that evening.

'A pint?'

'Aye, I wouldn't mind,' Harry said and they sat down in the depths of the corner and nobody came over and disturbed them. They were a bit nervous of Harry nowadays, Sorrel Maddison's right-hand man and nobody got in his road.

Stan came back with the beer. Harry, a small skinny man, he was only five foot two, had been fast, Stan could recall having seen him dribble the ball past three or four men. He had been good but it hadn't lasted. Nothing good, Stan thought, ever bloody lasted.

'I saw your Ruari play the other night.'

'Oh, aye? Like he was still at school. You'd think he'd find summat better to do. He thinks he's Jackie Milburn like.'

Harry nodded.

'Aye, well, I like the look of him so Mr Maddison and me we thought we might sign him up, you know.'

Stan blinked.

'For the team?'

'Why not . . . but give him a trial, a couple of years, and then we'll see.'

Stan downed the rest of his pint, he was so surprised.

'Another?' Harry offered.

'Aye. That would be grand,' Stan said, smiling.

Ruari was still up when Stan got home though his mam had gone to bed. Ruari watched him carefully to see how drunk he was, he might need helping up the stairs or he might only get as far as the couch but Stan, though bright-eyed, seemed more sober than usual.

'I saw Harry Philips in the Black Lion.'

'What did he want?'

'You. They want you to sign up.'

'Who, me?'

'Aye, you. Who do you think I'm talking to?'

Ruari hesitated. 'What?' he said.

'Is that all you've got to say when you're being given an opportunity like this? I have to admit I never thought you'd manage it,' Stan said.

'Mr Hutchinson said there was a scout from Carlisle and some other bloke from Teeshaven at the game tonight.'

'And you think they were there because of you?' Stan said.

Stan looked at him and Ruari knew what he was thinking, that Ruari was soft in the head to think he was that good, that any top First Division club other than his own would have him.

'And did any bugger say owt?' Stan demanded, staring at Ruari from cold eyes.

'No,' Ruari admitted, downcast.

'Well, then. Mr Maddison wants to take you on. What do you think to that?'

'I think it depends how much they're offering to pay,' Ruari said.

'How much? Lad, you've got to grab your opportunities with both hands. You're not that far off eighteen. You're going to be too old to play football if you have to wait much longer. I said we'd meet him at Dunhelm Hotel on Friday night.'

Friday night was a long time off, Ruari thought, and he couldn't help but notice that the man from Teeshaven, a man he hadn't seen before at the ground, came over when he was training the following evening. He was short and stocky and kept his hands in his pockets while he talked to Mr Hutchinson who ran the games at the shipyard and Mr Hutchinson introduced Ruari and he said he had come to make Ruari an offer. Ruari didn't know what to think or say.

He looked at Mr Hutchinson for guidance and Mr Hutchinson said would Mr Hodgkin excuse them for a second and he drew Ruari to one side.

'Does he mean it?' Ruari said.

'Yes, I think he does.'

'How come nobody did before?'

'You're just a late developer,' Mr Hutchinson said with a grin. 'Everybody's different. Two years ago you were just another lad playing football. Now . . .'

'Now what?' Ruari said, eager for praise.

'Now it's different.'

'Mr Maddison wants me, so me stepdad reckons.'

Mr Hutchinson's face darkened.

'Well, you have to make your own mind up and in the end it's down to what you want and the money.'

'How do I make up me mind, though?' Ruari said.

Mr Hutchinson looked at him.

'Well, you know, Ruari, they say that there are three things that matter in life.'

'What are they?'

Mr Hutchinson paused and then he said softly, 'Money, money and money.'

They went over and sat down and Mr Hodgkin made Ruari the kind of offer that got him excited. The money sounded good and Mr Hodgkin didn't make any special promises, he put the offer plainly.

'Think about it, Ruari, and let me know if you think it's a good idea. Then I'll come over and talk to your parents. They have to sign the contract as well as you.'

'Me mam.'

'Your mother then and we'll see what she thinks. There's no rush. Take your time. See if it's something you want. We want you but we know it would be a big move for you.'

Ruari stuttered his thanks and left.

Teeshaven was one of the local rivals and it was about thirty miles away, a bigger town than this and industrial with a chemical works and a steel works, on the coast but it had bigger shipyards than here. He was scared but he thought Mr Hutchinson was right. He would be a fool if he didn't go for the team which offered him the most money. He would be able to tell Jenna, once it was sorted out, and he would move and she could go with him and get a job and he would be able to send money home to his mam and everything would be wonderful. He was so excited, his dream was about to come true.

Jenna went to Farne House, Paul's home, for dinner. Her mam had tried to talk to her about coming in like that and Jenna had told her who she had been with and that was enough to make her mother happy and it was nice for her to feel that her mother approved.

She couldn't help being impressed when Paul had stopped her in the street the day after they had been out and said that he had been worried, was she all right and his father would very much like it if she would come to their house in the evening for a meal and somehow she didn't remember how to refuse. She hadn't known what to say.

'I know you go with Ruari, I know it was just . . .' Paul had hesitated. 'But we could be friends, couldn't we? What's wrong with that or are you busy tonight?'

She was never busy, she thought, she never got to do anything exciting and to be asked to their house and to something as posh as dinner was too much temptation.

'I won't get you drunk, I'll come and collect you and fetch you back.'

He had done so, shaking hands with her mam when he came to the door. Her mother thought he was wonderful, she could see. She only wished her dad was at home to see the lovely little sports car as it stood in the street at the front of their house. She was glad then for the first time that they had moved, it would have been too awful for Paul to have to come to their old house, she would have been so ashamed.

Farne House was a wonderful place, the kind that people went to at the end of fairy tales. It was big and stone and reassuring, the sort of house which wrapped you around like it was hugging you to it and she loved it from the moment she saw it.

It was nothing like she had thought their house would be. It was an old manor house, not a brand-new one like a lot of rich people had. The building was long sideways and the roofs came to three points with three storeys of stone mullioned windows. Paul showed her around the gardens. Furthest away there was an enormous swimming pool.

'There used to be a kind of orchard here, a nuttery.'

'A nuttery?'

'A place with lots of nut trees. My father had them cut down and the place cleared so that we would have somewhere to swim.'

He showed her around. It was wonderful, Jenna thought and must have cost a fortune to build. There were changing rooms and there was another building and inside it a sauna and a steam room, a plunge bath and showers, all things she had never seen before. She wondered if she would ever be invited to use them.

But also she kept thinking about what the nuttery would have looked like, the shade in the summer, the little spreading trees and the long grass moving in the warm breeze. Would it have had that wonderful smell like almonds had and how were nuts harvested? It was such a novel idea that she wished she had seen it.

The rest of it held half a dozen garages and a huge area for turning. Three Mercedes cars were parked on the drive. There was a very big lawn on which reposed large statues and a fountain which had a big green statue of what looked like a semi-clad nymph in the middle of it and water spouted from various places around the statue.

'It used to be different,' Paul said, frowning as he tried to remember. 'I think there was a Jacobean garden with herbs in it and things like lavender. My mother loved it and she was really upset when Dad changed everything.'

Inside the house was very big, the kitchen had narrow stone mullioned windows and deep thick walls and an Aga set in a huge arched fireplace. Jenna thought every woman must want a house with a big cream Aga like that one.

The walls were white, rough plastering in the big sitting room too and it had a huge open fire which made her wish that the weather was bad because she thought it must be wonderful when the rain was pouring down the four big leaded windows. It had a beamed ceiling, black beams and cream in between. There were lots of big leather settees which were bliss to sink into and little tables and a variety of modern paintings which were lines of pink and purple.

The dining room was her favourite room, the walls were covered in oak panelling and it had a flagged floor with rugs all laid out, and the table was oak too and long enough for a dozen people but laid with four places so the dinner was just because of her which made her feel very important, with the candles burning and their light reflected in the crystal chandeliers.

There was a white cloth, the kind which would have taken ages to iron, and starched serviettes and crystal glasses, three or four of them at every place setting, and there were flowers in the middle of the table, plucked from the garden no doubt and dying but they looked pretty.

Jenna felt shabby and rather silly in her cheap flowered dress. Mrs Maddison came downstairs at the last minute, wearing a very expensive frock. Jenna, working with clothes, knew the real thing when she saw it. Faye Maddison was tall, slender and had a tan, which proved she had been abroad recently. She wore gold jewellery, several chains around her neck and gold bangles on her brown arms. Jenna was also impressed because Mrs Maddison did not go into the kitchen, she offered drinks but the food was cooked and served by other people which Jenna had never seen before.

Jenna didn't like her. She barely spoke, nothing but courtesies and Jenna knew nothing about drinking and Mrs Maddison was no help, asking her in a flat voice what she would like and Jenna couldn't ask for champagne, it seemed so rude so she shook her head and stuttered that she was all right, thank you. Mrs Maddison merely turned away to pour champagne for herself which she opened without asking her son to. Usually, Jenna thought, men did things like that but Mrs Maddison opened the champagne with such expertise, a quick twist of the bottle and out the cork came with a discreet pop, that Jenna realized she must have done it hundreds of times before.

Mr Maddison came in at the last minute full of apologies like Jenna was somebody special. She was in awe of him, had heard stories about him, how he had started in the gutter and made lots of money with nightclubs and betting shops. It was said that he was a millionaire. Sorrel Maddison was tall and dark and seemed to tower over everybody but he was nice to Jenna that evening and she liked that he was so fond of his son that he would put himself about for her.

'What do you think of the house?' he said to her. 'It cost a fortune. I had to fight the planners at the council to change everything but I got what I wanted in the end because it was dropping to pieces when I found it, they were going to pull it down and build something entirely fresh. I rescued it if you like.'

Jenna smiled and agreed and Mr Maddison insisted on showing her over the house, including the six bathrooms all of which had gold taps and gold and white tiles, like something from Greece, she thought.

The bedrooms had thick carpets and built-in wardrobes and there was an exercise room in the cellar with things like a running machine, Jenna had never seen anything like that before, and down there in another room was a bar. There was another bar in the sitting room, which ran the full length of one wall and behind it was every kind of drink you could imagine. Jenna caught sight of herself in the mirror opposite before she sat down at the table to eat, badly dressed in comparison to everybody else and pale. She was so nervous.

They had wine. Jenna had never had wine before, except for the champagne she had drunk with Paul, she thought guiltily, and nobody talked about her being too young to drink it. She didn't know what kind of wine it was, just that it was so golden it was almost green and tasted of summer, gooseberries and butter.

The food was better than anything she had tasted before, salmon, chicken in some kind of pale cream sauce and a pudding made with raspberries and meringue. They had coffee outside. It was, she thought, a different world than the one she knew and she felt real gratitude towards the whole family. She didn't want to leave, it was as though she had come home somehow.

There were lights strung between the trees. It was like fairyland, Jenna decided.

On the way back she said to Paul, 'I had a lovely time.'

'I'm glad. My dad liked you. You can come again any time,' he said.

Jenna hesitated, wondering why he had said his dad and not his mam though it had been obvious his mother didn't care for her so perhaps it was nothing but the truth.

'I shouldn't really,' she said.

He stopped the car and for a moment Jenna was frightened he wanted to kiss her but he said, 'We can be friends if that's what you want.'

'It wouldn't be fair.'

'I don't mind, really I don't.'

'Thanks, Paul, that's lovely of you,' she said.

Her mother had waited up for her.

'Did you have a nice evening?' she said, ready to be glad.

Jenna couldn't remember her mother having ever been interested before in what she was doing. She told her all about it, her mother was enthusiastic and it was lovely just to sit there and talk about what she had done and for her mother to be so pleased. Just before they went to bed her mother hesitated, a foot on the stairs.

'Oh, by the way,' she said, 'Ruari came to see you.'

Jenna stopped in the hallway.

'Did you tell him where I was?'

'It wasn't a secret, was it?' her mother said.

'No, no of course not,' and now her evening was ruined. She couldn't sleep thinking of Ruari, wondering what she was doing.

# Five

Stan met Harry Philips before Ruari got there on the Friday evening.

'I wanted to see you first,' Harry said and he took from his pocket a great big roll of five-pound notes and pressed them into Stan's fist. 'Here,' he said, 'this is just as thanks.'

'But . . .' Stan wasn't usually given to stuttering. 'Nowt's signed yet.'

'No, but you're his dad, aren't you, as near as, and you can sign for him.'

'Aye, I suppose I can,' Stan said.

'Well, then, we don't need to wait for Ruari.' Harry Philips gave him a pen and showed him where to sign and Stan, sweating so much that it ran into his eyes and he could hardly see the paper, signed with a flourish and he thrust the big wad of money into his pocket. He needed a pint to stop the sweating and another to chase it.

Ruari was ten minutes more. He was late, Stan thought, and he could hardly sit still as Ruari came into the foyer of the hotel.

'Isn't this grand?' Stan said.

Ruari said nothing.

Harry Philips said, 'Sit down, Ruari. I would offer you a drink but I know you aren't old enough.'

'I don't want owt, thanks,' Ruari said.

Harry waited until Ruari sat down.

'I've talked to Stan here about it and we want you for two years, that's usual at this point and we'll see how you go. We'll give you twelve pounds a week—'

'You'll have to do better than that,' Ruari interrupted.

Harry looked at him. Stan glared at him.

'Don't argue with the man, lad,' he said.

'What do you mean?' Harry said.

'I've been offered twenty pounds a week,' Ruari said, 'and more if I make good.'

Harry Philips stared at him and Ruari was suddenly aware of how much he disliked this man. Harry Philips was almost sneering at him.

'Twenty pounds a week?' he said as though he couldn't believe it. 'That's a fortune for an untried lad like you. Who is it?'

'Teeshaven.'

'You can't go and play for them,' Harry said with a dismissive snort. 'You belong here with your own folk.'

'I belong anywhere they'll pay me,' Ruari said and in a way he wished he hadn't, in a way he wished he didn't have to say it but the truth of the matter was that he thought Mr Hutchinson was right and that it all boiled down to money in the end.

He couldn't afford to stay here just because he liked it and it was home when they wouldn't offer him the same money.

'I don't think I like your attitude, lad,' Harry Philips said and Ruari thought, he wasn't used to people speaking their minds, saying their piece, he expected to have everything his own way. Harry Philips' face had gone dark and his eyes had narrowed and his mouth was nasty and thin.

'If you offer me the same money I'll talk to me mam about it,' he said.

Harry Philips laughed and Ruari didn't like the look in his eyes.

'That's big of you, lad,' he said.

'So, are you offering me?' Ruari said because he couldn't see how they could do any less and his mam would be really pleased.

'No, I'm not. They're lying to you.'

Ruari was sure the look in Harry's eyes was supposed to make him feel small but it didn't, it just made him more determined not to go with North End.

'I won't sign, then, I'll take what Teeshaven is offering.'

'You can't take it. Your father has signed the papers and you're ours for twelve pounds a week now,' Harry Philips said and there was triumph, and it was mean, in his eyes. 'What Mr Maddison wants Mr Maddison gets and he told me to get you and I have so we'll not have any of this lip from you my lad or you might learn to regret it, especially when I have you in training.'

'Is that right?' Ruari said, suddenly hating him.

'Aye, it's right,' Harry Philips said, showing him the paper. 'You're ours now, we can do what we like with you, train you, not train you, play you, not play you, drop you . . .' He let his voice trail off.

Ruari looked at the paper and then he looked at Stan and then he looked straight at Harry Philips.

'That doesn't mean anything.'

'What doesn't?'

'His signature. He's not me dad, he's not me legal guardian so it doesn't mean owt, and I haven't signed. The only person who can sign with me is me mam and she's not here,' Ruari said and he got up and walked out.

'Yer mam'll sign. She'll have to and so will you,' Stan shouted after him. 'Come back here, you little shit.'

Ruari didn't want to go home, he hadn't told his mother about the meeting with Mr Hodgkin, he had wanted to see what Mr Maddison had in mind but he could see that Harry Philips and Stan had cooked things up between them, he wouldn't have been surprised if Philips had already given Stan a backhander and that was why Stan was so enthusiastic.

He had heard that such things went on in football and it would be naive to imagine people didn't go on like that but it was not just a hard game it was a hard business, he had not realized until this minute.

He hadn't thought either that he would be so angry, that he would behave like this, like he was much older. Behaviour had consequences, he knew it did. He made himself go straight home. He didn't want to bad-mouth Stan to his mam either, he mustn't do that, it wasn't right.

She had been out when he left, she worked at the local school, cleaning after the kids had gone home. Ruari had gone back as early as he could after work and changed into his best clothes because he knew how important it was that he should make a good impression even though he didn't like Harry Philips and couldn't bring himself to think about signing for North End, especially when Mr Hodgkin had made him what he thought was a good offer.

It was mid-evening now. His mother was sitting at the kitchen table when he got in. She glanced up and then looked hard at him.

'Where have you been?' she said.

Ruari pulled off his good jacket, put it over the back of a kitchen chair and sat down.

'Stan wanted me to go and see Harry Philips.'

She was really interested now, her eyes were bright.

'Honest?' she said.

'Aye.'

'You think they might take you on?'

'They offered to.'

She put her hand over her mouth in surprise.

Ruari didn't go on. Harry Philips had scared him. He didn't like to admit it even to himself but it was true and worse still somehow Harry Philips had made him think that when he was a bit older he was going to be a very unpleasant man, difficult and bad-tempered. He didn't remember his mam saying that his dad had been like that and she certainly wasn't so who was he like?

At that moment the back door swung open and Stan walked in. His face was red with sweat and fury. He came straight across the room and he walloped Ruari hard round the face and because Ruari hadn't been expecting it he fell over, the chair clattered and he went with it. It was a hard landing on the kitchen floor and he was dazed and couldn't think for a second so he just stayed there until he could.

There was no way to avoid whatever would happen now. Ruari wished he had had time to explain more to his mother. He got up gingerly and then stood for a moment and Betty stood too, eyes blazing, and taken aback at what had happened, Ruari thought, and then Stan said in a deceptively soft voice,

'You'll sign for North End.'

'No I won't,' Ruari said. His face hurt, he could taste blood and feel it running inside his mouth and it angered him.

'What gives you the right to hit my son?' Betty said, her face white.

I am only 'my son' when things are going wrong, Ruari thought and he wished he had handled things better though he couldn't think how.

Stan glared at her so much that Ruari was afraid of what he might do now, he was so angry.

'Your son,' Stan ground out the words, 'made me look a fool in front of Harry Philips. North End have offered him a perfectly good two-year contract and he told them he wouldn't do it and that I had nothing to do with it.'

There was silence. Ruari didn't want to talk about this in front of Stan, he wished he could have had a little more time. This was worse than he had anticipated. His mother looked at him, thinking, maybe hoping, that it was Ruari's fault because she knew as well as he did that most of the grief in their house was because of Stan and she blamed herself.

'Why didn't you tell me about this sooner?' she accused him. 'I'm your mother, am I not entitled to know what is happening?'

'I've been made a better offer,' Ruari said, looking at her. He could see now that she was very annoyed because he hadn't confided in her before, normally she would not have endured Stan touching him.

She was full of suspicion and why should she not be? Nothing good had ever happened to them without hard work and even then nothing like this.

'You,' Stan said, 'you would trust anybody. Have you seen anything on paper yet?'

'Mr Hutchinson voiced for them—'

'What is this, Ruari?' his mother said. 'Explain yourself this minute properly.'

'I've been made an offer by Teeshaven—'

'By a football club that all the locals hate,' Stan said. 'It's a stupid idea and I'd already signed him up for North End and he comes in and humiliates me and says I've got no right to sign for him, like I didn't matter, like I was nobody.'

'You turned them down for an offer of another club?' his mother said as though she couldn't believe it and her eyes searched his face and they were troubled.

'Yes, I did.'

'When there's nothing on paper?' His mam was suspicious. Ruari panicked. She was right, he had turned down a good offer right here where he lived. Had he been wrong?

'I've got the—'

'You're not going,' Stan said.

'You can't stop me.' Ruari could hear himself shouting and he was glaring at Stan, something he had never done before and he was amazed at himself.

'Aye, I can. Your mother won't sign and you won't be able to go. You'll stay here and I'll talk to Harry Philips and you'll go to him and apologize.'

'I won't,' Ruari said.

Stan made as if he was going to hit Ruari again and Ruari's mother put herself in front of him before he could stop her.

'It's up to Ruari, Stan. He has to make his own decisions,' she said.

'Is that right?'

'Aye, it's right,' she said holding his gaze. His mam, Ruari thought gratefully, had always been like that, always willing to take the responsibility for everything, it was hard but she did it.

'I thought I was the head of this household,' Stan said, 'it turns out I'm nowt of the sort. Well, I'll just take meself back to the pub, then,' and he turned around and walked out, slamming the back door after him.

Ruari listened to him clash the yard gate. He didn't know what to say.

'Mam, I'm sorry. I would have told you but it all just happened. I didn't get a chance.' It was not quite the truth, he thought with a flash of guilt, he had wanted to sort this out his own way.

His mother said nothing for a few moments and her face was white with fury.

'You have no excuse for this,' she said, 'you shouldn't have put Stan into that position.'

'But, Mam—'

'You have to do what's best for you, it's nothing to do with Stan or with me,' his mother said more softly. 'If you can get out of here you should but it sounds to me as though you don't know what you're doing. Have they made you a proper offer or is it all hot air?' Her voice was so quiet as though she was sure he was wrong but didn't like to tell him and she didn't look at him. He felt sick.

'I have the papers here for the contract. I need you to sign them.'

She was looking at him now all right and her eyes began to fill with hope. Ruari produced them and a pen, his mother looked through the whole thing and her eyes began to shine.

'Do you think it's all right?' Ruari ventured.

'It looks fine to me,' and his mother signed the paper.

Ruari was ashamed of himself in so many ways he couldn't think and his face burned.

'Mam—'

'We won't talk about it any more now,' she said with a brief smile and she went back to the sink to wash the dishes from tea.

'I need to say something,' he said.

He waited until she stopped as he had known she would.

'North End offered me twelve pounds a week.' He paused there but his mother said nothing. 'Teeshaven offered me twenty. If I'd thought you wanted me to stay here and take the lower offer I would have but I didn't think you would.' She still didn't say anything. 'If I was wrong, Mam, I'll take it all back.'

She dried her hands and came to him and then she hugged him to her as Ruari had known she would.

'You should take the better offer always,' she said. 'I'm proud of you, Ruari, you did the right thing.'

Ruari went round to Jenna's and banged on the back door. Her mam answered it and she seemed to draw herself up when she saw him. She didn't smile. She never smiled at him. She had never liked him. He didn't know why and then he thought, Yes, I do, she thinks I'm not good enough for Jenna, that's what it is. Maybe she'll change her mind now. He smiled broadly.

'Hello, Mrs Duncan. I wondered if Jenna was in?'

'Jenna has gone to a dinner party,' her mam said.

Ruari thought he hadn't heard her properly.

'Is she out?'

'She's gone to Farne House to have dinner with the Maddisons,' Jenna's mam said proudly and she closed the door.

It was suddenly as cold as if it was autumn and Ruari was not dressed for the weather. There was nothing for him to do but go home.

# Six

'That girl is common,' Faye Maddison said to her husband as she watched him pulling off his tie when they went upstairs to bed.

'Isn't she?'

'You looked as though you liked her.'

'I am hoping he finds somebody better than that but what is the point in trying to direct him, he won't take any notice.'

'You think she's a passing phase, then?'

'I'm hoping she's a passing something,' he said smiling grimly and he looked at her. She was sitting on the bed pulling a file across her nails and not looking at him. 'I'm sure that's what your parents hoped I was.'

She said nothing to that and he didn't expect her to. They had reached a truce of sorts. She didn't care who he slept with because she wouldn't sleep with him. He made the money and she spent it. They tried to do the best they could together for their son, their only child, and neither of them wanted a girl like Jenna Duncan, a badly dressed kid from a back street who couldn't even talk properly, to be his choice of woman.

It brought back uncomfortable memories. Sorrel was tired and didn't want to think about how things might have been or might be. He had sent Paul to an expensive public school, had hoped he would do well, go to university, be a doctor or a lawyer or anything really which didn't involve nightclubs, betting shops or the lower echelons of society where he dwelt most of the time. He was used to it but it was not something he wanted for his son. He should have known by now. Dreams were only there to be shattered. His were. Faye's were. They went to bed in a single bed each in the same room. They could have had separate rooms but somehow it would have destroyed the point, they slept together and yet alone, they had kept up the pretence of their marriage for so many years that it had in some ways ceased to be a pretence.

It had been for Paul, they had wanted respectability so badly, but tonight Paul had unwittingly made a mockery of their attempts and Sorrel was so tired now that he was glad to get into bed in the darkness and not think about anything. It was too late for all the things he had wanted except for his football club. It was the only thing that mattered any more, the only thing he had to look forward to.

Ruari waited for Jenna when she came out of work on the Monday. She didn't seem to have been around all weekend, he hadn't liked to go to her house again but had hung around in the streets and not seen her and he didn't like to go to the drapery department when she was working.

Then he had waited for her to come to him, surely her mother would say he had called but she didn't and he felt guilty about neglecting her and also he was desperate to tell her about his progress. He waited outside the Store until she finished. It was a cold dark day, like November, and there was a bitter wind screaming across Durham Road. She didn't see him, he could see when she left with a scarf over her hair that she had her head down against the wind and the rain. He shouted her name behind her. She stopped.

'Jenna?'

She looked guilty, she looked unhappy. He wanted to take her in his arms. There were lots of people about so that he couldn't even speak to her really and also he didn't want to put any pressure on her.

'Can I talk to you?'

'I have to get home.' She stared down at the pavement and then she turned around so that she had her back to him.

'Have you given me up?' he said.

The frankness of this stopped her. She didn't turn around but she didn't move either and he gazed at her thin back which seemed to shrink from the words.

'You could just tell me,' he said.

She said nothing and then her shoulders hunched and he thought she was crying.

'It cannot be that bad,' he said.

She didn't move. He went to her, around to her so that he could see her face, her eyes. Both were wet, her lashes were black, and all he could think of was that he loved her so much and it hurt. People hurried past, nobody noticed that she was crying.

'It is,' she said and her voice was harsh.

Ruari was frightened now.

'Why?' he said.

'I went with Paul Maddison,' she said.

The pavement was suddenly the only place for his gaze. He couldn't have lifted it if they had told him he was going to play for England in the next World Cup. He watched people's feet, they hurried and their trousers and stockings were wet with the rain, dark and the day was getting darker or was it just his imagination?

He didn't know how long they stood there, it must have been quite a long time because the legs going past lessened as though everybody had gone home while they stood. He always thought people were going home to more than he was, to more than his overworked mother, Stan's beery breath, a house that wasn't big enough, a back lane full of holes and a future which he had dared to think he could better.

He wanted to run. Jenna didn't love him any more, she couldn't have done or she would never have gone with Paul Maddison, and the side of him which said she was his was so angry that he felt he might hit her and though things were bad they could be worse. He could turn into the kind of man who thought hitting women helped. He had to remind himself that he was much bigger than Jenna and that she did not belong to him, not now, not any more.

'You could say something.' Her voice was even harder now, like the kind of sandpaper you would use on rough wood. 'You could tell me I'm a slut, you could be angry, you could shout, you could even ask me why and then you could judge me. You could say that I did it on purpose because you went to your stupid football game!'

'And did you?'

'Yes,' she said, 'yes, I did,' and then she ran away.

He went after her, not immediately, somehow he had to try and remember how to move so that by the time he reached her she had left the main street and when he tried to get hold of her she turned and pushed both fists into his chest and that was when he got hold of her so she couldn't get away and dragged her down a side alley and slammed her up against the wall. They were both breathing heavily by then and the rain was running down his neck.

'I don't love you no more,' she said, shouting against the rain. 'He does it better than you do and I liked it. I went to his house and we had salmon and they had this great big dining room and they had white serviettes and a white cloth on the table and a crystal chandelier.'

Ruari said nothing. They weren't touching any more but still she stood back against the wall like it was more of a friend to her than he was. And then she started to cry and it was different than it had been before, she started to cry like she'd never ever done it, hard and bitter. Her whole body shook and because there was nobody to comfort her she turned from him.

'Why don't you just go away?' she said.

'I'm sorry,' he said and then he turned her from the wall to him and he unbuttoned his coat and pulled her in against the warmth of his shirt and he put a hand on to her dripping wet hair. She cried until he couldn't distinguish between the rain and her tears. He was soaked.

'I'm sorry, Jenna,' he said again and she pulled away and she said, 'You stupid bugger.'

'Aye, I am.'

She drew back properly and she lifted her wet face, it was shiny.

'I'm going home now,' she said.

'But—'

'No. I'm going. Don't you come after me, it won't do you no good. Don't,' she shouted when he put out a hand. 'Don't.'

She turned up the collar of her coat as if it would make any difference and then she walked away into the rain.

Jenna had never thought that she would be pleased they had moved for more than the odd few moments when Paul had picked her up in the MGB but by this time she was quite ready to be somewhere else than Back Church Street, something she had not considered. She wanted, more than anything in the world, not to see Ruari daily, not to have memories of what they had had thrust into her face all the time and because they had moved she didn't have to. She was so grateful to her mother that she almost liked her.

She and Ruari never met after that. She escaped to work. She had taken to going out of the front door straight down the stairs from her bedroom in the morning without seeing anybody or having anything to eat. Her mam had been surprised at first but rather pleased that things had changed and when her mam questioned her as to whether she was seeing Ruari she shook her head and Jenna did not miss the look of satisfaction that they were no longer together.

She had never seen her mother so happy. She greeted Jenna's dad with wonderful meals and a kiss when he came home so he seemed happy enough. Presumably Ruari was still kicking a bloody football up and down the lane of Back Church Street day in and day out, Jenna didn't know and told herself she didn't care. She didn't even miss him.

She cried a lot in the toilet at work and had to repair her mascara and her mother gave her money for new clothes so she was always in the latest styles now. Her mother was determined that she should have a chance to marry Paul Maddison, Jenna thought bitterly.

It was soon full summer, the hedgerows were covered in willowherb, the breeze making the long purple stems sway. The gardens were pink with roses and the children were on holiday so on fine days the beach was littered with sandcastles and buckets and spades and little kids in bathing suits and parents with red and orange windbreaks at the top of the beach.

The tinkling bell of the ice-cream van reminded Jenna of all the summers when she and Ruari had played swing ball or cricket on the beach with the other kids. They were not kids any more, she wished the time back but wishing would not make it so.

# Seven

Ruari lay in bed in the late evening for a short while, listening to Stan's voice as it came up clearly from the floor below into the bedroom. It was cold and dark up there like it was the middle of winter instead of summer, it had rained for days, even now he could hear it, pattering off the roof. Usually he liked the sound. Now he didn't, it reminded him of his meeting with Jenna after she had gone with Paul Maddison and of the hours he had spent devising all manner of deaths for Maddison.

He didn't move until his mother's voice began to join in and it sounded feeble by comparison, wavering as though she was about to cry. His mother had never been feeble. Stan's behaviour had worn her down. Ruari tried to tell himself that he hadn't made it worse with his signing for a club thirty miles away but it was right. He had altered the delicate balance of power somehow in the house.

They began to argue. Usually it died down, Stan wasn't much good for argument when he had been at the pub so late, his voice was slurred and he had difficulty in getting his words out, but his voice was getting louder and louder.

Ruari slid out of bed and pulled on his jeans, he wasn't wearing any clothes, he hadn't had any pyjamas for years and had got used to sleeping in nothing but his pants even when it was cold, things like jeans and sweaters were much more important, and football boots – but he didn't want to go down there feeling vulnerable.

He didn't try to disguise the sound of his footsteps as he went down the stairs but his feet were bare so the carpet muffled the noise. Maybe they would be too caught up in what they were saying to notice but when he was low enough to see into the room Stan was glaring at him.

Stan, Ruari thought, but he had already known, was drunk. His face was shiny, beefy with beer. Had he stopped loving the woman who was standing with her back to Ruari and her head down? Ruari shook his head to alter these thoughts but they wouldn't go away. He wished he didn't know so much, understand how people felt. He didn't want to understand how Stan felt, only his mother.

She heard or at least sensed his presence. She turned around and in that moment, her face wet with tears and her eyes full of foreboding, Ruari couldn't understand how anybody could not love her. She had given everything of herself to them.

She had been beautiful once, he could remember when he had been very little, now her face was lined, she was too skinny, her bones showed everywhere, there were great bags under her eyes which nothing could lessen; she was ill-dressed and her hair was going grey. How could life do this to his lovely Mam?

'Go back to bed, Ruari,' she said.

Always she put everybody before herself. Women did that. How could men not love them for it?

'Aye, gan on, lad,' Stan said with a touch of nasty humour, 'listen to yer ma.'

'Who could sleep with all that noise?' Ruari said.

'We'll keep quiet,' his mother said.

'This is all your fault,' Stan said, 'if you'd made your mind up to sign for North End this could all have been avoided.'

'They didn't offer enough money,' Ruari said for perhaps the fifteenth time.

'What on earth were you thinking about? Did you think I would get a job in bloody Teeshaven?'

Ruari wanted to say that Stan never kept a job for more than a few weeks so it wouldn't matter anyroad.

'No, I thought I'd go on me own,' he said. 'They've said they'll find digs for me.'

'Mr High and Mighty,' Stan sneered. 'Not thinking about your family. Maddison offered me good money if you signed. Did you not think about that?'

'It would all have gone down your throat, you and the Black Lion are like that,' Ruari said, crossing his fingers to indicate closeness.

'Ruari,' his mam said, shocked even though it was the truth, Ruari thought. It mustn't be said, the truth could never be uttered, it hung between them all and he thought that made it worse somehow.

'You never let me be a dad to you,' Stan said.

'Oh, give over,' Ruari said, losing patience. Sober, Stan would not have said such a thing.

'You didn't. You never liked me. You went on and on even when you were a little lad about your dad. You didn't even know yer dad, how could you have remembered him? You were nobbut a bairn when he died. It was her.' He jerked his head at Ruari's mother. 'She filled yer head full of him. She didn't tell yer that three months after yer dad died down that bloody pit she had it off with me.'

His mother didn't even defend herself. Ruari thought of her, alone, grief-stricken, wanting to cling to the first person who offered, thinking she could bring back his dad with another man.

'Please don't talk about it,' was all his mother said.

'What for?' Stan said. 'I never stood a chance. Things would have been different around here if anybody had really cared about me. She never even gave me a bairn of my own. Do you know what that feels like?'

The trouble was, Ruari thought, like most other things, that there was some truth to it, just enough to make him feel guilty and wrong about everything. He wanted to say to Stan that he had made a mistake, that he should have gone with North End, that it would have stopped all this but it was too late now. This was all his fault and there was nothing he could do. He couldn't sign for North End, he couldn't make himself do it, there was something about it which was not and never would be right.

'I'm going,' Stan said and he even had sufficient grace to look ashamed and that was worse than if he had cursed and blinded and been hateful.

Going where? was Ruari's second thought. Where could he possibly be going at this time of night?

'It's dark,' Ruari said stupidly.

'Aye,' Stan said, 'I know,' and even more stupidly, Ruari wished he wouldn't go, wished as no doubt Stan also wished that he was a better man because he had to live with the person that he wasn't.

Ruari had liked Stan, had even wanted him to replace his dad. Ruari knew that in his mind he had glorified the man his dad was, that no man could replace the golden image in his head which his dad had never been, that no man had ever been.

Poor Stan, he had been on a hiding to nowhere right from the start, Ruari thought sadly. Stan had been the cavalry coming over the hill for his mam after his dad had died and his mam had been so broken up. Stan had rescued Ruari and his mother from loneliness and from one another and it had been so brave of him, Ruari thought. Now it was over. It didn't matter what anybody said or did.

'I've got somebody else,' Stan said, a bitter kind of pride in his voice.

Ruari was shocked to think that now he had found a reason to despise Stan and it was a release from love.

'Oh aye?' Ruari said.

His mother put a hand over her mouth so that she would not cry out, so that she would not offend the neighbours. Ruari wanted to hit Stan.

'You came between your mother and me,' Stan said.

'I never did.' Ruari's voice was unsteady because he felt guilt slay him.

'You did,' Stan said, 'right from the start, you never gave me a chance, it was always your mam and you against me. I never felt welcome here, never felt at home. I was never good enough for you. You always made me feel pushed out and second best.'

'How in the hell could it have been my fault?'

Stan didn't reply.

'And you've got another woman?' Ruari's mam said as though she couldn't believe it.

'Aye, I have.'

She stared but only for a second or two.

'Well, then, you'd better go.'

Stan began to move towards the door.

'No,' she said but it was a reflex action and she put both hands up to her face and then she turned away. Her back was so narrow, stooped, defeated, Ruari thought.

Stan seemed to pause but it was only for a second and it was as if he had willed Ruari downstairs, deliberately provoked a scene so that he would be able to leave. Ruari's mam didn't even look up, didn't say anything, didn't attempt to stop him or follow him or even cry.

She had been left before and even though the circumstances were different the result, Ruari could not help thinking, and it made him feel sick, was the same. She had seen this before, must be getting used to the brutality of such things by now if you ever got used to it which he doubted and maybe he was too because all he did was stand there while Stan walked out.

Stan didn't take anything but Ruari knew he wouldn't be back. There was something so final and yet so vulnerable about his leaving.

His hands shook when he opened the door but he didn't turn around.

There would be no funeral, no gravestone this time. Stan was disappointed not only that Ruari would not be playing for the local team but also because in a way Ruari had made him feel small over the business of signing or rather not signing. It had not just been the money, Stan had thought of himself as Ruari's father, had been happy to make the decision for him, maybe was even ready to be proud of him. Ruari had humiliated him in front of Harry and also in front of his mother and things had not been the same since and never would be again.

When Stan had gone Ruari had to remember that he was seventeen and could not cry. He was not entitled to but nothing could lift from him the terrible weight of what he had done.

'You mustn't think this is because of you,' his mother said.

'But it is. If I'd signed for North End none of this would have happened.'

'Oh, I think it might,' she said, smiling in spite of herself. 'I think all he needed was a good excuse. Sooner or later one of us would have given it to him. Don't blame yourself, Ruari, it was really nothing to do with you.'

Ruari tried to remember, when he went back to bed, what his mother had said but there was a nasty worm in his conscience which would not absolve him of guilt.

Ruari tried to talk his mother into going with him to Teeshaven but she refused.

'I don't need you to look after me, I never said I would come with you and you certainly don't need looking after, what you need is to get away.'

If she wouldn't come with him he couldn't go, his conscience wouldn't let him.

He started to think he would never get out of there, that he would end up going and begging that bastard Harry Philips to take him on after all that had happened because he wouldn't be able to go to Teeshaven or anywhere else and he would have to try and break his contract with them. He didn't know how people went about things like that.

'Me friends are here, Ruari, and it might not look much but I like this house. I don't want to move anywhere.' When he didn't say anything she said, 'If you stay here you'll never get a chance like this again and you've wanted it all your life, worked for it always. You must go, I want you to. It would waste everything if you backed out now.'

'I'll send you money, then.'

'I'll manage,' she said.

# Eight

It was not the nausea or even when she threw up or again when she fainted that made Jenna think she was pregnant. Somehow she knew. She felt as though her whole body was standing on some kind of cliff edge, that something was happening and everything had changed.

She tried to ignore it at first. And she knew why. Because if she was pregnant the baby was not Ruari's, it was Paul Maddison's, and she could not consider the possibility. She and Ruari always used something, they never took risks and she hadn't seen him at the right time. She and Paul had just done it, nobody had thought, nobody had done anything about it. She was pregnant and it had to be Paul's.

The shock stayed with her for days. She got to the point where she could not think about anything else, it took up all her time, all the space in her brain. She could not believe it. She could not believe she had done anything quite so stupid but in a way she knew why she had done it.

Glamour. The worst word in the language but that was why. She had never had anything like that in her life, never felt expensive fabrics against her skin or champagne on her tongue. She had never driven in a sports car and known how the wind rushes past. Was it wrong to want such things? She was sure it was and now she was paying the price for what she had done but why did it have to be so expensive?

She had betrayed Ruari and she had felt awful but now . . . now she did not know what to do. She had nobody she could tell.

Jenna had not expected Ruari to be waiting when she got back from work that late August evening. He looked wrong outside her new house, as though he had no place there and he was standing awkwardly as though the very stones upset him.

Jenna's face felt stiff. She attempted a smile.

'Ruari, how are you?' she said.

'I'm leaving.'

'Leaving?' Jenna stared at him. They stood there for a long time while the words sunk into the very pavement, she thought.

'Aye. I've been offered a job like.'

'A job? What sort of a job?'

Ruari looked as awkward as any ordinary lad at that second, she thought. In fact it was worse than that, he was embarrassed.

'Working, in Teeshaven.'

'What kind of job could you get there? Is it another shipyard? Can you move like that?'

'I've signed a contract for two years with the football club.'

Jenna stared at him.

'Are you serious?'

'They've taken me on. It might not come to anything of course but I'll work and maybe it will.'

Jenna was stunned. He was leaving not just his job and his house but the town. How on earth had this happened? How had things gone so badly wrong?

'What about your mam?'

'She won't come.'

Suddenly Ruari looked older. He stood up straight. He was six foot tall by now.

'They must think you're going to do well,' Jenna said.

'It's the only chance I've got.'

'Didn't Mr Maddison offer? Then you wouldn't have to go anywhere.'

'Aye, he offered,' Ruari was all awkwardness again, 'but it wasn't enough. The others offered more. Will you come with me, Jenna?'

'Me?'

'We'll manage. You can get a job and eventually we could get a house and . . . get married and . . . you know.'

His face was almost but not quite shining, he was so excited, so pleased, to have within his grasp something he had worked so hard for so long to achieve. He could offer her a life which any girl around here would have fallen on gladly, an escape. Who got that?

She didn't know what to say. The whole world was falling apart and she knew that for him to offer to take her when she had gone with Paul Maddison was a long way beyond what any lad around there would have done, it was not just big of him, it was monumental.

'But . . .'

'I don't care what happened, if it doesn't matter to you then it doesn't matter to me either. I can't believe you care for him like you cared for me. We can get past it.'

Jenna didn't know what to say. She wanted to cry, she ached to, she wished more than she had ever wished anything in her life that she had not got into Paul Maddison's car, that she had not ruined everything. She tried to say something which would make sense to him.

'Most lads don't make it,' she said.

'I know,' he said, 'it might all come to nowt.'

He looked past her as though he could see the shining future he had planned and made possible and then he looked straight at her, waiting for her answer, waiting for her to say that she wanted to be part of the dream.

There was silence for a while and then he said, 'Come with me, Jenna. Give me another shot at things, give yourself another chance. We can make a go of it, I know we can.'

'I cannot,' she said.

He was silent and then he said, 'I love you, Jenna, come with me, please.'

She knew how much it cost him to say it.

'I cannot,' she said again.

He didn't believe her, she could see, not even then but the shining in his eyes was beginning to dim, he was starting to think that his dream could shatter.

'Why not?' he said.

Jenna knew she owed him the explanation only she couldn't tell him why she had done it. She didn't know, didn't remember why, just that she had had too much champagne. Oh, you couldn't blame the drink, that was what men did, they blamed something else so they didn't have to take the responsibility.

It had not been the drink, it had been other things, it had been the idea of a better time, of some vague notion of the future which had to do with fun. Not even glamour or excitement, just fun, something better, some time when you didn't have to think about every penny you spent and how you could not afford it.

His dream had taken too long to come true, that was the problem and she had become impatient, had ceased to believe in it. She had spent too many nights in the back bedroom at her mother's house and too many days bored in the gloom of the drapery department of the Store, its brown walls and brown counters and fat middle-aged women coming in to buy corsets to contain their overflowing flesh had seen off the odd time that anything pretty had come into the Store.

Even the cheap things she could afford to buy could not fill the emptiness in her. She felt stupidly, like the nuttery at Paul's house, that everything good in her life had long since been torn away and replaced with tinsel.

And the back lane had eaten away at her trust in Ruari, more than anything in the world she had to get somehow beyond the back lane in her mind which she never really had done in spite of moving and maybe there was a part of her that had known Paul Maddison could do that for her.

If she were to be with him there would be no more back lanes ever. She would not escape just as far as Wesley Road but much, much further. She had not known until that moment how much she wanted to get away and if she had waited Ruari would have done that for her but somehow she had not been able to wait. She had settled for something far short of what she had wanted, like the girl who took the cheap engagement ring because it was offered now rather than waiting for the diamond she might get later when things were better, and there had been a part of her which had never believed that things would ever get better, that she and Ruari would go on and on in the grinding every day of the dark little houses until they died. She had panicked. She had learned in life that there was no point in waiting for what would never happen and that learning was costing her so dearly now.

'Oh, Ruari, I'm sorry.'

'Sorry?' He looked so hard, so accusingly at her.

'You shouldn't have assumed—'

'I didn't assume anything.' He was beginning to sound a little desperate, his words ran into one another at speed as though the more of them he uttered the more he could impress upon her that they had to get away. 'We . . . we're a pair, you and me, we belong together, you know we do. What has it all been about otherwise? I can't do it without you, Jenna. I'm not saying we'll ever be rich but it would be a chance of a good life.'

'I cannot,' she said. It was the third time she had said it, so it was almost like a chant now, the only thing protecting her, like in church when the more you prayed the better you felt, only she didn't.

His gaze finally wavered and she saw the defeated look come across his face though he fought with it. Ruari had always been a fighter.

'Why not? Tell me why you can't.'

And that was when Jenna thought she owed him some kind of explanation so that he would not go on hoping.

'I love Paul Maddison,' she said.

'You love him?' He couldn't accept that and why should he, he had always come first with her but now she had to make him believe it, it was the only thing left she could do for Ruari.

'Yes,' she said clearly, 'I do.' Like you said 'I do' in church when you were getting married. 'He can give me everything I want.'

He stared at her.

'What is it that you want?' he said.

And she couldn't remember, that was the stupid part, she didn't really care about Spanish holidays and gold taps and how many cars you could get on the drive and where your clothes came from, it was just sticking plaster for the wound and it wouldn't hold but it was too late now, she could never have Ruari and he would go away and she would be left.

He had so little conceit that after the first seconds of disbelief he gave up, she could see it. As though he had never thought he could have somebody like her, that it was a dream too far, that somebody was bound to break it, it was like those dreams you had just before waking, near the surface, with the sunshine butterscotch in the early morning, after the horrors of the night and suddenly you were relieved and you just knew everything was going to be all right only this time there was no relief from it. The dream tore in the half truth of what she said. It broke, she heard it somehow.

He knew that Paul Maddison could have her, why should he not, he had everything else. That was it, she could see it in Ruari's eyes. He didn't try any more. She had convinced him that she didn't want him. He didn't look at her. He walked away and she couldn't bear to watch him.

'Who offered more?' Sorrel Maddison had said.

'Teeshaven.'

Sorrel swore.

'The bastards,' he said. 'They can't afford it. What the hell are they playing at? They're bottom of the division, they have nothing but crap players. What is it, a last-ditch attempt? Hodgkin's losing his mind.'

'Gallacher'll never make it,' Harry said, 'he's just another stupid Geordie lad. He's not that good, I've seen him play. We've lost nothing. I heard Stan Robson left because of what happened.'

'Why couldn't he be loyal?' Sorrel said. 'How can a young lad like that up sticks? He's mad. And to think I tried to help him.'

And then it occurred to Sorrel that if Ruari Gallacher was really leaving he might take the girl with him and once rid of the lass Paul might meet somebody classy, somebody who could talk properly and knew which knife and fork to use when she sat down to dinner with folk like them. He had watched Jenna hesitate and tried not to despise her because it was something he had had to learn but he wanted for his son a girl who knew automatically such things. Was it such a lot to ask? Yes, it would be worth the sacrifice of a not terribly good footballer to get rid of the girl his son thought he was in love with. Sorrel was almost satisfied.

# Nine

Jenna went on seeing Paul and it was as though her instincts propelled her towards him. The burden of not telling anybody about the baby was starting to get to her and although they had not so much as kissed again she was panicking. He would bring her home from his house and leave her there and wave and smile and he seemed quite happy about it. One night in the early autumn when he had gone she turned to walk up the stairs and had only got two steps up when her mother's voice, strained somehow, said from the hall, 'Are you all right, Jenna?'

She stopped, about to say that she was fine, and then she heard the worried note in her mother's voice. Her mother didn't often show concern, Jenna had thought her mother was not sensitive at all to how she felt, caught up in her husband and her home and Jenna knew that her mother had been pleased she and Paul were going out together, even proud that her daughter knew the son of the football-club owner, the businessman who was so important, and Jenna had been pleased but her mother had realized something was wrong and the tears threatened.

'Is there something the matter?'

She did not realize she had not answered and her mother 'had enquired again.

'It's not that other lad, is it?'

Jenna turned. She felt really sick not just at her mother mentioning Ruari but as though he ought not to matter, as though she could not remember his name. It was almost as though Ruari had died, and he might as well have done, Jenna thought, because the chances were she would never see him again.

He had gone, she didn't know exactly when, and her gaze had searched the streets for him day after day for fear that he should leave because once he was gone everything was over in a different way than it had been and then her father had come back from work one day with the news that Ruari had left and since then Jenna had had to stop herself from running to Teeshaven to him, searching the streets and finding wherever he was lodging no matter how long it took and pleading with him to take her with him. She knew now that she couldn't go to him or after him. She would have to stay here and face the consequences of what she had done. She knew that she deserved it.

'No, it's nothing to do with him.'

'You were so very keen on him all that time that I did wonder . . . You are going to go on seeing Paul?'

This was the point, her mother was worried that the dream would not come true, that Jenna would not go on seeing a boy who was rich. Her mother, Jenna could have laughed, thought that if you had money things were easier, Jenna was beginning to realize that it set up a whole new kind of problem, it certainly had for her.

If money was not the root of all evil, then the love of it, the desire of it, certainly had been. Jenna broke down and then she sat down on the stairs. Her mother stood there at the bottom like it was something out of a film and could not possibly have anything to do with her.

'Has he finished with you?' she said faintly as though the knowledge would be too much to bear.

Jenna said nothing, she sat there, wondering how on earth she was going to tell her mother.

'I'm expecting,' she said.

She did not know how she had got the words out, she had lain awake night after night trying to think of how to coat the pill, of how to tell her mother so that something so hard to swallow would not sound quite so bad. She felt relief that she had said it, even that baldly.

Her mother stood there for so long that Jenna thought maybe she hadn't heard her except that her mother's face drained of colour and her eyes were fixed on Jenna's face as though the ceiling had just fallen in.

'You what?' she said.

'I'm having a baby.'

For a few moments it was as though her mother could not believe such luck, as though she would deny it or run into her newly decorated bedroom and shut the door and shut out Jenna and what was happening.

'Oh God, Jenna, you stupid girl,' her mother said in a breathy voice quite unlike her own. 'And he's gone. Well, he'll have to come back here now and you'll have to get married.'

Jenna sat up slightly. Her mother actually thought that the baby was Ruari's even though they had not seen one another all summer.

Her mother really didn't know anything about her life, was not interested, her mother was only interested in illusions, the idea of her daughter marrying above her socially. Perhaps it was the only thing her mother had left to dream about, she had married a man who worked in a shop, she had had only one child, and her sole triumph was this awful house in a terraced street, no wonder she had hoped for better, felt short changed, her life was so dull.

'No,' she said, 'it's Paul's.'

Her mother stood there as though she would never move again. Then she straightened and her lips sounded stiff as though she could not get out the next thing she said.

'Are you telling me you went with two lads at once?'

Her mother made it sound as though they were having an orgy, the kind of threesome you read about in dirty stories.

'I did nothing of the kind,' she said, 'and anyway . . .' She had been about to tell her mother that Ruari always used protection, that he was careful, that was Ruari, cautious. He had not been cautious about his career. Why had he been so careful with her? If he hadn't been she might have been with him now, fat-bellied and full of hope for the future, instead of which . . . Instead of which what?

She didn't know. His career, his bloody beloved football, it had meant more to him than she had and then she thought, that was not fair. He had asked her, begged her to go with him. I love him, she thought, I should have said yes, I should have deceived him and told him it was his and gone anyway. What am I doing still here? She wanted to get up and run out of the door and down the street after him, screaming his name. She had thrown everything away and she didn't seem able to retrieve it.

'It wasn't like that,' she said. 'It was just the once with Paul.'

And her mother was pleased. Jenna felt bitterly amused. Her mother could believe that she was not a slut and that was important, that perhaps even she had never gone with Ruari, that this was just a single slip and although it was shameful they would get through. Her mother, Jenna thought, did not live in the real world.

Jenna should have left it there, she knew but she couldn't.

'I loved Ruari Gallacher,' she said.

'So how do you know it's not his? Is this just wishful thinking, Jenna?'

Why did her mother not understand? She didn't love Paul Maddison, she would never love him, she thought his dad was a braggart and his mam was the kind of woman who knew nothing but how to spend money. And she had gone with Paul, like any fool.

'No, it isn't,' she said, 'me and Ruari had fallen out. It's nothing to do with him.'

Her mother sighed. 'Why do things always happen to us? I know women who have lots of children and things like this don't happen.'

'You're exaggerating,' Jenna said, drying her tears with the back of her hand.

'Have you told Paul?'

Jenna shook her head.

'You have to get married.'

Jenna couldn't go on. Her mother was wrong, she didn't know what Paul would do or say. It was such a disgrace to be pregnant when you weren't married. She felt so guilty. Besides, her mother hadn't met Sorrel Maddison.

If he decided there was no way Paul would marry her then there would be no marriage. And thinking about fathers brought her uncomfortably to her own. How would she even tell her father?

He would never think the same about her again and if Paul refused to acknowledge the baby as his she would be an unmarried mother. Her mother, and maybe even her father, would never recover from it. She imagined herself pushing a pram down the street and everybody talking about her, the whispers. She would have no life, she would be almost hidden away, there would be no future of any kind.

'I have to go and talk to Paul,' she said. 'There's no point in putting it off any longer.'

Her mother seemed pleased about this and then she looked at Jenna.

'However will we tell your father?' she said. 'He'll be so disappointed.'

He would wish she had done better, behaved better. He would never get over it, Jenna thought. Being the manager at the Store everybody saw him every day and he would have to face the whole community.

'We won't tell him,' her mother said. 'We won't say anything at all.'

# Ten

Teeshaven was not a top club any more though it was still in the First Division but its reputation had suffered, it had almost been relegated to the Second Division at the end of last season. Ruari hadn't thought about it or cared though he knew the position of every club in the First Division, it was the money that had got him, he thought cynically now, and he was slightly uncomfortable about it because Teeshaven was not doing well because it had bought the wrong players. Was he another bad buy?

They had found digs for him, a house in the heart of the town where three other relative newcomers were housed so he couldn't make a fuss over it but Ruari thought he had died and gone to hell. He had thought his mother's house was poor but it was poor and clean. His landlady, Mrs Johnson, was a slut.

She sat in her front room and smoked all day and ate cake, she was so fat that it hung in layers from her middle-aged body and even though her clothes were the kind of tent which covered up such things nobody could be deceived. She wore her hair up possibly because she didn't have to wash it that way, she wore a lot of make-up which was orange. She watched television most of the time, the rest of it she spent talking to her neighbours, hanging over the back gate to catch anyone who would spend the time of day.

The house was not exactly dirty, it was grubby, that was the word, the sheets on the beds were creased and worn, the mattresses were lumpy, dead spiders and flies sat in cobwebs above his bed and he didn't think the carpet under his bed — if he lost anything and got down on the floor he tried not to look — had ever been hoovered. The towels were thin and grey and the bathroom was cold and unfriendly, even in summer it never dried out and everything above eye level was lined with mould.

There was no fire in the back room where he would have sat had he ever sat in the house, which he tried not to. Meals were served in there, it smelled of limp cabbage and that was another thing. He was not used to bad food. Mrs Johnson couldn't cook. Everything tasted and smelled the same and it was all cheap.

There was margarine for your bread in the morning and jam so awful it had no fruit in it. The tea was watery and the milk was generally off so that he stopped using it. At night the meat on his plate was grey and anonymous and the vegetables were cooked to wilting. The potatoes were dark and hard and the crumbles that were pudding were not well enough done so that they were soggy and he couldn't tell what the fruit was.

His room was tiny and boasted no wardrobe. All there was for his clothes was a set of shelves open on the wall and sometimes he found mouse droppings on them. He told Mrs Johnson but it was obvious she did nothing so after that he kept most of his clothes in his suitcase beside the window and ignored what he thought was the sound of rodent scufflings in the night.

His window looked out over street after street and it was a noisy area. When it was windy his window rattled because it didn't fit properly and when the autumn set in the wind howled through his bedroom so that the curtains moved. Nightly people got drunk in the pub across the street and spilled out on to the pavement when it was late, shouting and swearing and often fighting. Windows got broken and sometimes the police arrived and in the mornings the pavements were covered in vomit and people had pissed up against the corner walls so that it stank.

Even so he could not be entirely unhappy. He didn't have to go to work any more and although he had not hated it, being able to be in the football world and to be paid to do it was enough. And having to do nothing but play it made a difference to his game, he could see right from the start.

He was full of energy now that he had no work to do, did not tire in training no matter how much was demanded of him and the coach started to praise him and he soon knew that he was the sort of person who did better on praise than on criticism.

There were several areas where Teeshaven was not as good as North End. Sorrel Maddison might have been an awkward bastard, Ruari thought, but he was a rich awkward bastard and he had put a lot of money into North End, Ruari had heard the stories about the wonderful dressing rooms and the training facilities.

Here they did not seem to have very much money and it meant that there were no particular training facilities and the facilities such as showers were basic. You had to take your own soap, even your own towel, and the kit was for everybody, chucked in the middle of the room in a heap so you just picked up what you could.

The pitch itself was reasonably well looked after but the rest of the place was near to falling down, the gates, the fences, the walls, and he soon saw why. There was no money. They had a lot of players who had been good but were now too old and they could not afford to buy experienced players so he could see right from the start that a lot depended on him.

The young players they did have were very young indeed and it showed. The club had taken a huge risk paying so much for him that he lay in his gritty bed at night and wondered whether they might not have made a mistake. The chairman and directors of the club were businessmen, not like Sorrel Maddison, they were not slick bastards, just ordinary people like solicitors and accountants, and while people like that made more money than a lot did it was not the kind of money which made for a rich football club.

He did not miss his home town though he did miss his mother and worry about how she was managing. From the start he sent her money and although she protested he insisted. He learned not to miss Jenna. A girl who did not want you was not somebody you wanted to think about so he shut her from his mind.

Once the football season started up and training began he got to know some of the other players, in particular the goalkeeper for the first team, Jack Eliot, who was from Carlisle.

He had moved here with his family when he was a little kid but he still retained a thick Cumbrian accent which comforted Ruari. Jack was big and solid and had been playing for the first team for two years and he had a reputation as a good goalie. He was determined that things would be better and helped Ruari by showing him around the grounds and introducing him to the other players. He asked Ruari to his home which Ruari thought was very good of him.

They lived in a pretty semi-detached house and he had a wife and two little girls, one three, one just a year old. His dad and mam lived nearby. They had come down here to work in the dockyards and his mam obviously missed Cumbria and talked longingly about how beautiful the Solway looked with the sun on it in the summer evenings. Ruari found himself envying Jack who appeared to have everything and made Ruari imagine how things would have been if Jenna had come with him. Maybe in time they would have had

children and his mother could have moved there and . . . the idea
faded. His mother would never have moved and Jenna was in love
with someone else.

On Fridays nobody was allowed to go out, it was the rule, Saturdays
the footballers went out together after the match. It wasn't Ruari's
problem, as he couldn't drink and didn't anyway, and he wasn't
playing for the first team. He would have to wait for his chance. In
the meanwhile he trained hard and watched and listened and did
what he was told and prayed to get into the reserves so that he
would at least be there at the matches and might be asked to play,
it was every reserve's dream.

Thinking about it, this was not what he had envisaged and he
could see now that lots of the apprentices had been around since
they were fifteen and some of them thought he was old for starting
and some of them resented his being there at all, especially when
he was almost but not quite local, the teams close to one another
hated rivals.

They didn't talk to him but huddled in little groups when he
was around, though it could have all been in his mind. He thought
they didn't like his accent and would pretend they didn't understand him and he had the feeling that they imitated him when he
was not there. They didn't like him coming in like this and being
better than they were – and he was, it was not just wishful thinking,
he could outplay them all, it soon became obvious. At first he was
embarrassed and then he was just pleased and within months of
getting there he could even outrun and outmanoeuvre some of the
top players.

Under the coaching he began to shine at every session and people
began to notice him. He had been haunted that he might get here
and not be good enough, show up badly in front of other profes-
sionals, but he hardly dared to think that his dream might come
true except that he did, there was a slow-burning excitement about
him, there was a little bit of him which was convinced he would
fulfil the ambitions he had set himself and make his mother proud
of him and also that he would be able to show North End and
Jenna Duncan what they had missed.

He could see that a great many lads never got a game, never
got any further, didn't make it as far as the first team or even into
the reserves, and his nightmares were full of his failure. What would
he do if he didn't make it? Almost everybody, he realized now,

didn't make it. He would have to go back and find some kind of job.

He decided then that he wouldn't go back, no matter what happened. He promised himself that he would be as good as he could, train as hard as he could, and hope for a match. The more matches he played the more he would be paid and then his mam could give up her job as a cleaner and he could afford to keep her even at a distance. He had to succeed here.

# Eleven

Paul looked surprised to see Jenna.

'You said you were busy. You're always saying you're busy, though what you have to be busy about I don't know.' His voice was a degree or so above freezing because he felt neglected, he had begun to want to see her often and it made her hope that what she had to tell him would not be badly received, she could only pray.

'Could I talk to you?'

He drew her into the sitting room. Sitting room. Even drawing room wouldn't have covered it, Jenna thought. It was massive and over the eight hundred years that it had been there it must have seen a lot of domestic drama. It was hushed somehow and yet she felt comfortable as though you couldn't surprise it at all, it had seen everything.

Jenna tried to ignore the room. Somehow this house was all caught up in her behaviour towards Ruari, she felt like a traitor, she had cared that the house was beautiful and it seemed so stupid now, so shallow, so pathetic, she hated herself. But there was no way round this, she might not tell her dad but she had to tell Paul so she looked straight at him and took a deep breath like a swimmer and then she plunged.

'Paul, I don't know how else to say this. We're having a baby, I know that it was only once and I know that it shouldn't have happened and I know you probably think it's got nothing to do with you, but I thought I should tell you. It seemed fair.' She looked up at him.

Paul frowned. He went on frowning for quite a long time so that Jenna grew impatient but she couldn't say anything. Then he looked uncomfortable.

'A baby?' he said. 'Are you sure?'

'Yes, I'm certain.'

'I thought there was something the matter, all these weeks you've behaved like I was a leper and then recently you just seemed plain weird.'

She said nothing. Paul looked almost apologetic.

'Jenna, you let me have you once and it was weeks and weeks ago—'

'I know that—'

'So you'll excuse me if I'm being blunt but Ruari bloody Gallacher must have had you hundreds of times. There's no point in you pretending you were a virgin when I had you because I know damned fine that you weren't—'

'I never said I was!' Jenna declared, stung.

'Now he's not here and I am so I get the blame. Does that seem fair to you?'

'I know it seems unlikely but . . . it wasn't like that with Ruari.'

'It wasn't like what?' Paul said, staring white-faced at her. 'Don't tell me you didn't do it with him because I know you did and you and him have probably been going at it for years.'

'We always used something.'

'And it couldn't have gone wrong?'

'It isn't that.' Jenna couldn't believe he thought she was lying. 'I didn't go with him at the same time. We fell out, at least . . .' She didn't like to say that she had been teaching Ruari a lesson, that he couldn't take her for granted, that she had felt she should come first, that for weeks and weeks they hadn't touched one another. 'Obviously I didn't go with him.'

'It isn't obvious to me,' Paul said. 'The very idea that you went with both of us doesn't bear thinking about but I put up with knowing you'd been with him. I didn't think you were going with us both but now . . . now I think you must've done, you're just that sort of girl.'

Jenna was suddenly very cold.

'It is your baby, Paul, it really is.'

'You think I'm an idiot,' Paul said and he was angry, she could see, and she could hardly blame him for that.

'No—'

'Yes, you do. You went with me because I'm rich, you didn't think about the fact that you were already going with somebody else, which shows what a cheap little turn you are—'

'That's not true! How can you say something so horrible?'

Jenna could feel anger and it was strange because she hadn't felt entitled to anger, she felt guilt, she felt ashamed, so where was the anger coming from in Paul's rich, posh bloody house where his father had so little taste that he had destroyed everything that was good about the place, taken out the lovely old things, cut down the nut trees and tarmacked the old-fashioned garden which had the herbs and lavender? She hated Sorrel Maddison, she really did.

'So why did you, then?'

'I don't know. I was fed up.'

'Oh, fed up,' Paul said. 'Well, in that case we won't worry. You were fed up with Ruari Gallacher so you went with me. You had nothing better to do, after all.'

She could hear the anger too in his voice and she wished she could have handled this better, God knew she had rehearsed it often enough, she wasn't getting it right and it made her panic. She couldn't think what to say and then he goaded her.

'Go on, tell me you love me,' he dared her.

Jenna couldn't say it. It wasn't true, it never would be true. She stood there in the enormous room which had no books, no nice ornaments. The curtains were like something in a hotel, right from floor to ceiling and shiny like silk and so full it was almost indecent with those flash cord things in gold around the middle of them, in fact the whole bloody place looked like a hotel.

'I didn't go to Teeshaven with Ruari because of what I'd done—'

'Well, that's noble,' Paul said.

'Stop it!' she said. 'Just stop it!' and her words echoed around the room. She shouted so loudly, it seemed to her it must have gone back all the hundreds of years to when the house first had people living there. Rows were like that, they didn't disperse, all the awful things that were said, they stayed in places like that and haunted it and gave it what it was and once things were said they couldn't be unsaid and she didn't care, she didn't care at all. She had tried to be honest with him and it wasn't working.

'I'm having your baby and I'm trying to tell you about it and you have no right to say that I'm bad and a liar and that it isn't yours because it is and I wouldn't say it was otherwise. You can't get out of this by denying it, the baby's a fact and if you don't choose to believe it's yours that's your problem.'

'If you don't want it I'm sure we can get rid of it,' Paul said.

'Get rid of it?' She stared into his narrowed eyes and she thought how cruel he sounded, his mouth like a straight line. He didn't want her or the baby.

'Yes, that's what people do in this enlightened day and age. You don't have to have it, if you are pregnant.'

'What do you mean?'

'I think you just think you're on to a good thing and that because I'm who I am that you can get me to marry you. Well, you can't.

I never had any intention of getting married and if I did have any marital intentions it would be because I chose and not because a little slapper like you thinks she can blackmail me into it.'

'Paul—'

'Tell me you love me,' he said again, 'and make me believe it.'

She didn't move or speak.

'I don't want you here,' he said, 'get out.'

Jenna went.

Paul had always been afraid of his father though in a way, gazing at him now, he was not quite sure why. Outside of the house there were stories about him and Paul had heard a great many of them, about how his father and mother had run away from a slum where his father lived on the Tyne when he was fifteen and made money on the markets in Newcastle and gone into various kinds of business and been successful where more educated men had failed.

He was sitting alone when Paul came to him. It was, Paul knew, his favourite time of day. If he was coming back at all it would be early evening. Often he would eat and go back out again but mostly he didn't come back before one or two in the morning so this was in a sense his treat. He was perusing the newspaper, a whisky and soda on a small table beside him. The French windows were open to the sunshine of the evening. The evenings were cutting short. It wouldn't be long before autumn was here for real and the leaves turned.

As Paul hesitated in front of him Sorrel folded his newspaper, put it down and regarded his son from steady eyes.

'Now then,' he said, smiling, 'what is it?'

'I've got a bit of a problem,' Paul said, sitting down and trying to remain calm.

'Right.'

He looked surprised, as well he might, Paul thought. Most things were sorted out without Paul coming to him like this. Paul wished with all his might that this would have sorted itself out in a less complicated and undignified way. He couldn't see why it had to happen to him, how unlucky was that? He had considered ignoring it, he had told himself over and over it was nothing to do with him, that it was Jenna's problem, that Ruari Gallacher had done it. He could take that way out, there was nothing Jenna could do, but the more he thought about it the less happy he was.

Paul couldn't think what to say. Time went by. He didn't want the open look on his father's face to die away and be replaced by anger. His father was scary when he was angry and Paul didn't know how to look at him, not because he was scared but because he knew that his father was disappointed in him, had wanted him to do something splendid with his life and so far he had done nothing but lounge about all summer. His father, to be fair, had said nothing so that Paul felt guilty and he was about to make it worse.

'If you don't tell me I can't help you,' Sorrel said.

'It doesn't have to be a problem. At least I don't think so but . . . I just had the feeling that if I didn't tell you, you might find out and . . .' he tried hard to smile into his father's set look, 'you wouldn't be very pleased with me.'

Paul remembered in detail the other times when his father hadn't been pleased with him. To be fair his father had never hit him, not like a lot of fathers, not like the majority, and Paul thought that was strange. His father had never even shouted at him, but Sorrel had such presence that he didn't need to. Paul knew too much about him for Sorrel ever to need to do or say anything.

His father had lived with violence. It was never spoken of but it was there. He had vague memories of being somehow in the street when something had gone wrong, somebody tried to take his mother's bag and his father had knocked the man to the ground, so efficiently that it had been a shock.

His father knew of such things and had, during the last few years, managed to keep them from his home and presumably from his life but Paul was afraid of the very air his father breathed when Sorrel was angry. He was unpredictable, that was it.

Sorrel waited and Paul reflected that his father very rarely lost his temper and that in a way it was his forbearance that people were afraid of because that forbearance held his temper at bay and only for so long, Paul had the feeling that men had gone beyond that forbearance in the past and paid dearly for it.

Paul shook his head. He couldn't say it.

'Come on, spit it out.' Sorrel's voice was softer.

He was so practised at these things. Paul was beginning to sweat and think of the house when he was a child resounding with the timbre of his father's voice, not at him and not at his mother, at other men in other rooms. Sorrel didn't look like a man who could be violent but Paul remembered him as a very young man, coming home bleeding, angry and resentful. He did not let people get away with things.

Paul sat there, wanting to cry like he hadn't for years. He was so embarrassed he could feel his face suddenly burn. He mustn't cry in front of his father, yet the water in his eyes stung so much that only shedding it would help. How had he managed such a mess? He felt more stupid than he had ever felt before.

'I'm not going to clip you round the lug, you know,' his father said, trying to smile. 'It can't be that bad.'

Paul vainly tried to smile, to ease the way, but to him now this man was not going to like what he had to say and his memory was providing him with the sounds of furniture smashing and loud voices and almost certainly cruel laughter.

'Look, Paul, anything you think you've done,' his father sat forward and his voice was gentle, 'whatever it is I've done worse myself and I'm not going to judge you, I'll try and help you.'

'I don't even know whether it's . . . whether it's anything to do with me.'

'It can't be so very terrible, then.'

Still Paul said nothing.

'The dinner's going to be ready if you don't hurry up.'

It was true, he could smell meat cooking even in here.

'Jenna's pregnant,' Paul said and he let go of his breath and sat back and waited for his father's temper to fill the room and make him want to be a hundred miles away.

Sorrel didn't say anything for so long that Paul began to think his father hadn't heard him but when he had the courage to look into his father's face, he had been right. The light had gone from his eyes. There was nothing but darkness and a kind of strange puzzlement.

'Jenna?'

'Yes. She came over to tell me.'

His father seemed completely taken aback.

'I thought she'd gone.'

'Gone?'

'Yes, with Gallacher. He has gone?'

'Yes, he's gone.'

'And so?'

'So.' Paul took a deep breath. 'She says the baby's mine.'

His father stared at him and then frowned.

'Does she now?' he said slowly and he looked as if he wanted to kill somebody. He sat back. Paul couldn't breathe at all now, he was so afraid.

'Right. I didn't realize your . . . relationship had got that far. You don't seem to me to be more than friends.'

His father was shrewd, Paul thought. That was exactly how it was.

'It was just once,' he said. 'We had too much champagne and . . .'

His father nodded.

'And Little Miss Duncan was as pure as the driven snow before you, was she?'

'No.'

'I didn't think so. She went with Gallacher, yes? They were very thick, isn't that the case?'

'Yes.'

'You know that lad's turned out to be something of a pain,' his father said shortly.

Nobody spoke after that. Paul didn't know how to go on or what to say to make things any better.

'So, is she a devious little cow?'

That was exactly it, Paul thought and then was obliged to be honest.

'I don't know. How do you tell?'

'He could be foisting it off on to you because he'd already decided to leave and didn't want the encumbrance of a woman who wants to marry him because she's pregnant. He has his way to make, his future to think about.' Sorrel sighed. 'I think the odds are that it's nothing to do with you.' He sounded comfortable with the notion, Paul thought.

'That's not what she says. She says she didn't go with him at that time, that it could only be mine.'

'It didn't occur to you that she was having you on or that now he's gone you're all that's left?'

'Of course it occurred to me,' Paul said, a trifle impatiently. He wasn't quite as stupid as his father thought.

'What have you said to her?'

'Nothing.' Paul couldn't look at his father.

'Have you said you'll marry her?'

'No, I told her I wouldn't, that it was nothing to do with me, and then she left.'

His father looked so relieved that Paul got up, he felt faint and needed some air. He went to the open doors and stood there and he felt sick.

'There's nothing more she can do,' Sorrel said. 'She can't force you to marry her and neither can her parents so you've got nothing to worry about. Why don't you just forget about it?'

'I don't know that I can.'

That was the trouble, Sorrel thought. The poor sod was in thrall to Little Miss Loose Knickers.

'Let me tell you something, Paul. You can have any woman you want, you can have more than one if you like, as long as you have plenty of money. They're simple creatures, you see. They're only any good in the kitchen or the bedroom—'

Paul gazed at the garden.

'I love her,' he said.

It was exactly the response Sorrel had waited for, had purposely evoked by his own words. At last he thought they were at the crux of the matter.

'You love her?'

'Yes.'

'How can you love a lass like that?'

'What do you mean?'

'She's a little scrubber from a pit row.'

'She's nothing of the kind.' Paul had turned around and was almost glaring, which was brave of him, Sorrel thought idly.

'But she doesn't love you?'

'She loves that bastard Ruari Gallacher. I've been trying for months to get someplace with her and I never did apart from that once and it was just because I got her drunk. I know it was stupid but it was the only way and if it was his she would have gone with him, I know she would.'

'What if he didn't want her?'

'He did. He never came near her after I went with her and the look on his face when he was around . . .'

'Maybe his instincts were better than yours.'

'I don't think so. I want her and I think . . . well, obviously, we have to get married, as soon as we can.'

Now they were getting to the heart of it, Sorrel thought. Paul, typically, wanted what he couldn't have, or what he thought he couldn't have. Maybe Jenna Duncan was clever and had played him and was ready for a second round with Paul since she had not got him to say that he would take her on.

'Have you considered other answers?'

'What?'

'You could get rid of it.'

'I don't really want her to have an abortion and she doesn't want it either and – and you can't. It would be . . . your grandchild, you couldn't want—'

'No, of course not,' Sorrel said smoothly, wishing Ruari Gallacher in hell.

'She says it was nothing to do with him.' Paul didn't seem able to get the words out without pain and he had read his father's mind which surprised Sorrel. 'She wouldn't lie to me and do you know why? Because she loves him. If it was his she'd have told him. She would even have gone after him.'

His father sighed.

'You have to consider this very carefully. There will always be girls who will try it on with you, who will know who you are and whose son you are and that you have money. Is that what this is? Because if it is then you want nothing to do with it. And if she doesn't love you . . .'

'I want her. I've wanted her since the minute I saw her,' Paul said.

'Aren't you going to shut the doors?' Faye said for maybe the fourth time. 'I don't want to put the lights on because the insects will come in but I want to read. Sorrel, are you listening?'

Sorrel was standing by the open doors beside the upstairs balcony. It was one of his favourite places. He loved the sound of the waves. He wished he was there now on the beach. Always there was another problem. He never got a day off, never a day free, he didn't suppose anybody ever did.

He was more disconcerted now than he had ever been. He was worried about Paul. Paul was in love with Jenna Duncan and whatever kind of awful lass she was he would not stop loving her.

He had never stopped loving Faye even though it was obvious that she didn't care any more about him, if she ever had which he doubted. He was lucky they were still in the same bedroom. She had long since insisted on single beds and he thought the worst way to spend the night was like this. What was the point in having somebody in the same room but not warm beside you? It was worse than having a room to yourself, lying listening to somebody sleeping, someone you had loved for so long and aware that you couldn't get into bed with them either for sex or for comfort.

All he could think of was the day they had bought the cottage in Tynedale, on the edge of a pretty stone village. It was the first thing they had bought, the first place he had taken her to after they were married, their first holiday, only it didn't belong to him then, he had bought it for her later, knowing how much the place meant to her. He could remember stopping the car at the bottom of the lane and walking up. She had slipped on the wet grass and he had caught her and they had laughed and he had kissed her.

The garden was overgrown and the wall which bordered it was falling down and he thought, That was the day I realized I would always love her, it was the worst feeling of my whole life because I knew she didn't love me and however many cottages I found for her and whatever I did to please her it wouldn't matter.

The cottage had tiny windows, two of them in the upper storey were rounded, so beautiful, and the stone was grey and square and regular and had been well put together. The cottage was high up a twisting narrow road which had no footpath and the houses clung to the sides of the hill as you ascended and it had a view of the village below and of the river ribbon silver in the bottom of the valley.

Beyond it the sheep huddled on the moorland where there was nothing but a few trees and the stone walls turned this way and that to accommodate the landscape and the cart tracks petered into nothing.

A lapwing rose up crying at them for fear they should disturb the nest. It came, dive-bombing them, unafraid or so afraid that it would do anything to distract them from what it had to lose, swooping over them endlessly and putting forth its pitiful cry until they had retreated sufficiently far so that it was not afraid of invasion.

He had lost everything he held dearest that day, in some obscure way she had found her freedom from him there and he had always hated the cottage from then on. Faye had not been able to understand why he never wanted to go there. He felt as though it belonged to her, it was full of things he didn't understand, open fires which she had to get going, a little pot-bellied stove which always went out when he touched it, books like *Moby Dick* which he found boring. There was no television, no telephone, it drove him mad, he felt out of control, he couldn't remember who he was.

The garden grew rhubarb and gooseberries, blackcurrants, great swathes of nettles and big purple buddleia bushes which the butterflies decorated in red and orange and black spots, wings fluttering as the summer progressed, and in late July the willowherb was three feet high on the roadsides and covered in dark pink flowers.

Every summer she would go there and cut him out of her life. She spent all the school holidays there until Paul objected when he was about fourteen and then she found him a friend to go with and that took care of that for another couple of years, she even wanted to go at Christmas when he wanted to fly away to somewhere warm. She could spend hours reading a book and ignoring him and more than anything in the world he hated being ignored. She made it so obvious she would much rather be alone.

She was rushed from there to hospital when she lost their second child. They had to send an ambulance down the blasted unmade rutted lane because she was too ill to go by car. He had begged of her to stay at home in the town but she wouldn't because the weather was fine at the cottage and she loved to sit by the fire and read.

I can see Paul about to make all the same mistakes that I made, he thought, and the only thing I can do is to stand around making what I hope are the right noises.

'Sorrel!' Faye sounded exasperated.

Sorrel drew back, turned around, closed the windows.

'You've been standing there ages not saying anything. What's the matter?' she said.

He hesitated. He didn't want to tell her, though she had a right to know.

'Paul thinks he got Jenna Duncan pregnant.'

'Oh no.' She put down the book she was holding and looked anxiously at him and his instinct was the same as always, he would have given anything to take that look away. 'The one who came to the house? She's not the kind of girl I wanted for him.'

'I wasn't going to tell you because I don't know what's happening. He hasn't exactly been frank about it and I didn't want you upset.'

'But they'll have to get married,' and then she read his face. 'No, you can't do that, you can't start insisting that he pretends it's nothing to do with him if he cares about her. This is his life.'

'That's why. Look at us.'

She stiffened, he felt her. He was sitting on her bed by now and wished he hadn't done so. He shifted a little.

'It was worse then. People felt obliged to get married,' Faye said. 'I suppose some still do. Does Paul feel like that about it?'

He wanted to say to her, 'Would you have married me otherwise?' but it was a pointless exercise because he knew that she wouldn't have and he thought if only he had bought Ruari Gallacher none of this would have happened. Jenna might not have gone with Paul and even though Paul cared for her Gallacher would have got in the way and everything would have been different. He had made a basic mistake. He couldn't tell Faye, she wouldn't understand.

'You have to stay out of it,' his wife said.

'He's going to spoil his life over it.'

'Yes, well, each of us does that in our own special way,' she said and that was when he got off the bed.

# Twelve

Paul couldn't rest. He had put forward all the hateful things he could think of about Jenna but it didn't help. The following day was Sunday. He stayed upstairs until mid morning. Then he ventured downstairs to find only his mother standing in the kitchen reading the *Sunday Express* and drinking tea.

'Where's Dad?'

'He had to go out, something went wrong. Are you all right?' She looked sympathetically at him. At that moment the back door opened and Sorrel came in.

'What was it?' Paul said.

'The betting shop at Easton, somebody broke into it. As though I would leave money in there on a Saturday night.'

Faye poured coffee and made toast and then she went upstairs and Sorrel opened the Sunday newspapers as he sat at the kitchen table.

Paul thought back to various Saturday nights when he was younger and his mother would count piles of notes on the kitchen table and they were broken into every few weeks over the weekends because people thought his father kept cash at home on Saturday nights that he had siphoned off so that the taxman would not get his hands on it. His father would buy jewellery for his mother with crisp notes, diamond earrings, ruby or sapphire rings. The groceries were bought with cash, his father would go around with great rolls of fivers in his pockets.

'I want to marry Jenna Duncan.'

'Oh God,' his father said, looking up from the newspaper and his toast. 'Look, Paul, you've seen what happened with your mother and me—'

'It isn't like that.'

'The more I think about it, the more I realize how like that it is. She didn't want to marry me, they made us get married because you were on the way and I knew that it was the wrong thing to do and now you are going to do the same thing.'

'She's having my child. Weren't you glad you had me? I'm going to ask her to marry me.'

'You'll be making a mistake.'

'I already made the mistake, now I have to try to retrieve what I can of it.'

His father said nothing but his disappointment was thick in the air.

'Maybe this is the right time to consider your future. What are you going to do with your life now that things are changing?' he said and Paul could hear the resignation in his voice and for the first time ever he felt sorry for his father. It was so important to Sorrel that his son should be a better man than he was, that he should not be involved in underhand doings or take part in the business. His father wanted other things for him, worked so that Paul could live differently.

Paul understood but he no longer wanted to move away from what his family did, he didn't know why, just that he wanted Jenna and he wanted to stay here with her and to carry on what his father had done and to work with him. He didn't want to go away and try new things.

'I thought I'd come and work for you.'

'Paul, you have brains. You don't need to have brains to do what I do, any idiot could do it.'

Sorrel's background and lack of education was privately a sore spot for him which was why he had wanted Paul to do something else and it was a stupid thing and he knew that you couldn't live through your children even though you might try. It never worked, they were the people that they were and it had very little to do with you.

'I wanted respectability for you,' Sorrel said.

Paul stared, not very surprising, his father thought. He had never said such a thing to him.

'I know it sounds silly but you've lived with me all these years and I've done a lot of things I'm not very proud of because I wasn't clever and I had to do what I knew in order to survive at a good level. I wanted to be rich. It isn't everything. You don't have to do that, you can have anything you want. Don't throw away the idea of trying something else before you've thought really hard about it.'

'I wanted to do something which would please you,' Paul said.

Sorrel felt worse then, he hadn't realized that.

'You shouldn't do it for anybody but yourself,' he said.

'Then I'd like to work with you,' Paul said.

★   ★   ★

'You changed your mind?' Jenna could not believe it.

'Well, no, I didn't really, I just stopped doing what I thought I should and did what I wanted instead,' he confessed.

'You want the baby?' She could not believe that either.

'I want you.'

Jenna was inclined to burst into tears, into song, anything which would be better than the way that she had been feeling over the past few days. She could not believe that Paul had come back. She had sat in her room and been unable to imagine what the coming months would bring, what the rest of her life would hold and she could not understand the mess she had got herself into.

There was nobody else to blame. She would have to work in the drapery department until she was fat and people stared and stopped talking to her and then she would have to stay in her mother's house until the baby was born and there would be no celebrations, no joy, her parents would not be able to talk about the baby and be glad. She was becoming very depressed at such thoughts when her mother had come into the sitting room, trailing Paul behind her and looking wooden-faced, as though she did not know whether to be pleased or not.

'The trouble is . . .'

'What trouble?'

He looked at her.

'I know you don't love me. I know you think you should do this but, Jenna, if you don't want this baby we can do something about it. We don't have to go through with it.'

'I would never consider getting rid of my child. Don't you want it?'

'I want it to be what we both want, it's not going to work if it's one-sided. That's what my parents did. It's not the way that I want to live. I know that if it hadn't been for the baby you would have gone with Gallacher.'

Jenna looked at him and she knew what she wanted.

'That's over now.' She stopped and decided to be completely honest with him. 'I don't think Ruari ever wanted me as much as he wanted football. I know it sounds silly but I think subconsciously I was aware of it and perhaps it was the reason I went to you. I think we could have a really good marriage. You're the person I want now and I want our baby,' she said. 'I want it more than I've ever wanted anything or anybody in the world so if that's what you want too let's get married.'

The weight looked as though it had lifted from Paul. He grinned and looked exactly like his father and then he hugged her and promised her he would make it work.

# Thirteen

Paul thought he was going to like working for his father and for the first few weeks Paul followed him around while Sorrel explained how everything worked and Paul began to enjoy being there. He was not interested in football but he found he was quite interested in how the club was run from a business point of view and once he had stopped thinking of it as a game and regarded it as a commodity he liked being there.

Sorrel spent almost all his waking time at work. It occurred to Paul that his parents did not give one another much time but he had no illusions about their relationship. They had been married for almost twenty years and presumably in that long the novelty wore off. His mother was good at spending money, his father at making it. His mother had lots of friends and went out every day, his father worked and never went anywhere socially.

Best of all, Paul discovered, his father loved the football club, he would have said it was the most important thing in Sorrel's life, and sooner or later every day they ended up there, usually in the evenings where Sorrel was content to be until nine or ten o'clock and often after that he would go to the nightclubs to check that everything was running smoothly.

Paul liked this too, he enjoyed seeing people spending money on roulette wheels and in slot machines and at bars and he liked the lights, the music, the way that the girls dressed up, the sight of notes being handed in and the thought that he was part of this.

The office at the football club was very flash, all pale expensive wood and modern chairs and desks in chrome. Drinks were hidden in a big cupboard and in there too was a large refrigerator for champagne, ice and vodka. The tea- and coffee-making facilities were of the best and his secretaries were young, beautiful, blonde, long-haired and neat-fringed with very short skirts and very tanned legs. They wore low-cut tops which showed off their breasts, and they had neat waists and slim hips.

His father had lavished money on the ground, on the buildings, on the new training area, on baths and showers for the players, everything he could think of was done so that the team would win.

The pitch itself was immaculately kept and everything around it was spotless, his father was a stickler for perfection, it had to be right, the groundsmen kept it so and the first team played in white and each time they played everything was new. He only had one level, Paul thought with some pride, the top as far as the club was concerned.

When he had taken it over some five years earlier it was in debt but it was not in debt any more. His father did not back losers, not that he was aware of. He had a great manager, he had bought good footballers, they had finished near the top of the division at the end of last season.

It was mid-evening and they should have been at home having dinner but his father was bored at home and Paul had got used to doing without dinner. Sometimes midweek he would be there for Jenna's sake or he would take her out but weekends were the most important for work.

Sorrel poured more whisky for himself and thought. It was autumn, his favourite time of all. He had been born in November and had always imagined that this was why he preferred the autumn, otherwise it seemed silly, the dying back of everything, the onset of winter, and then he realized that it was nothing to do with any of that, it was because it was the beginning of the football season.

He liked the idea of starting new things, especially somehow at this time of the year. Because of the football he looked forward to the leaves falling and the nights darkening. To him it was the excitement of the new football year. Each year was a new opportunity and he had made some good purchases over the summer and he had a good team and with enough encouragement, training and general pampering of the best kind they might make it all the way this time.

One of his friends, Cecil Meredith, who was as unlike him as any man could be, Sorrel thought with a grin, had introduced him to a new club. It was not far from where he had been born and brought up in Newcastle.

It was strange how he loved to go back there, he liked to recapture the idea that his mother was still living there, waiting for him in the tiny house by the river; in his mind she was always there, she had not died and left him when he was ten. Thinking about her was a painful process and yet the familiarity of it brought comfort to him.

Many of the streets had not changed and he would leave his car and walk around a little, remembering the smells of the river and the sounds which came from the houses, the accents and the women in the streets were just like his mother had been. He did not think that he would ever stop missing her. She had been dead for over twenty years yet the sound of her voice and the prettiness of her face were as clear in his mind as they had always been.

Cecil was a well-respected businessman. The new club was just the place for tired men to retreat. There was a billiards room, a bar and other rooms where if you were keen enough you could lounge in a big leather chair and read and smoke and drink brandy. There was good food and great wine and best of all there were girls who danced for you and there were several bedrooms, discreetly away from the rest of the place.

In particular was one girl called Joanna. She reminded him of a girl who had lived near him when he was a small boy, she would put her nose in the air and not speak to him because her dad was something important, or she thought he was.

Living in that street, Sorrel reckoned, he couldn't have been anything very much. Anyway he liked Joanna. She had red hair and blue eyes and small perfect breasts which were high and tilted and when she undressed for him her body was creamy in the lamplight. He liked the way that she sighed when he had her. He didn't pretend to himself, the sighs cost him money but he didn't really mind.

Jenna had to be married in white, that was the custom and nobody said anything and in fact she wasn't getting any fatter. Faye Maddison had suggested that she and Vera and Jenna should go shopping for a bridal gown. They went to Fenwick's French Salon in Newcastle and various other expensive shops.

Jenna lost all sense of reality there because it appeared she could have anything she liked, nobody cared about the money. Although it was traditional for the bride's parents to pay for their wedding, since her parents had no money and Paul's father had plenty of the stuff he and Mrs Maddison were not mean about providing for this wedding.

She was beginning to learn that once you were involved with them the Maddisons took you for theirs and everything was looked after. It might feel slightly uncomfortable in some ways but Jenna thought she might as well enjoy what she could. She put all thoughts of Ruari away from her and concentrated on what she had and the wedding dress which they chose could not have been more beautiful.

It was a miniskirt as was the fashion with long sleeves and a neat veil. Mrs Maddison ordered flowers, they went to the top hotel in the area and booked almost the whole place and Jenna realized that even though she and Paul were getting married in a hurry, he was Sorrel Maddison's son and everything would have to be of the best.

In the end her mother invited all the family on both sides. Who Paul invited, other than a couple of his school friends, she had no idea. The other people there were the business people of the area and there were a great many of those.

They were married in the local parish church within sight and sound of the sea and it was full though neither of them had set foot in it other than Easter, Christmas, weddings, christenings and funerals for years.

The vicar was very nice about it in the circumstances, Jenna thought, but she noticed him afterwards talking to Sorrel Maddison so perhaps there was more to it than that and Mr Maddison had given them some money towards a window or such. Certainly the church seemed very grand that day and it was difficult not to be happy.

Each pew had a posy of roses at the end of it, she had a bouquet of the same, the wedding meal was a sit-down do though buffets had become fashionable. It was lavish, lots of champagne, the hotel decorated from top to bottom, they had a holiday booked in the Seychelles, she had enough clothes to last her for months and she managed to get Sorrel aside and thank him for what he had done.

He seemed embarrassed which was a strange emotion for such a man, she thought. She didn't like him. He didn't seem to her like a father at all, she felt dangerous when she was near him but not for herself, she was inside the castle walls. Beyond them there were troubles but she was safe because she was now a Maddison. She didn't think he liked her, or it was worse than that, she was beneath his notice, but she kissed him and thanked him. Loyalty, she thought, that was what he was good at.

Sorrel could not help thinking back to his own wedding that day. Perhaps because this was the first wedding since which had mattered to him.

They were both Catholic back then so it had to be a church wedding. Nobody had any money, they were very young so nobody came except her parents, and two local people as witnesses. The baby had already showed and there was no meal, no celebration, they went back to her parents' house and then he went to the market stall where he was selling clothes to make his living.

They had run off to begin with but her father had somehow found them and persuaded them that a wedding must happen but Faye was eight months gone with Paul when it took place. She was seventeen and he was just sixteen.

He would have preferred Jenna to be married from their house but it couldn't be. He couldn't deprive Jenna's mother of the occasion. She had bought a blue outfit which Sorrel thought looked appalling but then Faye wore something very much the same except it was in cream and the women wore hats and Jenna's dad was all done up in morning dress as they all were.

He was just glad to get it over with. It was not what he wanted for Paul, he was worried that Paul's marriage would go the same way as his parents' had, he wished Paul could have chosen somebody with a bit of class, had some other kind of life, but there was nothing you could do about such things and regretting it would not make anything different.

# Fourteen

Jenna would have preferred a little house of her own. She didn't realize that to begin with, she was so impressed now that she was married with the lovely old house where the Maddisons lived that she thought it was something she would find easy. She had bad morning sickness and it could last all day. She tried various things, the best was supposed to be somebody bringing you a cup of tea and a biscuit before you got up but Paul was always gone early.

There was nothing to do. Mrs Maddison ran the house so that other people cleaned, cooked, washed and ironed and most of it happened without anybody noticing which was amazing, Jenna thought. Mrs Maddison also went out every day.

She played tennis, she went downstairs to the gym they had, she had coffee with friends and she somehow assumed that Jenna would get on with whatever she was getting on with and it was so lonely that Jenna could not believe it. She found herself going back to see her own mother for something to do but her mother was decorating the lounge and the place was upside down. Also the smell of paint made her morning sickness worse.

Because the business was concerned with the football club there was always a lot to do at weekends and the clubs and hotels took all Paul's time during the week. It did not stop in the evening like normal men's work. She didn't like to complain. Everything they had was of the best, she could have gone out and bought whatever she liked, the trouble was she didn't need anything except things like baby clothes and a pram and a cot and she would have been happier if Paul had gone with her for these things.

She spent a couple of happy days choosing things and thinking about what they would do with the nursery.

Sometimes Jenna would be in bed when Paul came home. One night she awoke as he got into bed and the clock beside her said three.

'Wherever have you been?' she said sitting up.

'We had some trouble at one of the clubs. There was a big fight.'

'Are you all right?' She sat up as he peeled off his clothes, wearily, threw them on a chair and climbed into bed as though he had been thinking about sleep for a good long time.

'It's nothing to worry about, we have bouncers, it just got a bit out of hand, that's all. The place got smashed up and we had to get the police.'

He didn't seem worried. He turned over and went to sleep. Jenna lay awake for ages afterwards, thinking about what would happen if Paul was hurt.

He got up at the same time to go to work, though, it was just after six. He rushed about having a shower.

'Could you make some tea for me? I feel sick,' she said as he came into the bedroom.

'Haven't got time, sorry. I'm late.'

'How can you be late? You just came home and no club is open this early.'

'I have to make sure everything is all right from last night. I dare say my mother will make you some tea if you ask her.'

'That means I have to get out of bed, which defeats the object,' Jenna said,

'Sorry,' Paul said and pushed on his jacket. As he was about to leave she said,

'Aren't you ever going to have a day off?'

'Yes, Sunday. Dad's taking me out somewhere. It's a surprise,' and he smiled at her and was gone.

Jenna felt even worse after this. Had he no time to spare for her at all, even on his one day off?

On the Sunday morning off he went and she felt resentful that he should leave her. She felt very tired that day, not wanting to do anything in particular. Faye was at home and Jenna felt better knowing that somebody else was there even though they didn't do very much together. They had lunch and then Jenna lay down on the sofa by the fire and fell asleep. When she awoke she lay looking at the lawn which was covered in autumn leaves. It would be Christmas in no time, her first married Christmas. What did they do at Christmas? She supposed they would be busy, hotels and clubs were the places people went to for entertainment, especially at such times.

As she lay there Faye came in.

'You've been asleep ages. Are you feeling all right, you look awfully pale, would you like some tea?'

Jenna sat up when the tea arrived and let Faye give her a piece of chocolate cake. Halfway through the tea Jenna dropped both cup and saucer she had just picked up. Tea spilled all over the turkey rug, the cup and saucer bounced and she was gasping for breath beyond the pain.

Faye was not the kind of woman who went around assuring people it would be all right. She moved just as far as the telephone which hung on the wall and within seconds she had called an ambulance. Jenna waited for the pain to ease and when it didn't the tears fell unbidden down her face. At the same time she felt the warmth between her thighs.

'I'm bleeding.'

'Oh God,' Faye said and put an arm around her.

Faye left her briefly to throw on some clothes. She seemed to be gone such a long time but it could have been no more than a minute or two and the ambulance came shortly afterwards. Faye put the rug from the sofa around Jenna and then the men came and they would not let her walk anywhere. She felt stupid but beyond anything she felt pain.


Sorrel had told the office that nobody was to bother him, he had planned a special outing for Paul. He had not expected Paul to be competent in business, he had been so pleased that Paul listened to what he said, did as he was told but was ready to move on in so short a space of time to projects of his own. Sorrel had said nothing so this new car was his gift to Paul to acknowledge that he was doing so well and he wanted nothing to get in the way of this moment for them both.

'Where are we going?' Paul had said.

'Wait until we get there.'

Paul said nothing, just sat and they drove up the coast and towards Newcastle and beyond it to a certain garage and there they got out of his father's car.

'Are you buying something new?'

'Not exactly.'

'Is it something for Mum?'

'She would be here,' Sorrel pointed out.

'A surprise for her?'

'No.'

'Well, it can't be for me, I've got your MGB and the old Volvo for when the baby comes and I don't want Jenna to learn to drive until after the baby is born, I think it's too dangerous, so what is it?'

Sorrel took him inside and there the manager was waiting, smiling and there stood a Ferrari 250 GTO, red as only Ferraris are and sparkling and new with that wonderful smell. The smell was the best thing about new cars, Sorrel thought. He took the keys from the manager and handed them to Paul

'Congratulations,' he said, 'welcome to the firm.'

Paul's reaction satisfied Sorrel. The boy obviously couldn't believe it.

'But, Dad, I haven't done anything yet.'

'You've shown that you have a lot of ability and that's the most important thing of all. Get in, let's take it for a spin.'

They did. They drove all around the coast and when the cold night drew in Sorrel took his son to the club in Newcastle where he had first met Joanna. He went there often, they knew him, in fact only people they knew were allowed in.

He didn't think until he got into the bar and then Paul stopped. Sorrel didn't know why he stopped at first and then he realized and grinned. Dozens of beautiful women stood around the bar, tall, shapely and blonde most of them, models, actresses, would-be actresses, women with ambition. Paul stared.

'Just choose what you want,' Sorrel said, 'it's yours.'

Paul looked at him.

'Do you mean . . .' he said and stopped.

Sorrel knew why he stopped. He remembered when Faye had been pregnant. It had never been the same somehow after that. The idea of another person taking over his wife's body had nauseated him and after she was a mother he found that he wanted the person that she had been, the person who was all his.

He was shocked by his reaction but he wanted a woman with a flat stomach and high breasts and slender thighs. Faye had put on weight when she was pregnant with Paul and had never lost it. Here he could choose the body that he wanted and so could Paul and undoubtedly as he saw the fight go on in Paul's eyes his son would struggle and then decide.

'Well?' he prompted.

'The one on the left at the end,' Paul said and Sorrel looked at her. The girl at the end of the bar was an excellent choice, long yellow hair and a gorgeous figure. This one looked unattainable. She was the one he would have chosen.

It was an illusion of course. None of the women who came here were that. They wanted men with money and men with money wanted them. The gamble was for how long, would it be just for the night, would it be a week, a month, would there be jewellery in it for them, perhaps a car, maybe even better than that, a flat in a good area and a monthly income so that they could give up the shitty little job they were paid to do and in return all they had to do was be available occasionally? It was not much to ask, he thought, though he had never settled for one girl like that. He didn't see why any man would when there were so many.

Paul went to the girl. She did not seem to be looking at them but that too was false, everybody in the room knew who Paul was, who his father was. She smiled. Paul knew what to do instinctively, Sorrel thought, and he watched Paul order champagne.

Sorrel left him to it. He went to the back of the club and to the room where Joanna was waiting for him. Their arrangement was such that he would see her on certain nights and this was one of them. He knocked softly on the door and she opened it and then she flung herself into his arms.

From the hospital while she sat waiting Faye tried to get her husband and Paul on the telephone but there was nobody at the office and it was growing late. She even tried Sorrel's secretary at home but she had no idea where he was, she said she hadn't seen him, he had left, he had just said he and Mr Paul were going out, he didn't know when they would be back and they weren't to be disturbed.

'But I must find him,' Faye said. 'It's a family problem, very important, and he must be told.'

'I'm sorry, I can't help you. I don't have a number for him.'

'But you must have.' Faye was sure her husband had to be available in case something went wrong at any of his numerous business concerns but all she got from his secretary was a stony silence and she realized that the woman would not help her no matter what the circumstances.

She kept ringing the house but there was no certainty that Sorrel would answer the telephone, he rarely did so as though it was nothing to do with him and most of his business acquaintances would know better than to ring him there. Surely if he went back, seeing nobody there he would do so but the telephone rang out every time she tried it.

Faye didn't want to go back there for when he did arrive home, she wished now that she had had the presence of mind to leave a note but at the time she had thought of nothing but Jenna, she felt that she was some kind of talisman, that as long as she was there this would prove to be a false alarm, that Jenna would be all right, that the bleeding was something that happened to lots of women, as she was sure it was and that in the morning it would be better.

Rain was starting to fall. She had telephoned Jenna's parents as soon as she got to the hospital and tried to explain as well as she could and of course they insisted on coming to the hospital and she was glad of them. She had not thought she would be but somehow when she saw them coming up the hospital corridor the relief which flooded her made her want to cry.

They were so badly dressed, they were so poor. Mrs Duncan was a short fat woman, amazing how some people had beautiful children. Mr Duncan was terse-mouthed and he was little too and stocky, probably his ancestors had all been pitmen. Mrs Duncan was white-faced and crying and Mr Duncan didn't look directly at her so she went to them. Mrs Duncan insisted on seeing Jenna and went in, Mr Duncan hovered and then said, 'Is she going to be all right?'

Faye didn't believe that she was when nobody was reassuring, when there were no sighs of relief, she knew exactly what this was like, this was what had happened when she was having her second child. She tried to force the memory away from her while she reassured him. Why should she not? He sat down with a sigh.

'I knew nothing about this, you know,' he said.

Faye tried to look across the corridor where other people were sitting waiting and looking much the same.

'Nobody told me.'

'Would it have helped if they had?'

'Did you know?' he said.

'I think Jenna was so ashamed and she cares about you so much—'

'Her mother knew.'

'That's different.'

'Aye, well,' he said bitterly.

'I think she wanted to do better for you.'

He looked at her.

'Better than your family?' he said.

'Definitely,' Faye said and smiled dimly.

'Aye, I wish she had too, she was going with a nice lad when your son happened along with his flash car and his flash suit.'

And his flash father, she added silently.

She had been amazed at how personally Sorrel took it when their second child had died. She hadn't thought men ever reacted like that. She hadn't thought he would, as though it was his fault, and in a way it was. He was never there, he was always out making money, he was obsessed with the idea of security, of making enough so that he could look after his family, like he could hold everything off with cash and she had a very small child and no help. In some ways they had not got past it. Would Paul and Jenna get past this?

The evening wore into night, the rain poured down and they sat and waited. Faye had always thought that three o'clock in the morning was the worst time but she realized tonight that it wasn't so. Jenna lost her baby at four o'clock in the dark, when there was no prospect of light for months to come and then she wanted her mother. Faye went home.

The windscreen wipers were of some comfort somehow, something normal. The house was empty. She didn't realize until she got there that she had hoped he would be there, she hadn't really thought he would but she had hoped. She sat in the car, unable to get out somehow and then managed to open the car door and walk across the gravel and open the door.

She went into the sitting room and put her feet up and dozed on the sofa. She was awoken by the slamming of the outside door. It was daylight. Nobody came into the room and why would they, she thought sitting up, dazed but beginning to remember?

It was early morning, light filtered through the clouds. She soon heard her husband's footsteps upstairs, there was a long pause and then he came back down again and he shouted her name and then Paul came down and they came into the sitting room.

'Where's Jenna? What happened?' Paul said.

Faye stood up, collected her shoes from where she must have kicked them off and said, 'She miscarried.'

There was silence. She didn't question them, she didn't ask anything, she just walked slowly out of the room and into the hall. Paul went after her.

'Miscarried?'

'That's what I said,' and then she walked up the stairs and into her bedroom and closed the door behind her.

'Dad—'

'No, you go to the hospital, I'll talk to your mother,' Sorrel said.

He followed her upstairs. She was standing in the bedroom, not doing anything, just standing.

'Did you have to do that?' she said.

'Do what?'

'I'm too tired for games. I know very well now where you were, you were at some wretched club in bed with some floozy. You must have been, you didn't come home at all. Did you have to introduce your son to such . . .'

He said nothing and she looked at him and she sat down on her bed.

'I just wish I had known, could have got in touch. Your secretary was of no help though I'm sure—'

'She didn't know where I was.'

'Well, all I can say is you have a strange sense of priority.'

'The girls there are clean,' he said.

'Clean?' Faye looked at him. 'That's not a mind you have there, Sorrel, it's a sewer.'

'At least I'm realistic. Don't you see what is happening? It's the same thing all over again—'

'It is now. They stood a chance—'

'Oh, come on. It was all over when she said "I do".'

'If Jenna can't have any more or she doesn't want him there'll be no grandchild. Have you thought of that or don't you care about that either?'

'Just because we lost our child . . .' he said and his voice faded as she turned away from him. 'Lots of women miscarry and go on to have other children.'

'He wasn't there,' Faye said. 'She went through all that without her husband. I just hope whatever girl you were screwing gave you a good time.'

'It's more than you ever did,' Sorrel said before he could stop himself and she got up off the bed and came across the room so fast he didn't have time to move before she cracked him over the face. It was the first time she had touched him in fifteen years.

Jenna had never felt so ill and when it was over, when they told her that the baby had died, she felt nothing. She lay in her hospital bed and watched the autumn rain pour down the windows. She was in a room of her own. Sorrel had come to the hospital and made a great fuss and she was now in this palatial place with flowers everywhere at the very time when she would much rather have had some company. It was so clean and so white that only the heat saved it from being close to a refrigerator but she had already learned that there was no point in arguing with Sorrel, he didn't listen to what anybody said.

Paul had been pale-faced when he came in.

'I'm so sorry I wasn't there. Dad insisted on taking me out and we just forgot the time, got carried away.'

'It doesn't matter,' Jenna said, not caring whether he was with her now it was too late. She felt so bad, she was so tired she didn't even want to talk. 'It wouldn't have made any difference.'

'I will never, ever leave you again, I swear it.'

Why was he beating himself up about this, she thought, it was not his fault that his father had tried to give him a treat, even though she thought he could have let her know?

He was inconsolable, she was touched, she hadn't thought of him like that. She thought he had taken the baby for granted but now that there was no baby – how would she get used to the idea? – he was grief-stricken.

Sorrel also seemed most concerned. She didn't realize he wanted a grandchild so much but then he would, a man like that who was concerned with business wanted people to carry it on and no matter how unimportant she might think that, it was obviously a big part of his life, and then she remembered how keen he had been that Paul should go on and do something other than go into business with him and knew he was just upset.

He sat down on the bed and kissed her hands. It was a strange gesture, as though he was acknowledging his responsibility and that wasn't fair, she thought, it wasn't his fault, he had done everything he could to help once he had known she was pregnant.

'Is the room all right?' he said looking about anxiously as though there might be something wrong or a speck of dust somewhere.

Stupidly he made her feel better, he was so out of place there, in his expensive suit, watching the door as though some dragon might come for her and he would slay it in an instant. Jenna couldn't help but smile.

'The room is fine.'

'Jenna, I'm sorry we weren't there,' he looked her straight in the eyes and his eyes were so very blue, so very dark, 'especially I'm sorry that Paul wasn't there. I wanted to buy him a new car, he's worked so hard lately.'

She could vouch for that, Paul had hardly been at home for weeks. She had grown used to it.

'And then we went to this club in Newcastle and . . . well, you know.'

'I know,' she said.

It was odd. He was like a little boy, charming, repentant.

'We came in with the milk bottles,' he said and pulled a face. 'You won't leave, will you?' he said.

And then she realized. Sorrel was used to being left, perhaps his parents had done it, he expected people to leave, even lived his life taking for granted they would and moving on in case they did and before they did. How odd and how very uncomfortable.

Jenna wanted to look away but she couldn't because somehow he held her there.

There was a flash of understanding between them and then she said softly, 'I have nowhere else to go.'

Sorrel smiled at that and he kissed her forehead and then he got up.

'I should go to work. If you need anything just tell them,' and then he was gone and somehow she felt cocooned by his concern and it was a very warm feeling.

Paul was only amazed that his guilt didn't fell him, that God didn't strike him dead. He waited for his sentence and when nothing happened he sat by Jenna's bed and burned like somebody condemned to the stake.

The trouble was the blonde girl was experienced and he had never had anyone but Jenna. Now as the guilt began to wash, to move from him a little, he tried to justify to himself what he had done and his memory gave him Trudie on her knees before him, her blonde hair hiding who she was. He had imagined Jenna like that. He had even tried to push her head down so that she would take him into her mouth but she had always refused just by shaking his hands from her head.

Had she not done that with Gallacher? Was the boy genius a prude? Was he sexually naive, unimaginative or was it just that Jenna gave as little as she could to her husband because she didn't love him and only her sense of duty had got her to him. She had married him because she could not bear the talk and her poverty and the look on her parents' face.

Whatever else it was it was not love. And even while he assured her that he would never leave her again he remembered the look in her eyes when they had sex. She would turn her face away and wait until it was over, as he was convinced she had never done with Gallacher. She never said anything, she never took the lead, she never caressed him or kissed him voluntarily.

He knew now that his father had been right to take him to that club or he would have done what he had seen a great many other men do of a Friday or Saturday night, pick up a prostitute from the street or get drunk and stupidly pay just anybody for what they weren't getting at home. The truth was that he was gagging for it. Last night had been the best night since he had been married and he could not bear it. When Jenna finally slept he went out into the corridor and cried.

Sorrel didn't expect Paul to go into work that day, he should stay with Jenna, but Paul turned up mid morning, lurching into Sorrel's office at the football club as though he was drunk. He probably had a hangover, Sorrel thought, but surely he hadn't been drinking again this early in the day.

He slammed the door.

'I feel dreadful.'

Sorrel lifted his head from the figures he was studying and looked up.

'It's mixing your drinks that does it. You should stick to one type.'

'Not about that.' Paul sounded irritated. 'I feel guilty.'

'You're married, get used to it,' his father said.

Paul said nothing for so long that Sorrel was inclined to think he had left the room and was back to looking at the papers in front of him and then he saw that Paul was at the window. It was a fine view, he had built it that way so that he could see the sea.

'You couldn't have done any more than was done for Jenna.'

'I could have been there!' Paul was shouting. 'I was shagging a blonde in a back room while my wife lost our baby. Doesn't it matter to you?'

Sorrel didn't answer.

'I love her,' Paul said. 'Don't you understand?'

'And does she love you?'

Paul didn't answer for a few seconds and then he looked down at the floor and he said, 'We're married and . . .'

'Last night had nothing to do with your marriage and you had a good time.'

'I shall never do it again,' Paul said.

'Yes, you will. Lots of times. You were just unlucky, that's all.'

There was silence. Then Paul said softly, 'I feel so awful, so guilty.'

'Yes, well, that's how most men feel most of the time,' Sorrel said.

Paul felt like a drug addict or an alcoholic. He lasted that night until about half-past nine and then he couldn't stand it any more. Jenna was still in hospital and his parents were at home and he was alone so he got into his new car and drove to the club and there he had Trudie and a bottle of Scotch to himself all night.

When Trudie finally slept he made a decision. If she would let him he would rent Trudie a flat, somewhere pretty so that he could go to her whenever he wanted. It would be something completely separate from his marriage, he would be a better man for it. He would not always be bothering Jenna for sex and things would be much easier.

Jenna could not believe that she had lost her baby. Her first instinct was to get out of bed and run away, preferably as far as Teeshaven and tell Ruari Gallacher that it had all been a mistake, that the time between now and when she had gone to bed with Paul was just a nightmare, because that was how it felt. She wanted to cry, she wanted to wake up, she wanted Paul not to sit on the end of the bed like a man who is about to be executed and doesn't really care at the outcome but most of all she wanted to go back to being pregnant, she wanted her baby.

She felt as though she would never come to terms with her guilt and that she was being punished for what she had done. She felt that she owed Paul for getting him to marry her when she was pregnant and now the reason for it had gone. When she felt better, when she could think more clearly, they must try harder, they must work at their marriage and maybe in time she would give him a child and they would be happy. She went home and there Mrs Maddison looked after her.

She had not been looked after in such a way before, her mother hated it when people were ill, she did not know what to say about the baby and would come to the bedside for a minute or two in the hospital, pat her hand and tell her the next one would be all right when all Jenna could think about was the child she had lost and how it was her fault and how much she missed Ruari. After she went home her mother did not visit at all as though everything was said and done and they could move on.

Jenna thought about what her life could have been, she dreaded going on with this one but Faye was good to her and she got out of bed the day after she reached home. Faye was sitting in a chair in the conservatory and got to her feet.

'You shouldn't be up.'

'I'm bored.'

'I was just going to bring you some tea.'

'I can't face any more tea,' Jenna said and made her smile but she liked the way that Faye fussed and made her drink warm milk and she sat in the conservatory watching the flowers and was astonished to think that it was still autumn in the garden. A few leaves had drifted on to the lawn. Faye came back to find her in tears.

'My baby. I was making plans.'

Faye cuddled her.

'I know, I know,' she said.

'All the things we bought . . .'

'I've put them in the attic. You won't see them.'

'I feel like such a lot of time has passed but really it's nothing and yet such a lot has happened to me. I feel like one of those twigs that gets caught up when there's a lot of rain and the river rushes away to Sunderland. What on earth can I do now?'

'Drink your milk,' Faye advised her.

Paul came home early and Jenna wondered for how long the look on his face would persist, like his guilt had overwhelmed him. She determined to put Ruari from her mind and to go forward and make Paul happy.

# Fifteen

There was training at the ground in the morning, just running and stuff like that, it wasn't difficult, in fact it was so mindless that Ruari was bored, he would have been a lot happier if it had involved work with a ball rather than this idea of general exercise, it didn't suit him but he did it because that was what they did at this club.

He went with some of the others to a local billiard hall and played snooker in the afternoons. Other lads when they began to make money playing football bought themselves a car but Ruari spent nothing, he got the bus to the ground and saved his money. He wanted to pay the deposit for a house as soon as he could and for his mam to be able to stop cleaning.

One autumn day his mam came to see him. He had told her that he would travel back but she knew that he didn't want to do that so she got the bus, it must have taken ages, he thought.

He didn't want to meet her at his digs, he knew she would be concerned because it was not clean and he was not being fed properly as she would think of it, so he met her in town and took her out for a meal and she chatted and tried to look happy but he could tell that something was wrong, so after she had been cheerful and asked him about his playing and he had said everything was fine he gave in to the look in her eyes.

'What is it?' he said.

'What's what?'

'Oh, Mam, I know you too well. Summat's the matter.'

'Nothing,' she said and she drank her tea.

'Summat up with somebody?'

The look on her face didn't bode well.

'Ruari . . .'

'Hell, I wish you wouldn't say "Ruari" like that and then stop. What's happened?'

'You did know that Jenna married Paul Maddison?'

He wished he could say that he didn't want to know, didn't want to hear but it wasn't true.

'She was pregnant, Ruari, and she lost it.'

The words were said in such a rush that there was no way he

could shut them out though he dearly wanted to. It hurt more than leaving her had done. It hurt more than anything had ever hurt before. It made him think of Jenna standing in the rain and how she had told him about Paul and how awful it had been.

'Don't you see,' his mam said, 'that was why she married him. It didn't mean she cared about him.'

'And you think that makes it better?'

'Wouldn't you rather have her a better person, than to think that she left you for him because he had more money?'

'She did! She did go with him for his money.'

'It was a mistake. Everybody makes those.'

'You don't know that. She was impressed with them, she liked the way they lived and I couldn't do that for her, I couldn't provide things like that.'

His mam said nothing.

'I will now, though,' he said. 'And one day I'm going to go back and better them because of what they did to us, the way they tried to take advantage, the way Paul Maddison took my girl. I'm going to go back and sort them out.'

'You mustn't,' his mam said. 'That would make you just like them.'

'And I'm going to save up and buy you a house—'

'Ruari, I don't want a house. I don't want anything except for you to live your life and find something which matters to you and I think you're doing that. I like being among people who know me, I can afford the rent, I go and play bingo, I have tea with my friends. There's nothing I want. Don't save your money for me, buy yourself a car, find yourself somewhere to live. I know you don't like your digs even though you've kept quiet about it and I know how unhappy you've been. You'll meet somebody else, believe me you will.'

He felt like saying to her that she hadn't, that she hadn't gone on to meet somebody who cared for her. She had got tangled up with a hard drinker and married him and look what had happened to that but he couldn't say anything to her, he knew what she meant, that he must get on with his life and try for things. Well, he would now.

When his mother had gone home and he had gone back to his digs he couldn't stop thinking about what Jenna had done and how she had let Paul Maddison have her without any kind of protection. How could she have been so stupid? And why? Maybe she had never cared about him really, maybe she hadn't wanted the idea of a child with him whereas with Paul, because he came from a family who had money and because Sorrel Maddison could do anything he wanted, she had felt safe giving herself to him and not minding whether there was a baby.

It wouldn't go from his mind for the next day or two so he was almost pleased when Mr Hodgkin told him he would be a reserve for Saturday's match against Liverpool.

Ruari had not realized that he was going to go immediately into a cold sweating panic over such a thing. He wanted to run away. The chances were that he wouldn't get to play anyhow, nobody had told him he was any good but some reserves didn't get a chance like this. Also it meant he could be replacing a first-team player, John Simons, who had been injured a few games back and had been playing badly.

Ruari thought he had got used to being involved in the club, that he was used to the noise that the fans made, sensed the anticipation, but it was not like that in the end. He wanted to throw up.

Jack sat with him in the dressing room, it was an away match which made it worse, all that having to travel and a strange place and another ground. Jack was encouraging and Ruari couldn't believe that Jack could be so calm, that they were not all getting up and running away. He had never imagined it would be like this. There was another reserve going with them, a player who had been with them for two years and had played several times already that season but when it came to it he was terrified.

The wait before going out on to the pitch was one of the worst times of Ruari's life. Somebody was actually throwing up in the toilet, he could be heard, another was walking up and down, sweating, one or two talked quietly and Jack, seemingly unconcerned, listened to the manager's pep talk and then waited silently so Ruari did the same.

He had not known that Mr Hodgkin would make him feel good before he went out. Mr Hodgkin told him he could do it, talked to him using his name a lot, smiling so by the time they were ready to go Ruari had stopped being nervous. When he was on the pitch he was almost numb with amazement.

There were thousands of people around watching and he felt aware of each one of them. The noise was deafening, the pitch was huge and he was only too well aware of the other side, the other players, in particular one little man, whom in his terror he didn't recognize, coming to him and telling him that if he touched the fucking ball he'd break both his fucking legs. Ruari believed him.

And then the game began and it all changed. He had never even as a little kid imagined it would be like this. He had come home. He was meant to be there. How extraordinary. The football field had seemed so big and now it didn't and he could see where he was meant to be and it seemed to him as though the fans, even on the other side, were there for him.

Suddenly it was the simplest thing in the whole world. All he had to do was get the ball and pass it to the player who was nearest the goal and even at one point when he was just outside the penalty area he could see Phil Wilson was in a better position and he passed it cleanly and swiftly and Wilson scored.

The place erupted. His ears couldn't take the noise. Phil was clapping him on the back and Ruari realized that even though Phil had made the goal he had made the goal possible and every player on his team knew it and every player on the other team knew it too and they were scowling at him.

He had never thought to be a part of anything so exciting and to be a part of something like this, it made him aware of all those minutes and hours and days in the back lane, all those years had come down to this moment and as he stood bathed in glory it began to snow, small hard white flakes which turned the scene into one of those ticker-tape parades he had seen on television when people celebrated a great event in an American city. It was only for a few moments as though the very weather was pleased with him.

At half-time Mr Hodgkin had turned into Father Christmas, jolly, glowing, red-cheeked, full of praise. It had been the only goal scored.

'We need another,' Mr Hodgkin said. 'One's not enough, you know it isn't. There's nothing worse than a team that's one goal ahead and relaxes. Absolutely nothing.'

Ruari sat in a daze until they went back on and almost immediately and to his disappointment Liverpool scored and the crowd went up again screaming and the screaming and shouting and swearing and bawling seemed to crash and echo all around the ground.

He took it personally. He was very upset that they had scored and that the little man who had threatened him kicked him hard on the shin and the anger moved him forward. It seemed to move him forward faster than other people, he could get past them somehow and even though there seemed to be a lot of them in the way he wouldn't have it, he could dribble and swerve around them and he could get ahead of them and from way down the pitch he could see the goal.

He had heard people talking of footballers who could see the goal clearer than other players did, that it seemed a shorter distance, that the goal to the best players was a huge thing, that it was very big indeed and that the distance between the goal posts was as big as the heavens.

Suddenly there was nothing in the way that couldn't be got round, there was nobody in view between him and it and when he had run far enough and outrun them he paused to see which way the goalkeeper thought he was going to go and he turned his body so that the goalkeeper took his dive one way, he twisted his body ever so slightly and turned his foot and the ball, not wet, not leather but suddenly about as heavy as a balloon, soared like a coloured kite on a beach into the sky.

It seemed to him to go in slow motion from his foot, across the top beyond the grass, beyond the green, into the sky which was blue behind the big white flakes of the snow which had started up again and were square and momentarily dazzling. He could taste snow in his mouth and he could see the ball, like a bird, like one of those seagulls which soared high above the North Sea, and then it began to fall ever so slightly and while the world stood still and the goalkeeper went the other way towards the ground it buried itself in the back of the net as accurate as the gull that dived and lifted its trophy, the shining silver fish from the sea.

It seemed to Ruari that the world had stopped completely. The players didn't move and for seconds together there was silence and then the whole arena erupted and it was ecstasy. He had never in his whole life felt anything like it. Great waves of feeling came off the crowd and lifted him so high that he was weightless.

It was the final goal.

When they came off the pitch Ruari couldn't believe what had happened. He hadn't thought you could feel like that about anything other than Jenna. It was exactly the same thing, he had felt it before but he had forgotten and now it hurt because she was not there and she should have been there to see what he could do with the gift which he had worked so hard to improve and it was bitter-sweet, the gift which had cost him the girl that he loved.

Already he had begun to come down but once in the dressing room with the other players laughing and teasing him and Mr Hodgkin, who looked like he was going to cry, he was so pleased that the image of Jenna was wiped momentarily from his mind.

He had a bath and got changed and when he came out to get on the coach his mother was there and his mother really was crying and she came over and cuddled him and kissed him and she said, 'I knew you could do it. I'm so very proud of you.'

He hadn't known she was going to be there, Mr Hodgkin had organized a car and paid for a hotel room and Ruari was pleased so the good feelings started all over again. They went back to the hotel and Jack ordered champagne and Ruari could hardly speak for the feelings.

Later, when Jack had gone off and his mother had long since gone to bed the other players were drinking in the bar and they came over and offered to take him to a nightclub.

They weren't supposed to do this after a match but he thought Mr Hodgkin would turn a blind eye because it had been such a good day. He didn't want to go but he didn't want to stay there and go to bed, he didn't want the evening to end because he was convinced there would never be another like it and indeed there wouldn't, it would never be his first match, his first goal, the crowd on their feet like that in recognition of what he could do.

'The newspapers'll be full of you,' Phil said as they walked out of the hotel.

'Of you,' Ruari said.

Phil smiled.

'You're the new boy,' he said.

'It doesn't necessarily mean I'll get to play again, though, does it? When John comes back—'

'He won't be back for the next game, I shouldn't think,' Phil said.

'There are other substitutes.'

'There are but they didn't just make two goals against a fantastic side,' Phil said.

Ruari had never been to a nightclub, but he was recognized on the door and nobody was going to deny him anything that night.

Liverpool was the place of dreams where the Beatles had been discovered playing at the Cavern. It had more atmosphere, he thought, than anywhere he had ever been, and there was no antagonism against the visiting players, at least as far as he could see and if there was fighting in the streets between the fans he was shielded from it completely.

The place they went to was very high class, he could see that because it was quiet, hushed, thick-carpeted, low lights and at the bar were the kind of girls that most lads only dreamed of. He thought about Jenna then and resented so much what she had done to him.

He didn't drink very much though some of the others did. He now felt as though he had a responsibility to look after the body which had given him pace and strength and vision but he was beginning to come down, to lose the high which the game had given him. He kept running it back through his mind but each time it played a little duller and a little further away and he understood then that there had to be another time and another game.

The girls at the bar seemed to know what he had done and were there, talking to him, and one in particular looked a little bit like Jenna though she had a Scouse accent, he liked it, it sounded so sexy, so gravelly. He danced with her. She smelled of expensive perfume, just a little so that you wanted to get nearer, and later, when it was very late and his so wonderful day was almost completely gone, he kissed her in the shadows and she was not Jenna and the day slid slowly to the floor where it crashed around him.

He went outside. It was still snowing. Phil for some reason followed him. Ruari was surprised. They had not been friends before now and only Jack ever thought about him.

'You all right, kidder?' he said. 'You haven't had too much to drink, unlike the rest of us?'

Ruari shook his head.

'It'll happen again.'

'What will?'

Phil waved a hand.

'The goals, the crowd, the feeling.'

'It's nearly gone now.'

'It won't ever go completely. You're lucky, think of all the thousands of daft sods who wish they were you tonight. They all hate you.'

It made him laugh.

'Maybe it was just a one off,' he said.

'Well, it had better not be, because Hodgkin will have your balls if it was,' and they laughed again, 'and thanks.'

Ruari looked at him.

'What for?'

'For the goal, you daft sod. You didn't have to pass it, you could have taken it yourself. You'd never scored before. Who would give up the chance?'

'I didn't think.'

'Yeah, you did. I saw you look at me before you passed it.'

'You were in a better position.'

Phil smiled.

'Dozens of other footballers would have taken the chance on themselves. It takes a particular kind of unselfish player to do such a thing, or just somebody so gifted that they see the whole team as one.'

'Bloody hell,' Ruari said, 'what did you have to drink? You sound like a teacher.'

'Come inside,' Phil said. 'A piece of advice before then. Take the little blonde to bed before you explode.'

'I don't think she wants me to.'

'Yeah, she does,' Phil said.

And sure enough she did. They went to his hotel. In a way it put Jenna back a pace, several paces, in fact. There had never been anybody but Jenna and stupidly, he had thought, there never would be. What lad only ever had one woman? He had been daft, he had been naive. He had thought they were going to spend their whole lives together but Jenna hadn't thought that, Jenna had gone to Paul Maddison.

Ruari actually cried. He hadn't done that since he was a little kid and Stan had belted him for something. He couldn't even remember what now but it must have been something bad because he remembered it.

The blonde girl touched his shoulder. He was buried in the pillows and he didn't think she knew, or maybe she did.

'You all right, Ruari?' she said.

'Aye, I'm grand,' Ruari said.

And he knew why he had cried because the blonde was not Jenna, nobody ever would be Jenna, and the only way he could create the same feeling was on the football pitch, scoring goals, and he didn't know whether he would be able to sustain that.

The flat which Paul rented for Trudie was only ten minutes away from his home. He had not intended that, he had thought he might find something in Sunderland on the sea front or in the middle of Newcastle so that it would be well away just in case somebody saw them but in fact the flat that she liked was the top floor of an old building which looked out across the countryside and she liked the view there. It was nothing like he would have chosen but he could see how pleased she was so he agreed to it and they even spent wonderful stolen time furnishing it. He had not thought he would like buying a bed or a sofa or wine glasses and several times in Bainbridge's or Fenwick's in Newcastle they had to hide to avoid seeing people they knew, friends of his parents or neighbours, his father was so well known that it was difficult to avoid being caught. That was part of the pleasure. Half a dozen times they emerged from a shop giggling.

All he did there was go to bed with her and drink wine. There was nothing domestic about it after the furnishings. He kept her, they went to bed. She didn't cook, they had fish and chips or cheese and biscuits. Sometimes he watched television. He didn't want to be part of her life, he never asked her what she did when he wasn't there, he didn't care. He didn't know whether she had family or friends or who else she spent her time with.

The sex with Jenna was something they began doing because she wanted a child. He didn't care any more about such things, he was starting to think that he had never really cared, that he had married her out of guilt.

Babies were horrid wet things which shrieked and he avoided small children, he was not interested in them. He made sure that Trudie was on the pill so that there would be no complications and he did nothing more than service his wife because she seemed to become obsessed with the idea that they might have another child. He found it boring but necessary, perhaps everybody's marriage was like that. He had stopped regretting that he had married her, he had ceased blaming himself for her miscarriage, he just got on with his life.

He left the club and was not very surprised when his father commented on it.

'No, well, I've been busy.'

'Doing what?

Paul did not meet his father's gaze. It was half-time on a Saturday afternoon. He had begun going to the football with his father though he still couldn't see the point of running up and down a pitch, back and forth chasing a bloody leather ball but because his father was so involved it was difficult not to be and his father insisted on his being there at least most of the time so Paul endured it.

This day was mid-season and it was raining hard. That was the trouble with football being a winter game, the weather was usually foul and he would sit there thinking of how he could have been huddled over the fire at Trudie's and when the game was done he would go there, pretending he was somewhere else. His father didn't seem to mind if he took time off because God knew they worked almost all the time.

The home team had scored, they were a respectable two goals up at half-time and his father was in a good mood. They had left their seats and gone back into the office as Sorrel had an important telephone call to make and he said,

'I want to talk to you,' so Paul had no option but to follow him.

'You don't go to the club any more,' Sorrel said when the telephone call was over and he looked directly at his son.

Paul was not confused. He did not pretend that he did not know what his father meant.

'I've set Trudie up in a flat,' he said. 'Why are you asking when you know?'

'Because I don't know. I haven't been spying on you—'

'You guessed it, then. It's a long-standing affair. Plenty of people have them. She gives me what I don't get at home. You do the same—'

'I haven't set anybody up in a flat.'

'No, well, I expect it's because you get bored quicker than everybody else. I'll bet you've lost count of the women you've had over the years.'

He had said something significant, Paul thought, when silence followed this remark.

'I kept looking for . . . whatever it was when I saw your mother. It never happened again. I've grown used to the idea that it will never happen now.'

Maybe he was right, Paul thought, frightened, that falling in love was only really something you could do when you were young, that if it went wrong you could be alone for the rest of your life in that way. And since the mood seemed right he asked what he had never dared ask before.

'Why hasn't she left?'

'I don't know. I used to think she didn't want me because she had a lover, I waited for your mother to leave after we lost the baby but there was never another man.'

'Maybe it was the money.'

'She could have had any amount she wanted and really she's never been much of a spender. She's had the same car for six years. Nobody could call her greedy. I don't even know why I care about her so much. It isn't as if she's especially interesting.' Sorrel smiled against himself. 'I think it's something to do with the way she turns her head. Nobody else does that. It was the first thing I noticed about her. She was fifteen and I was just a kid and I was working a market stall and she was walking across the Market Place with a friend. And she turned her head and looked at me. Things were never the same after that. I wanted her so much as a part of my life.' He sighed. 'Well, I certainly got that.'

Ruari played again and then again and each time he was on the pitch he scored. When they won they got extra money and they got extra money every week until he came to expect it and he determined to leave Mrs Johnson's, buy a house and a new car, but at the moment it all went satisfactorily into his bank account aside from what he sent his mother.

It was funny, when she did come to see him – because he didn't go home, she insisted on spending the money he had sent her and would take him out to tea at lavish hotels and buy him supper in Italian restaurants and he would put her up at good hotels. She didn't want to give up her job, she said she would be bored, she was thrilled at his success and he was pleased that she seemed happy at last.

Whether it was tact on Mr Hodgkin's part or because Ruari had not much experience when they played against Dunelm North End he was not included in the team. He thought probably Mr Hodgkin judged it would be very difficult for him to go back there so soon after leaving under a cloud and that he wouldn't play well because he wouldn't be able to concentrate so he didn't go.

He wanted to tell Mr Hodgkin that he had grown up a lot and that it wouldn't affect him to do it but he hadn't yet the confidence to be sure and since Mr Hodgkin was the one making the decisions it would have been awful to have let him down, so he didn't say anything and it was a relief in a way not to have to do it so maybe Mr Hodgkin had judged it well.

It wasn't the only time he didn't play, there were other people who had to be given chances, but Ruari gradually began to play more and more often and every time he played he scored and Teeshaven began to do better and better.

The money worries were disappearing completely and all he had to do was play football. It was so simple really.

The newspapers were full of Ruari's name by then and of his

girlfriends and of his social life. He and his team mates very often went up to London and stayed there and went to clubs. He learned how to dress fashionably and then he bought himself a car and the fans started to recognize him, shouted for him.

It seemed to him, all of a sudden, when he had played a particularly good match against Arsenal and scored three times, that the street was always full of people, staring in at the windows, hanging around the door, and he decided to move. He was tired of the awful room, the bad food.

He tried to talk his mother into going with him but she was determined to stay where she was. She let him pay so that she could go on a modest holiday with a friend and that was all and he would lie in bed at night and wonder what on earth he was doing when he had nobody to work for, nobody to come home to.

In the end he bought a modest house, it was a cottage in a tiny village on the Yorkshire moors, nothing like anybody else had but he had lived in a town all his life and he liked to go back to it when the day was over and he could take taxis or stay at a hotel if he didn't want to, but once the novelty had worn off he was lonely there and hardly ever went, he stayed in hotels or with friends, he couldn't bear the silence when he walked into the house. There was something so impersonal about it that he came to dread being there. It was the idea that he liked of having somewhere of his own, the cottage did not matter to him at all.

Ruari began to take for granted that he would play, even when Simons came back on to the team during the first season. He only came back for two games that season and both times he didn't score. Ruari hadn't thought much about what it was like when you failed. Simons had a wife and two small children, Ruari had seen them and already there was talk of a transfer. He felt bad for Simons. He hadn't realized until then that when somebody won somebody else lost, sometimes several other people.

The reserve who had been with him somehow quietly melted away during the second year and the next they heard he had gone to Guildford to be a butcher. The very idea made Ruari lose sleep and shudder. He could end up as a butcher, getting up at five, starting at six, finishing at seven in the evening, spending three hours a day washing out fridges, chopping up lambs. It was enough to turn you into a vegetarian and that wasn't funny at three in the morning.

He was injured soon after that, it was his knee, a weak point, and then he was afraid. Every footballer feared injury, it was such a rough game, but he was only out for a couple of weeks and then back and fit so he didn't worry about it. From time to time it bothered him but as long as he was careful and trained well and kept fit it didn't stop him losing more than the odd game.

He was no longer the new boy. By the third season he felt confident and sure of himself. The first time they played a game that season he didn't score, and it was against Sheffield Wednesday at home so he should have, he felt the responsibility and even Mr Hodgkin said to him, 'Having an off day, are we, Gallacher?'

It was faintly ironic, Ruari knew, but the truth was that they relied on him and the pressure was beginning to feel heavy. Mr Hodgkin saw his face.

'I'm only teasing you, son, you're doing brilliantly,' he said, 'and we won.'

That was it, they had won without his help somehow. Ruari was unhappy about that, he was used to being the best, he didn't like not coming top, he hadn't thought until then that he was so competitive but he trained harder, ate properly, slept properly and didn't drink and in the next game he scored.

Everybody knew who he was by that time and he went out one weekend after Christmas in London and in the pub a big young man came to him and called him 'a fucking Geordie' and Jack had to pull Ruari outside because Ruari turned around, fists clenched.

'You don't hit him.'

'I wasn't going to hit him.'

'Yes, you were. You can't afford it. He was probably paid by a newspaper.'

Ruari stared.

'Paid?'

'What wouldn't they give to see you fall from grace, to see you in a national rag socking somebody in the gob and ending up in court. Mr Hodgkin won't stand for it, so you don't do it.'

'I'm not that famous.'

'Hey, you almost are,' Jack said. '"Wonderboy Strikes". You have to be aware of it, OK? The newspapers don't mind seeing you with a different girl on your arm every week or the fact that you go clubbing in the big city, they'll accept that but they won't accept you being aggressive.'

'It would have been self-defence.'

'It doesn't matter. The public doesn't remember that, it only remembers the pictures of him bleeding and you going into court.'

'All right. I'm aware of it.'

Jack hesitated.

'I said I know.'

'Aye, I know you did.'

'So?'

The street was dark, it was late and Ruari resented Jack. It was like having a bloody older brother, always interfering and then he caved in.

'I'm frightened.'

Jack moved back slightly in surprise, Ruari thought.

'Of?'

'We're going home next week.'

Jack nodded, Ruari could only just see him in the shadows of the town.

'I want never to go back to play and now I have to.'

'Yeah, well, you knew that.'

'I told meself it wasn't going to happen.'

'She's married,' Jack said, as heavily as if he was carrying a sack of coal.

'If you tell me there are plenty more fish in the sea I'll hit you,' Ruari said.

Jack laughed and his laughter bounced across the street at the buildings opposite and re-echoed at his side.

'It had to happen sometime and you can count on it that Hodgkin knows the time is right. You can go back there and show them,' he said.

'I want to but what if I don't score?'

'Oh, Christ, yes,' Jack said, 'the end of the world is nigh.'

'It's all right for you,' Ruari said. 'You don't have to score.'

'No, I just have to stop ten other blokes on the far side from scoring. Neither do you, not every time.'

'It's what I do.'

'Well, then, go back there and score, do it for the bitch who left you.'

He pretended that it was just another game, that it was nothing to do with Jenna, or Paul Maddison or Maddison's bastard father or Harry Philips, but the funny thing was that when Ruari saw Philips as they came on to the pitch he went cold with temper, remembering how he had tried to manipulate Stan and how Stan, who was never the strongest man on the planet, couldn't handle it, and he thought Philips had known how weak Stan was, how poor they were and had done it on purpose to get Ruari cheap.

The anger had lasted him through seeing his home town again – actually he didn't see it, he just looked blindly through the coach windows, he didn't really see the fans or the town or the flash dressing rooms, all he saw was that rainy day when Jenna had told him that she had gone with Paul Maddison. He saw it over and over and it was silly really because it was what passed for a spring day in the north, freezing cold and very bright.

He just sat there in the dressing room and waited for the game. Other people were nervous, other people paced, threw up, couldn't eat. He was focused, he didn't even hear what Mr Hodgkin said, he just waited.

He went out on to the pitch and the home crowd reacted. Nothing had ever happened like that before. They booed and shouted and swore and even threw things on to the pitch and shrieked his name and called him traitor and arsehole and bastard and a good many other things which thankfully he couldn't make out and the home team grinned or glared depending on what they thought of him, and Ruari stopped at one point and wanted more than he had ever wanted in his life to run away, to go back down the tunnel and into the dressing room and hide against the huge roaring and spitting and cursing of the angry fans.

It was one of the scariest things he had ever experienced, so many of them, like a tidal wave. He couldn't breathe, he wouldn't be able to play, and then he managed to look up and there was a single seagull soaring. He thought, stupidly, that it was the same seagull which turned up all the time somehow, like a lucky mascot, a charm. Ridiculous how your thoughts just carried away.

There it was up in the blue sky, all elegant and white and perfectly in control, and all he had to do was to follow it, to take control and he went cold and knew that he could do it. He had come back here to show Sorrel Maddison, to show them all what he could do and he was not going to waste the chance, he was not going to be intimidated by a lot of sheep or by any of the North End players who were more experienced. He could feel the hate coming off them and coming off the crowd and suddenly he didn't care.

He thought about Jenna and how she had let him go and none

of it mattered any more. He was here because he was good, he had a right to be here and it was his home, it belonged to him. He could own this place, this pitch.

He could remember as a small boy hoping that one day he would be allowed to play here. This was not what he had envisaged but he knew that this was how it had been meant to be. He was master here and nobody was going to get in his way and spoil it, he had sacrificed too much to make a mess of it.

The kick-off came, the match began, the players moved and he could see that he was going to have the whole thing all to himself like a great big box of sweets that you got at Christmas, a selection box, that was it, where you got a Mars Bar and a Crunchie and a tube of Smarties and a bar of Dairy Milk and on the outside you got a game and his mam would sit with him by the fire on Christmas night and play snakes and ladders or whatever game it was with a dice and the back of the box and they would sit at the kitchen table and do the jigsaw she had bought.

He was just as happy here as he had been during those Christmases which had been the best of his life. Just him and his mam. Stan was never there, he was always out drinking and Ruari realized now that nobody could take such things away and nobody was going to take this. His mam was there watching, and no doubt she had bragged long and hard about her lad to her neighbours and this was his chance to make the whole thing memorable in all the best ways. He wouldn't let his mam down now.

Phil got the ball after a bit of scuffle and passed it to him and after that he just ran with it, like he had done so many times before. He knew how to do it, he knew the others couldn't get anywhere near, he was too far from them, too far in front, too far away and the goal was as big as the North Sea, it was the biggest space that he had ever seen. The gull didn't even flap its wings when he scored the first goal. He sank it not just neatly but totally, the goalkeeper didn't even see it coming past him.

The second was just before half-time and the two players from Dunelm North End who had been sent to see him off didn't get anywhere close before he netted it. The third was just after half-time and was a gift to another player, Selby, who acknowledged it afterwards with a clenched fist.

The fourth was another Phil goal, they did it so often that they almost took it for granted now and were, Mr Hodgkin had said, grinning, 'the well-oiled machine of the side'. The opposing team didn't score at all. Teeshaven were too fast and Ruari was too quick and too accurate.

The triumph Ruari felt made his head reel and spin but there was something bitter in it too and he could not help looking for Jenna in the crowd. Had she thought about him, was she aware that he was even in the game or did she care so little that she no longer noticed? She would not be there, he decided, why on earth should she be? She must know he was playing and that would be enough to keep her away and even though she had married the chairman's son it would not bring her there.

That night the others went home, but Ruari stayed and after he had been partied at a hotel by his mother and her friends he bedded a blonde with a local accent. He liked the way that she said his name, it sounded just like Jenna.


'We lost.'

Paul practically howled when he got home. Jenna already knew. She had known and dreaded Ruari coming back to North End even though she told herself it was not a proper homecoming at all, it was just as part of a team, for a few hours and would affect nothing and she tried not to let it get to her but it was hard.

She was hearing stories about how good he was. There were photographs in the newspapers of him all the time now, looking older and well dressed and always with a girl on his arm. He was 'a rising star'. She tried not to listen to the tide of publicity which began to follow him but it was impossible not to notice.

'Four goals,' Paul said, 'four.'

Jenna was about to point out that Ruari hadn't scored them all himself but it would have been a pointless exercise. He had set them up so it was the same thing really.

'We lost four-nil. My father is furious. Ruari Gallacher could have done it by himself, in fact he just about did. He made our players look like little lads. Harry was catatonic by the end of the match. He may never recover.'

Jenna wished she could have gone somewhere to get away from this. Paul had obviously forgotten all about her connection with Ruari. Paul, since they had lost the baby, was also very attentive. Jenna could no longer accuse him of neglecting her. If he couldn't come home he telephoned and she could hear by the clearness of his voice that he was being honest with her. Two or three nights he would come back at three or four in the morning but she knew that it was part of his work to be at the clubs late and sometimes to socialize and she did not complain.

They were trying for another baby but nothing had happened. Month after month Jenna bled with monotonous regularity. Paul even took holidays. They went to Spain and sat on beaches and ate good food and swam in big blue hotel pools, it was the kind of life she had thought she wanted, the best of everything. Now it meant nothing, now that she could not conceive the idea of never having a child seemed to fill her whole life. She had lots of other things, of course, everything, as the saying went, she thought, that money could buy. It was cold comfort.

Her clothes were expensive, she learned to drive but the trouble was that nothing held her attention now that she was not pregnant with the child which had cost her Ruari Gallacher. She had thought she would despise it but she ached for a baby and nothing had happened. She had to try to think of other things because she had the feeling that when you wanted something so badly nothing ever did happen.

'I could go out and get a job,' she suggested one night when she and Paul were alone in their bedroom. That was another thing, they were rarely alone. If they went out Paul liked a crowd though she did not become friends with any of his friends somehow and in the house his mother was often there and sometimes even his father and he would bring friends back and drink. Jenna privately thought that Paul drank far too much but at least he didn't drive when he drank.

'I pay enough tax as it is,' Paul said, 'it wouldn't be worth it.'

'Could we move, then?'

'Whatever for? I thought you liked being here.'

Just when she felt her mood slipping into self-pity Paul, who had just got into bed, looked at her.

'If you really want to move we can.'

'No, I don't, I was just . . .' I was just the spoiled kid, she thought but there was a part of her which thought they might manage a lot better if they didn't live with his parents but he so obviously liked being there and since they could not have a house like this on their own it seemed small-minded to insist.

'We could buy a place to go at weekends.'

Jenna kissed him for the thought, she was so grateful. Really, she thought, she only had to ask and she could have anything.

'Your busiest time is the weekend. We'd never go.'

'We could, though. We could buy somewhere abroad, if you like. Spain, maybe.'

'Spain?'

'Why not?'

'It isn't practical, I can't go there by myself and I don't see the others coming and you don't even have time to take a weekend off.'

'I will,' he promised, 'and we'll go somewhere nice.'

Sorrel and Harry didn't speak after the match. They each tried not to blame the other. Sorrel knew that if he had behaved differently they would have secured Ruari for the team and Harry just felt stupid at the way that he had attempted to manoeuvre Gallacher and had failed and they both blamed Ruari Gallacher for being so much better than anybody had ever dreamed he would.

'I never saw a lad come from nowt at seventeen, going on eighteen, like that,' Harry said two weeks later when their team had finally won against Newcastle and they thought the balance was somewhat restored.

'They must do it all the time,' Sorrel said comfortingly.

They were sitting in his office and this was the first time they had spoken of it. He had had the board to contend with and had made polite noises. Footballers came and went, he had said, Gallacher was just having a good season. He could be injured – in fact in his best dreams that was what happened. Gallacher got hurt and was consigned to the wilderness with a team in the Third Division and his career was over.

Neither of them said that they wished they had done differently, that was football, you couldn't win them all, you had to use what judgement you could and you made mistakes, it was just that to make such a mistake in their own back yard was seemingly stupid. There was worse news the following week. Ruari was chosen to play in the under-23s for England. They didn't talk about that, it hurt too much.

'Would you like some Scotch?' was what Sorrel said and Harry looked gratefully at him.

Sorrel poured generously into short squat glasses and then he said, 'I've thought of a solution.'

'What's that?'

'We should buy him back.'

Harry took his glass carefully and looked above it at his boss.

'He's worth a small fortune.'

'They have no money. He's the only really decent player they possess. If they could get sufficient money for him they could buy two or three mediocre players and that's what they are, a mediocre team.'

Sorrel took a good slurp out of his glass. It was ten-year-old malt and excellent.

'It would make up for a lot of things,' Harry said.

'And the lad would be back where he belongs.'

'What would the fans think?'

'At first they would hate him, they wouldn't forget that he left here when he could have played for us but after he scored his first goal wearing our colours he would become their hero. You know what they're like, fickle, and they have short memories. And in a way we'd be getting our own back on what he did to us, in the nicest possible sense, of course,' Sorrel said and he grinned.

Harry sipped appreciatively at his Scotch and sighed.

'They need to sell him before their whole bloody ground falls to pieces,' he said. 'And we could win with a player like that, we've already got half a dozen good people, all we need is a really good striker, somebody who never misses.'

'I'll talk to the board about it, get them to agree,' Sorrel said.

# Sixteen

Mr Hodgkin looked narrowly at Ruari as he came into his office and Ruari thought back and wondered if there was anything he had done wrong because Mr Hodgkin never looked like that at him and then he realized it wasn't exactly at him it was in spite of him somehow because Mr Hodgkin's eyes were still warm on him.

'Sit down, Ruari,' he said.

That was a bad beginning. You never got to sit in Mr Hodgkin's office. Mr Hodgkin sat down too. That was even worse. Mr Hodgkin didn't look at him for several seconds during which time Ruari tried to think of all the awful things that could have gone wrong and of anything he had done lately which might condemn him to criticism.

'We're in debt – the club, I mean, the club's badly in debt. We've been losing money for a long time and we need more good players. We have one or two but we don't have enough of the right quality. The . . . management doesn't have enough money, we need a very big influx of cash from somewhere.' He stopped there.

'I know things are difficult,' Ruari said, trying to better it.

'Yes, well, the top and bottom of it is that we've had a very good offer for you. We didn't seek it though to be honest we were thinking about it.'

He stopped there. It had never occurred to Ruari that he could be sold and now that Mr Hodgkin had said it he sat there and his whole body turned cold. He felt as though the office floor was giving way and there was an endless chasm beneath it and it made him feel dizzy and sick. He couldn't even say anything, he had to concentrate on trying to keep his breath even.

'You're worth a great deal of money and although we don't want to get rid of you we can't think of another solution to our money worries.'

There was silence. It was almost on Ruari's tongue to say that they couldn't but of course that wasn't true, he was a contract to them and they could do what they liked. He wanted to get up and run out of the office, to run home to his mam like he was a little kid who had just been bested in the school-yard.

He could object, of course, he could complain, he could say he wasn't going but these were good people and they had given him his chance when nobody else saw the potential, they had looked after him, had paid him more than anybody else would have and they needn't have done that.

This man had seen his ability and put money behind it such as nobody else had or might have and they had looked after him. He could think of lots of clubs he might have gone to where his talent would have been spoiled or neglected or just not come to fruition as it had here. They had treated him like valuable china and because of it he was now worth a lot of money and because of it he had to go.

'Can I ask where?'

The question seemed to make things even harder. Mr Hodgkin looked down.

'Dunelm North End,' he said.

Ruari didn't believe it.

'I can't go back there,' he said, unable to stop himself. 'I won't. Do you know what this means?' but of course Mr Hodgkin didn't, how could he?

'Ruari—'

'I can't go back there, it's . . . it's a horrible place, it . . . I've got a house here and friends and . . . and a life. I'm not going. You can do what you like to me, I'm not going.' He got up from his chair and slammed out of Mr Hodgkin's office. He didn't think anybody had ever slammed out of it before but then maybe Mr Hodgkin had never given anybody such a reason.

He tried to talk himself into it, he would get good money out of it, it was time to move on, did it really matter so very much? But it did.

He didn't say anything to anybody, he had the feeling that if he didn't talk about it he would wake up from the nightmare, it couldn't be true or real, not when they had all tried so hard and had managed to establish something so good.

Nobody said anything more for several days, none of the directors, or the chairman, an accountant who was a decent man and fatherly and the least like Sorrel Maddison that any man could be and Ruari was glad and grateful for that. They didn't even send him to talk to Ruari and Mr Hodgkin said nothing more.

Jack was more to the point when Ruari drove over to his house and they were by themselves. Jack's wife, Nora, had taken the two little kids away, she was a tactful young woman and she could see there was something the matter and that it was something Ruari didn't want to talk about in front of her.

'You're bigger than the club,' Jack said, moving around awkwardly on his new white leather sofa.

'What do you mean?'

'I mean all the stories are about you, every time anybody breathes out it's about you. The whole thing is about you. The club has to be more than one player. You have to go.'

'Well, thanks very much, Jack,' Ruari said really annoyed. He had thought Jack would be horrified, would be sympathetic, might even talk to Mr Hodgkin for him, though now he came to think of it, it was a long shot and even daft for him to think such a thing.

'Oh, come on, you know it's true. You're the only really good player we've got.'

'That's not so, you're good and Phil and Pete and—'

'Yes, but not like you. Players like you come forward once or twice in a generation. It wouldn't matter what position you played, nobody can teach you anything, you were born knowing it and it shows. You make everybody else look slow and daft.'

'That's not true,' Ruari said.

'You're good with both feet, you don't have a weak foot like other people, you play like some men paint and some men write, you've got it all, you bastard. You're faster than everybody else, more skilled with the ball than anybody else, sometimes in a match you hardly touch the ground.

'I've never seen anything like it. I've seen you come down the field from nowhere and leave everybody standing watching, like they didn't have legs, you're so fast. They don't know where you're going or how you do it, it's a natural God-given thing, it can't be taught. You outplay everybody so that they don't understand. You were born to do this and now you have to move on because this club cannot sustain you, it hasn't got the players to match you any more.'

'They'll be able to afford to buy other players when I go.'

'Yes, they will.'

'I have good reasons for not wanting to go back there.'

'I know you do,' Jack said, 'but you're going to have to go.'

'How will I manage? I can hardly go and live back with my mam, can I?'

'I don't suppose she expects it.'

Or wants it, Ruari thought. His mam had got used to being

on her own and he thought she liked it, knowing he was doing what he wanted, where he wanted. He felt like he would be intruding if he went back to the little terraced house.

'The fans hate me.'

'They won't hate you when you belong to them. They resent you for having left but once you get back there it'll be different. You're one of them—'

'Not any more. I hate the place.'

'How can you hate it?'

'I do. I never wanted to go back there and live. I thought if I was being sold it would be to Manchester United or – or Arsenal—'

'In fact anywhere else would have done.'

'Even bloody Newcastle would have been better than this.'

'Oh no, it wouldn't,' Jack said. 'You couldn't go to Newcastle, some poor Geordie bastard would bang you over the head.'

Ruari couldn't help smiling slightly at that, which was what Jack had intended all along.

'You won't be there to moan over,' was Ruari's other complaint.

'No, I know. Just think how I'll feel when I play against you and I have to try and stop you putting the sodding ball into the back of the frigging net,' Jack said.

Paul stood in the doorway of his father's office in the football club. Sorrel hadn't heard him and looked up almost instinctively.

'Oh, I didn't see you there.'

Paul didn't come inside, he stood there but Sorrel could see that there was something very wrong.

'What's happened?' he said.

'My father's turned into a sodding idiot,' Paul said.

Sorrel sat back in his chair. There had been a time when his son would never have said such things to him and he was amazed even now that they had been working together for some time and worked well together.

'I had to find out from Harry,' Paul said and he came inside and slammed the door so hard that it shook and he stood there glaring at Sorrel. 'Why didn't you tell me?'

Sorrel understood now.

'It wasn't anything to do with you. You aren't interested in football.'

'I'm interested in my wife.'

'Oh, don't be soft,' Sorrel said dismissively and would have gone back to his papers.

'You're bringing him back here?'

'I've bought him.'

'You didn't consult me.'

'Why would I? Paul, you know a great deal about how to run the clubs and the betting shops by now. There is nothing you know about football which is valuable in spite of having spent most of your Saturdays at the ground for the past two seasons.'

'It can't mean that much to you that you would buy him and bring him back here.'

'I've always wanted to,' Sorrel said. 'I've always regretted letting him go. It was a mistake and as far as football was concerned it was a major mistake and I flattered myself that I knew talent.

'I was mean and because of that for the sake of a few quid a week I could have had him and didn't. Now I can, it's that simple. They're broke and I can afford him even though it's costing me so much more than if I'd signed him up to begin with that it makes me want to retch. Now, is there anything else?'

'You don't like him, that's why you want him back, because he bettered you.'

'He did, yes, and he was a lad. Men with brains, influence and vast experience have tried to better me and they've never done it but that little bastard . . . he was seventeen and he got away.'

'And do you think you're bettering him now?'

'No, I'm big enough to admit that I made a mistake. I want his talent for my team. I want my team to win. Is that basic enough for you?'

'This club cannot matter more to you than your family. You don't like him.'

'No, I don't like him, what I know of him, which is nothing personally. I think he's a jumped-up little shit for the way that he behaved in the first place but he has magic feet and I admire that. I know it's nothing but instinct but I like it. And for that I'm prepared to put up with him and I feel like I've won because I know that he doesn't want to come back here and I can make him so I'm feeling a little bit powerful and if it's pathetic I will learn to live with myself.'

'But Jenna—'

Sorrel looked patiently at him.

'That lad has had more lasses than you've had hot dinners. What the hell makes you think he remembers a nice little lass like Jenna?'

'A nice little lass? Your daughter-in-law is a nice little lass?'

'Aye, she is,' Sorrel said. 'She's a grand little lass and it's more than could be said of most others. And you should look after her better.'

Paul said nothing to this, he walked out.

Ruari drove home through the rain in the early summer. It wasn't a long way but it certainly felt like it, like another world, like he was going back and things would be just as bad or even worse than what he had left.

There was a wind behind the rain but the E-type Jaguar, which he had finally bought because he had fallen in love with it, was low and long and most of the wind and rain went above it and it was a good car so it cut whatever didn't go over the top as it had done on other nights when the weather was vile. He had long since ceased to notice such things but tonight because he was coming home the car seemed buffeted as though in some peculiar way it wanted to turn back just like he did.

It seemed to him the least public way of returning. He had told his mother he would wait a day or two and now he had changed his mind, there was no point in putting things off so he had announced his return only to Sorrel Maddison's secretary and she had booked him in at a hotel.

It was evening but not yet dark when he reached the outskirts of the town and although he tried very hard not to he could not help driving into the area which had been his home.

The houses were still there, long rows of them dropping down steeply towards the sea. He left the car some way off and walked. It was dusk and he was glad of that. Even here or maybe especially here there was a possibility that he would be recognized. In the near darkness he was just another tall slender young man, rather better dressed than everybody else but nobody could see and he kept his head down and stayed in the shadows as best he could.

It had not altered as much as he had thought or even hoped and the details of his childhood came back at him, the fish shop on the corner was still there and the unmade back lane where he had spent so many evenings. He was still able to imagine he could hear the sound of the children playing in the street as he dribbled the ball up and down the lane.

He had reached their house now, the back of it, the yard. It seemed smaller but it was not really and the lights were on in the kitchen. He stood outside until it was quite dark and even the dogs had gone home in the rain and then he walked slowly back to his car, trying not to think about Jenna. He had promised himself he would not. There was nothing to be gained from it.

He wasn't going to go and see his mother tonight, he had wanted to see the place privately so that he could come to terms with how he felt and he was not going to go and stay there, she had not even tried to talk him into it. She understood perhaps better than anybody how his fame could ruin things and neither of them wanted it to spoil the little house which was her home. She would come and see him at the hotel when he let her know that he was there.

He began to walk back up the street and was suddenly confronted by a gang of boys. In the lamplight he could see that one of them had a knife and the knife was pointed at him. It was almost funny he thought that he had to be attacked for the first time in his life in the street where he had been born and brought up and left years ago. There were half a dozen of them so it was far too many for him to handle. The one with the knife clicked his fingers and Ruari was in the act of taking his wallet from his jacket pocket when the boy next to the leader said, 'Bloody hell, it's Ruari Gallacher.'

This was not necessarily good news, a lot of people round here hated that he had left, did not know or care that his choices had seemed slight, they regarded him as a traitor in the war between the different clubs.

There was nothing more important than cash in his wallet so despite the fact that the knife disappeared and the boys moved with the excitement of nervousness and were not as far as he could judge hostile any more, their eyes beginning to shine, he pushed the wallet at the leader.

'Here, take it,' he said, surprised and rather pleased at how they had reacted, watched them hesitate, shoved it into the boy's hand and then he strolled off as nonchalantly as he could manage just in case they recovered and decided they wanted to damage him. He waited until he got to the end of the road and then he ran, reaching his car by taking several short cuts down narrow alleys. He had long since lost them when he reached his car.

'Jesus,' he said, grinning in derision and breathing heavily, 'and you call yourself fit.'

He drove through the middle of the town. It was still raining. You never forgot how much it rained here, how even in the summer like now it rained so very often that if there was more than one fine day together people got excited and sat outside their houses, those who had no garden would sit on the front street rather he thought as Americans sat on their porches except that here you were right on the pavement but it was a sociable thing to do too because people passing would stop to chat. There was no chance of that tonight, the rain was relentless and gave the town a cleaner look than he felt sure it normally had.

It wasn't a big town, he had forgotten that too or maybe when you were younger it looked bigger. It wasn't as big as Newcastle or as small as Durham, as industrial as Middlesbrough or as busy as Sunderland but it had pits here, though a lot in similar places had closed. These were the big coastal pits, some of which employed thousands of men.

The town was big enough to boast a very classy hotel and it was here that he was staying. He would feel safe from the crowds and as anonymous as he could be. It was set in big grounds and had a long winding drive so had been some kind of country house in the century before this one, he thought. Somebody had lived here lavishly at one time.

He parked neatly at the end of the building and walked inside and there was a reception desk and the usual dog-leg staircase. He had been in lots of hotels like this one. The receptionist looked up with a ready smile, recognized him and smiled even more.

'Good evening sir,' she said and pushed the register towards him and when he had signed it she gave him a key. 'If you would like dinner—'

'No, thanks, I'm fine.'

'Room service?'

'Possibly, later. Thank you.' Ruari took the key and his suitcases and made off swiftly towards the lift while she was still offering help with his luggage.

When he opened the door of his room he let go of the suitcases, closed the door and sighed. It was the biggest room in the hotel, he had no doubt. It was massive. Sorrel Maddison had ordered it. Best of all when he went over to the window it had a great big balcony and not far beyond it was the sea and the moon was out there giving light. He had forgotten how beautiful it was.

It was the sound of his childhood, he thought, opening the doors, the best sound, the one he always went to when things were wrong and even when they weren't, and now the sea was wonderful. He missed it. There were a lot of things he didn't miss but he missed this, it was the only thing which was better here than anywhere else on earth. The waves were parading up the beach in spectacular style. The rain had stopped and he stood there in the darkness and watched the sea.

He had thought he had left nothing here but he was wrong. Somehow everything had been left here, all the things he had wanted to forget, all the things which he had thought he had bettered returned to him as though the time in between had counted for nothing. He was tired, he told himself, that was all it was and he missed everything and he wished he had gone home except that he didn't want to burden his mother and her tiny house with reporters and people looking through the windows, it wasn't fair and he knew she had been relieved when he had declined her offer.

The following morning Ruari awoke and couldn't remember where he was for a few seconds and then knew. He was back in North End. From beyond the window the seagulls were kicking up a fuss and in the next room a couple were shouting at each other. He phoned down and ordered tea and toast and bacon and eggs then went into the bathroom and stood under a warm shower for a long time.

When he had eaten he felt better. He opened the windows. The sea was calm, the seagulls had stopped squawking and you could see way out to the horizon. It made him feel like a little lad again. The Farne Islands were not a long way off. He could remember being taken there in a boat and being sick and the wonderful birds, the kittiwakes fighting in the sea, the puffins were his favourites, sound-less, their wonderful wings beating in the air and how he had loved their spectacular orange beaks.

St Cuthbert had lived on Inner Farne. Cuthbert had been his favourite saint as a child, who could live in such a place and survive and yet it was so beautiful on a day like this? What would Cuthbert have done for warmth, sustenance, when it was comfortless as it so often was here in the north? It had always seemed to Ruari that the Farnes and Lindisfarne in particular were full of God somehow.

Maybe when you really had God you didn't need all the rest. He had long since given up on God. He couldn't remember his last confession. He was ashamed. He didn't want to go anywhere that day, officially he was not there but the newspapers would soon know and after that there would be no peace so he did nothing, he sat on the balcony, it was a beautiful day, warm and almost still, he read, he had meals sent up and he talked to his mother on the telephone.

In the early evening the telephone shrilled. He left the sunshine and went back inside and picked it up. Tony Evans was in reception. What the hell was he doing there? was Ruari's first reaction. Tony Evans was North End's best striker, a tall good-looking confident young man. When they had met in matches Ruari had always wanted to knock his teeth down his throat, he was such an arrogant little shit.

Tony came up, smiling, holding out his hand and saying, 'Welcome to North End.'

'I'm from here,' Ruari reminded him.

'Are you really? I thought you were from Manchester. I was going to show you around.'

'That's nice of you but I'm sure I can find my way.'

'I was only being friendly,' Tony said. 'I tell you what, I'm going to a party tonight. Why don't you come along?'

'I don't think so.'

Tony looked at him in a curious manner.

'Oh, I think you might want to,' he said, 'I think it's probably expected of you.'

'Really? Why would that be?'

# Seventeen

Jenna had gone over in her mind many times the way that she and Ruari would meet again but none of it stood up to what actually happened. It was early summer. The trees were bright green from all the rain and the dark stones of the house were covered in sunshine. They had been looking forward to a lovely day. It was Paul's birthday.

It started off misty and then the sun got out and was hot. There was to be a party at the house and all their friends had been invited. Faye and she had gone to London for their clothes and Jenna was happy with what they had chosen, Faye had a pale pink dress with flowing sleeves and a square neck and she was wearing yellow and orange with thin velvet ribbons.

The food was laid out in the garden on big tables and people flocked to the front of the house. The guests had arrived. Jenna could hear the sound of champagne corks popping and then she heard Tony Evans's Lotus Elan as it roared up the street. He was late as usual.

When it stopped she could even hear the sound of the engine dying away and of Tony's voice, always louder than everybody else's. He was North End's playboy, lots of girlfriends, drank champagne and had aspirations to be rich. He owned clothing shops in Newcastle and wanted to open a nightclub. Sorrel thought he was a very enterprising young man and encouraged him in his business ventures and even invested in them, Jenna thought.

As Tony idled up the path toward the house she caught sight of him moving through the garden and beyond the beech hedge. He was wearing an expensive cream suit. He had somebody with him. No doubt one of the other footballers. Everybody had been invited.

The other man was taller than Tony, black-haired, Jenna could make him out now. He was wearing a grey suit and a white shirt, he had cream skin and there was something about the way that he moved, flowing and yet contained, that she recognized in that instant from the way he had spent his childhood learning to control a ball in the unmade back lane among the puddles outside their houses.

Her head told her it couldn't be, that he was still not home and she had been safe from this, but her heart knew him in an instant. It was Ruari.

She panicked. Had he been invited? He wasn't supposed to be here yet surely. They came into view, chatting, Tony smiling like an idiot. He would not know how very embarrassing this was going to be for everyone, or had he done it on purpose? She began to think that he was just stupid but whichever way it was it was unacceptable. Sorrel would have a fit.

Tony was gesturing with his hands. Everybody was looking now, had stopped talking. There was silence throughout the garden so that she could hear the birds singing, feel the slight breeze which came off the sea.

The people gathered here were used to footballers but Ruari they thought of as some kind of traitor because he had been a local boy genius who sold his talent to the highest bidder. He had left and gone to their deadliest rivals and now had deigned to come back.

From the corner of her eye she could see Sorrel, the way that he brought his shoulders up and then let them back down; he watched without blinking as Tony brought Ruari across the garden and into their midst. Sorrel ignored Tony. He didn't care how rude it looked, she could see. His gaze went to Ruari like an arrow and she knew then that he had expected Ruari back, had even perhaps planned it like this.

'Mr Gallacher,' he said, 'how nice that you could join us.' His voice was like early morning frost.

Ruari smiled. It didn't go anywhere near his eyes, it was the thinnest smile that Jenna had ever seen. They were, she thought, the nearest thing to gladiators out of a Roman arena, eyeing one another. How strange.

Worse still somehow Ruari had changed almost beyond bearing. He was not a boy any longer, she looked in vain for anything beyond his appearance which was familiar and could find nothing. That was a shock. He had always seemed so young to her and vulnerable, it had been one of his best qualities. It was gone. He was taller, she thought, and his eyes were like iced puddles in the back lane when they were children, so blue that they were almost black with a silver sheen.

'Mr Maddison,' he said, 'good evening.'

He didn't even sound the same. There was no local lilt to his voice, it was cool, flat, nothing like the footballers she was used to. He looked and sounded so classy, Jenna thought, pleased, and then realized that she was on the other side. How strange, she hadn't known. And the boy genius carried an aura with him, she had seen it slightly in other men but it was so well defined in Ruari, as though he knew exactly who he was, that he was the best, sure of himself, so confident.

She had observed it many times watching him play on television, he saw more than other men, he saw the goal, he saw the ball, he saw the spaces where you would not think there were any and he could move very fast, it left other footballers rooted, it brought the crowd to their feet.

He was poetry she could see, not just on the field but off it as he moved and did not move and every woman present knew it and there was something about it which was devastatingly attractive. She was horrified. He had been hers and she felt cheated somehow. He had gone and this man was in his place, famous, objective somehow, calculating. There was nothing left of the boy she had loved.

It was difficult even to take your eyes off him and he knew it though he didn't mind or didn't care, he accepted that other people were drawn to him, looked at him, it had become part of who he was. And he was successful and if there were women in the room who weren't aware of the attraction of all that, Jenna couldn't see them. They were staring.

Then Ruari saw Jenna and he smiled and the second smile held no more warmth than the first. He covered the space between them in a second. Funny that. All that time and yet he was in front of her.

'Hello, Jenna,' he said, 'how are you?' So simple, so direct, so cool as though he wanted everybody to see that he no longer cared for her or for any of them.

Somehow it broke the spell, the music started up, trays of champagne were carried around, people began to talk. Jenna extended a hand and he took it in slender fingers. His grasp was light but firm as though he shook hands very often and didn't think about it.

'Ruari,' she said, 'how nice to see you. How's your mother?'
'She's fine.'

Ruari looked beyond her, as though he was bored. Jenna felt a pain cross her chest that was almost physical. And then, to her relief and also to her alarm, she saw that it was the band he was looking at.

'Perhaps you'd like to dance,' he said.

Jenna wanted to run away but she did not know how to refuse and he took her by the arm. He had such a good grip on her that she would have had to make a fuss to get away. The music was slow. He took her into his arms and Jenna wanted more than anything in the world for Paul to come across and claim her. She was so humiliated.

'How's your marriage?' he said, looking her in the eyes.

This was taking frankness too far, Jenna thought, and she was amazed that he should say such a thing. Had she been wrong about the way that he looked? Was it all a show? Did he not realize how bitter it made him sound? Did he not care?

And to her horror she realized that it proved how he felt about her. That he felt anything at all amazed her. She had thought he was a different person but underneath the gloss and the success he was just the same. She was uplifted at the idea that he even cared and downhearted for him that he had not moved on. She wanted him to find somebody else but dreaded it.

'Fine. What about you?'

'Oh, I didn't marry. The girl I loved gave me up for a clown with a nice car.'

She concentrated on not crying, on not running away though she badly wanted to. People would talk, Paul would be angry at such a display. She had been right, he had not got over it. Her heart beat hard and she wanted to grab his hand and run out of there with him. That made her want to cry more.

She had worked so hard to be Paul Maddison's wife, to greet him with joy when he came home and be pleased, and her world had shattered in those few minutes since Ruari had walked into the garden. It made her want to weep, as though everything she had gone through with Paul and with the baby and with his family counted for nothing at all, her marriage evaporated like early morning summer mist.

She drew back slightly and his fingers stopped her from going any further from him. The trouble was she liked the feel of his hand on her back just as she had always done, the pressure, as though it was the only thing which mattered to him, having her there so near. It made her wonder why they had been apart for so long. Did he feel again that incredible attraction or was he taking revenge here? She didn't know and she didn't want to know, she wanted to run away, to run back to Paul, to have Paul rescue her. Where was he?

'I have a nice car now. Maybe I could compete or does my back-ground get in the way?'

'Don't.'

'Are you happy?'

'Don't you want me to be?' She looked up at him but she couldn't see him very well because her eyes were wet. 'When you love people don't you want the best for them?'

'I never heard anything quite so stupid,' he said. 'Paul Maddison is an idiot.'

'There are worse things for men to be,' Jenna said.

'You're right,' he said, 'to be called a genius is much worse.'

'It's what you are.'

'Einstein was, Mozart was. I play a game for my living. It makes people feel better to think they've seen genius, but it's just a talent. I'm very good at it and so are a dozen men every few years and people always think they're the best because they want to be close to something like that, they want to be part of history, to have seen the best even when there's no such thing. It makes them feel good, makes them feel part of something. I'm just a football player. I don't even enjoy it any more.'

Jenna hadn't thought of this.

'Why not?' she said.

'Because when I play badly they curse me and scream and spit and when I play well they think it's them doing it, that they make the difference, and they don't. I have to score goals, I have to do it all the time and I'm told what to do. I'm here because I was told to be, I'm Sorrel Maddison's puppet. He bought me.'

'But you're . . . you have so much.'

'I would have given it all to have you. I wish I had known what it was going to be like. I would have stayed in the shipyard.'

Jenna stopped dancing and when he let her go she moved back a little way. She wanted to run like she had when she was a young girl but everybody was watching so she smiled and pretended nothing was wrong.

She felt like she was burning, as though nothing in her life mattered any more. She wanted so badly to go back to her room now but it was not late enough, people would remark, maybe they would even remember.

She remembered, only too well, and it seemed to her as though neither she nor Ruari would ever escape the back lane. Maybe nobody ever did escape the first years of their lives, they spent the whole time trying to get back there to whatever joy or misery they had first known, perhaps wanting to change everything. She wanted to change what she had done so much, more now than ever.

Paul appeared as the music ended and he looked straight at Ruari and he said in soft tones, 'Keep your bastard hands off my wife.'

'Paul!' Jenna said in a loud whisper even though nobody else was within earshot.

Ruari said nothing. He was in no position to take on the Maddisons. He was miserable. There was nothing to bring comfort to him on cold wet Saturdays, when the fans, full of brown ale, were screaming abuse at him because he hadn't scored.

It had been a very long day. When Paul put an arm around Jenna and led her away he was only glad at the idea of going back to the hotel. It was almost like going home, going back there, it was such a relief. He was looking forward to seeing from his balcony the place where he had been born and brought up and the sea and then he would remember what it had been like when Jenna had been his, when she had loved him.

It would not have been so bad if he had not been able to remember and stupidly it was not really to do with how she felt under his hands, beneath him, it was to do with her voice calling him down the back lane. There had been other girls much more beautiful beneath him and in other ways, girls with silken limbs and warm eyes, and he had liked them all, had even, he thought, been in love once or twice but they were not Jenna.

As he went back to his hotel, when he drove through the town, he saw the fish shop on the end of the road and suddenly he could smell the chips and the vinegar running through them and the warm acid smell was the best in the world, he knew.

He was that boy again, making music with a football and avoiding the way the road went up and down in the back lane, the puddles with rainbows in them and Jenna coming back with the fish and chips for her family and the day dark with rain and the sea behind it all crashing to the shore. It was never like that any more and if she didn't know it then at least he had the memories.

When it was late he stood there on the balcony, thinking of how when he was young he would watch the sun go down, the sea darken until you couldn't see the beach any more and the sand grew cold under your feet if you ventured down there. He and Jenna on the beach with the bitter North Sea which even in

August had not warmed through but it was theirs, the beach and the sea and the little town and the back lane and the lights coming on as the day drew towards its end, he in his little house and Jenna next door, never together but never apart. It had not been as good as that again and now he was beginning to believe that it never would be.

Maybe it was all you could expect. Maybe some people never had that. Why should they? Maybe he had been lucky in that Jenna had loved him once and he had had so much since. He had been able to help his mother, the little she would let him, with nothing more than a stupid ability in his feet which somehow connected to his head. It was not intelligence, it was not education, it was nothing more than instinct. It had not given him what he had wanted, what he had planned, but maybe it wasn't supposed to.

He went back inside, the air was chilled even in early summer here, he thought fondly. He opened a bottle and poured himself a glass of wine and he stood inside with the doors shut. Even then you could hear the sound of the sea. It was enough to comfort him, enough to sleep by.


Jenna was so angry with Paul that she left him at the party and went upstairs. It was not long before he followed her into their bedroom.

'How dare you do that?' she said.

'I don't trust him.'

'What about me? Don't you trust me? People are going to talk if you behave like that. You've got nothing to worry about. I don't care about him. It was finished a very long time ago.'

'Was it? It didn't look like that.'

'Then what on earth did it look like? We danced.'

'He couldn't take his eyes off you and you . . . you watched him from the minute he arrived.'

'I didn't know he was going to be here, it was a shock, that's all. Somebody could have told me.'

'The bastard wasn't invited.'

'I imagine he would feel obliged. All the other footballers were here, after all, and your father looked to me as though he knew.'

'My father turns everything into business.'

'I think he likes them, wants to invite them. Your father's very sociable,' Jenna said.

Paul laughed. 'I've never heard it called that before.'

'What do you mean?'

'You don't know what my father's like, you don't see anything. He doesn't care about anybody, all he really cares about is his bloody football club. He can't stand Gallacher but he had to come back because he's so good and because it was the best thing for the club.'

'And isn't he right?'

'I don't care. I don't want the bastard back here dancing with you and coming over all smarmy and clever.'

'It means nothing to me,' Jenna said and even as she said it she realized what a lie it was. Ruari would always matter to her but he, like Sorrel and Paul, cared more for other things and she was not about to make any more mistakes with men, she had learned her lesson. She had the feeling that Ruari only wanted her now because she belonged to somebody else and he had to have everything he wanted, he had always been like that, maybe they all were. It was easier in some ways because he was nothing like he had been and that was the feeling that lingered with her. Between them she and Ruari had destroyed the boy and girl they had been.

It was only two days later that Ruari telephoned her at home in the early evening. She was alone. She was nearly always alone. Faye went out with friends and did not ask her and anyhow they were older and Paul was never at home at that hour. She had taken to drinking gin and sitting in the garden and reading and she was just coming in for her first gin and tonic when the telephone rang and she answered it.

'It's me,' he said, 'can I see you?'

She was astonished at his nerve.

'Certainly not,' she said.

'Why not?'

She didn't answer that, she was suddenly so frustrated.

'Are you busy?'

'No, not really.' She cursed herself instantly. Could she not lie to him, could she not manage? She tried to remind herself of how remote, how different he had looked and even the sound of his voice was different but there was enough of her that cared so that she wished the telephone call would never end.

'Come to the hotel. We could have a drink. It's been such a long time.' When she said nothing he said, 'I'm sorry for the way I behaved, I haven't seen you in so long, it would be nice.'

'How can I do that, everybody would see, and besides . . .'

'There's nobody about and you could come in the back way. Please. I just want to talk to you. There's no harm in it, Jenna, please.'

She went. She tried not to but it was no good, she could not help it somehow. It was a lovely summer's evening and she was quite alone as she almost always was. All the friends they had were couples, most of them by now had children and in the evenings they went home to one another or to their babies and it hurt, the being left out, the wishing she had the same kind of thing. She was starting to think she would never move on from where she was now, so she went.

Reporters were camped out at the front, she could see half a dozen of them lounging in the shade, chatting, bored no doubt that nothing was happening. She parked her car around to the side in among the trees in the shadows and she met no one and slid around by the side of the building and up the back stairs which the staff used and nobody saw her. She held her breath trying to remember which floor and which number and she prayed that there were no cleaning ladies about or any of the guests in the long corridor, thickly carpeted, which she had to negotiate. She banged on the door and he opened it. She took a deep breath and tried to keep her face in a polite smile.

It was the first time she had tried to look at him objectively. It wasn't simple. He wore expensive clothes and wore them well and easily and he was tall and in very good shape as a sportsman would be at his age. His hair was as black as a raven and his eyes were icy blue. His voice was soft and only a slight lilt betrayed his northern origins. He was sure of himself but in a polite way. He wasn't loud or boastful or difficult. He didn't greet her with kisses or try to get hold of her or launch into explanations, he just asked her to come in and it was a lovely room, full of light which it would be from the long day and clear sky. It was the best time of the year.

The first thing she noticed in the room was the double doors which led on to the balcony and the view he had of the beach and the sea. It reminded her of a good many things she thought she had long since forgotten, she could smell the beach and because of it the back lane somehow and all the things that they had forfeited. How on earth, she thought for the thousandth time, had things come to this?

She went out on to the balcony and watched the view and wished that she had not come here and thought of how she had nothing to stay at home for, Paul was never there and . . . if only we had had a child, if only the baby had lived, everything would have been different, she thought. Paul would have loved a baby and I would have had something so positive in my life I wouldn't be standing here like any idiot wishing to have back the past when I know very well that I can't do anything about it. He didn't follow her out, he stood inside and she could feel him hesitating as though he was nervous, as though he half wished he hadn't asked her there or wasn't there himself and yes, he must wish that, that he was back at Teeshaven where things must be less complicated.

Still he didn't say anything and the silence went on until finally she felt irritated that he had got her there and apparently for no reason and she grew tired of the view and turned and he was standing behind her watching her carefully and he said, 'Would you like a drink? There's champagne.'

She shook her head but, maybe just for something to do, he went over and took the champagne from the fridge.

'Don't open it for me,' she said.

'Don't you like champagne?'

'Not particularly.'

'Only rich people dislike champagne,' he said.

'You must have drunk gallons over the years.'

'I have.'

She watched him open it expertly with a quick twist of the bottle and like good champagne it popped discreetly and he poured it into two tall glasses and then he handed her a glass. Jenna moved into the room and took it. She sipped it. It was very good, cold. The summer evening light spilled in at the window. She didn't know what to say and she thought how strange that was, whatever had they talked about, it had always been so easy.

Ruari smiled slightly.

'Come and see the view.'

'I know the view and I've just seen it.'

'That's why,' and then he went out on to the balcony. Jenna followed him. A warm wind was coming off the sea, most unusual. It made her think of how things had been when they were very young and it was the last thing she wanted to think of. She tried to concentrate, looking out to sea as though there was something interesting on the horizon.

'How's Paul after seeing me yesterday?'

'Oh, don't let's do that,' she appealed and he looked at her.

'You didn't really ask me over here to resurrect it all, surely. You must know why I married him but I do care for him now, I do love him.'

He turned and Jenna saw the anger in his face in spite of the way he tried to hide it and then his eyes sparked and he said, 'How dare you talk to me about love after what you did to me?'

Jenna was astonished. 'You're still angry? After all this time? We're different people—'

'Rubbish,' he said and he looked at her.

'You're very different,' she said.

'You know nothing about me other than what you see in the gutter press. I'm exactly the same as I was. Talk about ruining things for people. How is your marriage?'

Jenna had to stop herself from throwing her champagne at him.

'You already asked me that. There's nothing wrong with my marriage,' she said.

'No? Where are the children?'

The pain that went through her was physical and she had to put her glass down on the little table beside her.

'I lost my child after you left. Didn't you know? I miscarried late and badly and I don't seem able to have any more. You hate me?'

'I did know and I'm sorry. You could have come to me then,' he said.

Jenna stared at him.

'You knew?'

'Of course I knew but I thought you'd married Paul because you wanted him. You told me that was why. I wish I could hate you,' he said evenly, still looking at her and he looked all over her face as though he wished to imprint the look of her on his mind. 'I've always loved you. After a while it becomes bitterness, that big empty nothing that nobody else can fill. It's sort of like gangrene. And I always think with every woman that comes along that she'll rescue me. Do you love Paul now, have you sort of grown into it? I think you must, you're still with him.'

Jenna could hardly breathe.

'Certainly,' she said.

'You bloody liar,' he said and that was when she threw the champagne over him and she thought, Yes, I did it on purpose so that he would get hold of me because that was what he did. He kissed her until she wanted him so much that she pushed hard from him, breathing as though she had been running a long way. He let her go. Jenna wanted to cry, the tension between them was so taut, and while she stood, fighting for breath so that she would not disgrace herself, he realized how upset she was and that was when for the first time since he had come back she saw a little glint of the boy that he had been because he tried to defuse the situation. He smiled slightly into her eyes and said softly, 'Stop chucking champagne at me, it's expensive.'

It made her laugh, which was what he had intended all along she thought.

'You taste wonderful,' she said.

'Is that an invitation?'

'Of course it's not.'

'Anybody would after Paul,' he said.

'You're being nasty about him. I'm very fond of him.'

'Oh God,' he said.

'He's nicer than most men. A lot of women would kill for a husband like Paul.'

'You sound like somebody forty,' he said. 'Comfort, what you're used to, when in fact you lie in bed at night and—'

'Don't,' she said, 'it isn't true.'

'Isn't it?' he said, idly. 'There goes another of my dreams.'

Jenna looked at him.

'I have missed you so much.'

He took her into his arms again and this time she let him hold her because that was all it was as though he had divined it was as close as she would allow him. She felt right for the first time in years, her eyes closed against his shoulder.

Nobody was like him and though she had tried to make Paul as important if not more so it had never worked. She cared about Paul, she would not have betrayed him, but this man was her soul mate. She knew it was a stupid expression and trite but she felt that she would have wasted her whole life if they had not known one another.

'You think I can't love anybody else?' he said, when she made as if to let go.

'That would be . . . conceited and . . .'

'Yes, but it's true, isn't it? You don't want me to.'

'I wouldn't act like that.'

'You were pregnant, that's why you let me leave.'

'I had to.'

'You could have pretended it was mine.'

'I wouldn't do that.'

'I would never have known. If the baby had looked like Paul would I have known? He has the same colouring as you.'

'I would have known. I couldn't do that to you.'

'No, but you could do worse and you did just by staying there instead of coming with me.'

She stared at him.

'That wasn't how it was.'

'Oh, I see. You did it for me. You let me go and stay away from you and you married somebody you didn't really care about that much and you kept us apart all this time because you thought your kid might look like Paul.'

'It was his child.'

'Parenting isn't just biology, you know, Jenna.'

'I would have deceived you.'

'Honesty is a very overrated thing,' he said.

Jenna smiled and drew well away from him.

'What?' he said.

'You're so intelligent.'

That made him laugh.

'Oh yes? It was my body you wanted me for.'

'It was indeed,' she said. 'Can we try to be friends?'

'Friends?'

'It's all that's left. I married Paul. He's . . . attentive and kind and I have no right to betray him. He did nothing wrong, he married me because he cared about me and because he wanted our child. It isn't his fault it went wrong. As far as I'm concerned this is for life.'

'Things aren't for life any more, everything's changed.'

'I will never leave him, so don't go thinking it. Please let's try to be civilized about this. I don't want you and Paul at logger-heads. There's no reason for it to be. Now either we are friends or we never meet again, I never speak to you again. Which is it to be?'

She watched the fight go on as his face worked and he looked down to hide it and then away for distraction. She waited for him to make the decision and then she said, 'We were friends first. You were always my best friend.'

And then finally he said, 'All right, I'll try.'

★   ★   ★

Jenna did not see when she pulled out of the hotel gates the car that was parked there, nor did she notice the camera which was taking photographs of her in the car park.

Ruari was awoken by the sound of the telephone. He fumbled, half still seeing the dream, he was at his little house in the country by himself and wishing Jenna was there. He took a deep breath and said hello and Jack's voice, angry and loud said back, 'What the hell are you doing?'

Ruari sat up. The clock by the bed said half-past nine. He squinted at it thinking it must be earlier than that, he was still half asleep and wasn't reading it properly.

'What do you mean? I'm not even out of bed yet.'

'You're all over the newspapers. I told you, how many times did I tell you, to be careful?'

Ruari sat up further.

'I don't know what you're talking about.'

'You and Jenna Maddison. There are photographs of her leaving your hotel. The owner's son's wife. Are you completely out of your mind?'

'Jack . . .'

'They are having a field day with you. Do you know what Sorrel Maddison does to people who cross him? What on earth were you thinking about? No, don't answer that. It's perfectly obvious what you were thinking about and it wasn't football.'

'I don't . . .' Ruari couldn't imagine what he was trying to say. 'Hang on a minute.' He put down the receiver, got out of bed and padded to the door. Outside were a whole pile of newspapers which he had automatically ordered the day before, he always tried to know what was happening. Now he had made a mistake. He turned over one after the other, there were thick black headlines, things like 'LOVE TRIANGLE' making it sound smutty and photographs of Jenna looking so beautiful as she walked to her car, her long blonde hair, her expensive clothes, her small serious profile.

'Oh shit,' he said.

'You went to him?'

Jenna was trembling. Paul was angrier than she had ever seen him.

'I just wanted to sort it out. I don't want you and Ruari fighting—'

'Fighting? Look at the pictures of you.'

'Paul, this is the nineteen-seventies, women are allowed to go to men's hotel rooms without everybody thinking they're going to bed together. Or is that just your mind? I can see that the tabloids are happy with it but I didn't think you were that foolish.'

Paul had come back from work. He looked dishevelled, Jenna thought. He had been out all night, something had gone wrong somewhere, she couldn't even remember what and he had not been home to shower and shave and change as he so often did. But he had seen or been shown the newspapers and he had come back to accuse her. Jenna only wished that Faye was there, not that she would have been much help but at least she would have diluted Paul's presence. She didn't get up on Sunday mornings and rarely put in an appearance before lunch.

Jenna had been sitting in the conservatory eating tea and toast and thinking how well she had handled Ruari and thinking how right she had been, it was all any of them could hope for now and it wasn't much but in some ways she had got Ruari back and if it could be kept as she wanted then they would be able to meet and be friends, and in some ways stupidly she had thought it would be like it had been when they were very young and there was the shore, the sea, the sun and his presence.

She had seen flashes of his kindness and who he had been and all she wanted was to see him, to be around him, it would be enough. She was almost happy until Paul came in and threw the newspapers at her. She sat there, gazing down at them, and she wondered why everything had to be spoiled. She could not even be friends with Ruari, somebody had turned it into a circus, the newspapers were making yet more money from something which wasn't true.

'You went to him,' Paul said again as though she hadn't spoken at all and his voice was very loud and raised. 'How could you be so bloody stupid?'

She resented his language and the way that he shouted at her but the look on his face was frightening. She had never been afraid of Paul before but he was glaring and she was uncomfortable and wanted to get out but she had the feeling he would not let her past if she even got up.

'He asked you to go there, didn't he?' Paul guessed. 'He wants to start things up again.'

It was unfortunately the truth but Jenna wasn't having that, it wouldn't help.

'No, he didn't,' she said calmly, 'he just wanted to sort things out so that we could be friends.'

'Friends? Look.' He waved yet another newspaper under her nose. 'What on earth do you think my father will say now?'

'I think your father has more sense than the tabloids.'

'How it looks matters.'

'And doesn't how it is matter? I want this to work out, I want us to be happy.'

Paul started to laugh. It wasn't a good sound, it was low and harsh and upset her.

'How can you be so naive?'

'He's here, Paul, it's a fact and I wanted us to get round it and I went to see him to sort things out and we did, he's quite happy to be friends—'

'Is he indeed? Oh, well, that's all right, then.'

'It will be,' she said but after Paul had finally been appeased and shut up and even sat down and had some coffee without spouting off again like that Jenna knew that he was right and that it would be difficult for the two men ever to be civil to one another because of her.

Sorrel was so angry when he saw the newspapers that he couldn't think. He didn't like his family being caught up in his business ventures but when he got home and saw Jenna and Paul sitting in the conservatory his better sense stopped him from going in there and then Faye had appeared and he was able to go into the kitchen and hide there while he calmed down.

'Yes, I've seen it,' she said before he had a chance to say anything. 'Let it be, it's for the best. Shouting at her isn't going to help.'

He sat down and she buttered toast for him as she hadn't done for years and put it in front of him and poured coffee.

'We don't need the scandal,' he said.

'You should have thought of that before you brought him back here.'

'I did it for the club.'

'Of course you did but even you must have known there would be repercussions. He was her childhood sweetheart, what on earth did you think would happen? If you don't fuel it and Jenna doesn't see him in private again it will die down. All you have to do is wait.'

Sorrel could see the sense to this but he was furious. He felt as though the whole plan had been ruined by a bastard like Ruari Gallacher and he couldn't think what to do. He had just paid out the biggest fee he had ever paid for a footballer. He had no doubt that in time Ruari would be worth it, he had already made more column inches for the club than anyone before, but the price of his son's marriage was too high for him to stomach. He wanted to kill Gallacher.

He knew that Ruari wasn't stupid. He had not forgotten how Ruari had turned down the original offer and gone to Teeshaven for a better fee, how he had not taken any notice of anybody, and he had seen Ruari in front of a camera and he was just as articulate as any other man. Sorrel had come from a back street himself, he knew that such places could make success and intelligence run hand in hand as well as any university. Neither did he believe that Ruari would purposely cause problems here. You never shit in your own nest, he knew. So had he or hadn't he? The sight of Jenna sitting in the conservatory with Paul made him feel slightly better but he was not a happy man.

'You asked to see me?'

Sorrel looked up. Ruari Gallacher stood in the doorway of Sorrel's office and it was like a bad dream. Of all the millions of men in the world that Jenna could have chosen to have an affair with surely she didn't have to choose this one, Sorrel thought. Was she or wasn't she? He didn't know and he wished he didn't have to care.

He felt weary. Not just tired. For the first time in his life he understood how old people felt. It was the feeling constantly that just one more small thing would push you so far over the edge that you would end up in the kind of hospital bed from where the only direction was the crematorium.

Paul's apparently working marriage had been the single bright spark of ambition left in his life and this bastard had caused it to break down and then Sorrel thought, No, this is partly my fault, firstly for not taking on Gallacher originally and secondly for insisting on having him back because although he had what was undeniably the finest footballing talent of his generation Sorrel knew that his own motivation had been partly − he didn't like to think what percentage of it − revenge.

He didn't like to be bettered and Ruari Gallacher had bettered him at the age of seventeen. To be bettered by a lad who although he showed promise had given no real indication of how brilliant he would turn out to be had made the bile rise into Sorrel's mouth. He had never forgotten it. He had been ready to better the lad and now the lad had bettered him for the second time.

He was not a lad any longer. He was still very young but Ruari Gallacher stood in the doorway of Sorrel's office so self-confidently that Sorrel wanted, for the first time in his life to say, 'All right, you win.'

'Ruari. Come in.'

Sorrel got to his feet. He usually did it because that way he looked down on people but he found himself looking straight into Ruari's eyes which was a shock, had he seemed so tall at the party or was it just that Sorrel was noticing different things and he had to stop himself from saying stupidly, 'You've grown,' like he was Ruari's father and was seeing his offspring fully fledged, and it was even worse because they had not met properly and known one another when Ruari was a boy. For the first time Sorrel wished they had and that somehow he could have helped and he had the most horrible envy, which was ridiculous, since Ruari Gallacher's father was long since dead down the Black Diamond pit, of a man who could produce such a son. So as they stood there facing one another like soldiers Sorrel was moved by the idea and held out his hand.

'So, are you settled nicely into your hotel?'

Ruari took the hand and smiled though the smile never moved above his mouth.

'I'm fine, I'm used to being on my own,' he said and it was so obviously untrue that Sorrel wanted to break his neck.

'Do you play chess?'

'No.'

'What a pity. You would be a grand master by now.'

Ruari said nothing. He didn't even move uncomfortably like any decent man would who had done such a thing to anyone, not to the man who employed him. It occurred to Sorrel that Ruari Gallacher was not a decent man, that he had none of that left, fame and success had taken it from him and he cared for nothing. He could look Sorrel straight in the eyes like this and it was Sorrel who broke the gaze.

'I got you back here to play football, not to play silly buggers.'

Ruari looked angry. Really, Sorrel thought, he was a first-rate bastard.

'I know that you . . . you had some kind of relationship with

Paul's wife but it's a long time ago and I wouldn't have brought you back here if I had thought you assumed you could . . . pick it up where you left off, so to speak.'

'Relationship,' Ruari rolled the word around on his tongue, 'is that what you call it?' His look was unblinking as though he had waited a long time for this. And in that moment Sorrel thought of Jenna.

She had that starry look about her, the bright shiny look that women had when they were involved with a man other than their husband and he couldn't stand it. He thought of the possibilities. Was there anything he could offer Ruari to go away, to leave her alone?

Sorrel was tortured with the idea of Ruari running off with the woman his son loved. It would be like somebody running off with Faye and dreadful as their marriage was he did not think he could go on if she walked out and left him.

That was what men like them did, they got women to marry them and then left the marriage like it was a deposit from a dog on a doorstep. Marriage, he thought savagely, who had ever thought it was a good idea, it was nothing more than control, a way of herding people into little houses and closing the door on their lives.

And men fought past it and some women did too and some gave in and some . . . some loved so hard, so truly well that they endured it. Was Jenna like that, would she give up her life and her freedom for this bastard and he felt as though it was all his fault.

'You made the tabloids and you've made me very angry. I've dealt with better men than you. If you don't leave her alone I will make sure you do. Do you understand me?'

Ruari frowned.

'Mr Maddison—'

'She's married to my son and it may not be a marriage made in heaven but it's legitimate and he cares about her. I don't care how many women you have but leave Jenna alone for all our sakes.'

'I haven't—'

'I don't want to know about it, I just want you to stop.'

'We had a drink—'

'I don't care what you had. It's finished, do you understand me? Well?'

Ruari's shoulders went down.

'She told me we might be friends—'

'No. You don't see her. If you see her at a function of any kind you keep your distance. If you ask her to your hotel or you try meeting her on the quiet I will know. I'm watching you. Now get out.'

# Eighteen

The football season began in September and from the very beginning Ruari hated it. There were some parts of it he should have
liked, he should have liked the immaculate training facilities, the
way that the ground was kept perfectly, that the changing rooms
were almost newly built. Everything was of the best but he had to
face Harry Philips, who was still the manager. When they came face
to face for the first time he said, 'Now then, Gallacher. Home at
last, eh?' Harry was the worst thing a man could be, Ruari thought,
he abused power, he might even enjoying hurting people if he held
a grudge and he held a grudge here. His eyes were almost starry
that he had control of the young man who had turned him down,
he had gone away and become rich and famous when he could
have done that at Harry's beloved North End. Harry, Ruari thought
with an inward shudder, would never forgive him. Would he take
revenge? What could he do? Ruari didn't think he could legitim-
ately do much and it would be a fight between his base instincts
and his love of the football club because if he upset Ruari too much
would he then not get the goals he so badly wanted, the way that
North End might do so well, so much better with such a striker?

'Yes, sir.'

Philips' eyes widened.

'You called Hodgkin sir?'

'Isn't that what you get called?'

'They call me Boss. Quite different.'

'Yes, Boss.'

Ruari didn't smile. He wouldn't. This man had treated him badly
and now he felt as though he was in his power though it was a
different game. This man had seen him as a beginner and maybe as
somebody to break before he moulded him. Now it was too late,
the mould was set and who had set it had made a good job. He
would do what it took to mollify Philips, obey him, listen to his
advice, show respect but if Philips went too far . . .

Philips looked down and Ruari thought, with some relief, Yes,
he cares more about the game than about what we did to one
another. Finally, after a very long pause Philips looked him in the

eyes and said, 'I wanted you back here and not for the reasons you think. You think I'm going to hang you upside down and shake you until you drop and I could but I'm not going to. You're the most naturally gifted player I've seen in a long time and I was a fool not to secure you long before I did and then a bigger fool not to make sure of it.

'I think we've both changed. I brought you here to score goals. I'm not going to say I don't care how you do it because I care how all my team conducts themselves on a football pitch. We don't do mucky, we don't do underhand like a lot I could name—'

Ruari wanted to interrupt here and say that neither did the team he had left but he didn't want to sound defensive or like a kid crying for home so he didn't.

'You're a clean player, a good lad and you're a bright spark. I underestimated you. I didn't realize some lads are adults at seventeen. I should have remembered your father.'

'You knew him?' Ruari was interested now, he couldn't stop himself.

'Aye, I did. We were mates, we played football on the same team when we were school kids. You didn't know that?'

'No.'

'There's a lot of things about me that you don't know. I'm a disappointed man so I'm going to say this to you, Gallacher. Don't let me down, don't disappoint me, because if you do then you'll look back on this conversation like drowning sailors look on a millpond.'

'I always do my best.'

'I know you do, that's what you're doing here. You didn't want to come back?'

Ruari was surprised by the question.

'We paid a lot of money for you, Gallacher, and we expect to get our money's worth, so no pressure, eh?' He gave a ghostly grin, it woke Ruari up from his sleep with a shout that night when he dreamed it.

'I said I'll do my best.'

'You'd better,' Philips said. 'If you don't I'll make you wish you had.'

It seemed ironic to Ruari that the first game of the season should be against Teeshaven. Last year he had scored three times against Dunelm North End. Now he was in different colours and working against them. It was lucky that he didn't see his former team mates though he and Jack had already met several times in the past weeks as Jack was determined to sort out what he called 'this mess'. Ruari in what spare time he had kept going back and staying with Jack and Nora because he didn't want his mother to see how difficult everything was because she would worry, but he needed support of some kind and he could go to Jack and Nora's when he had time off during the week, even stay overnight and take the kids to the park with Jack and sleep in a bed which was not in a hotel. He didn't go to his house, somehow he couldn't bear to, and when he thought hard about it he realized that it was because in some remote part of his mind he had seen himself there with Jenna. What an idiot he was.

'It isn't a mess,' Ruari insisted when Nora had taken the children to bed one night that autumn and he and Jack were sitting over a beer.

'You should have refused to go there in the first place,' Jack said unhelpfully.

'How could I? You encouraged me, even.'

'I don't know,' Jack admitted, 'but I wish you'd found a way. I don't like how this is going.'

'It's nothing to do with you.'

Jack glared at him.

'It's to do with me when you're all over the bloody newspapers. Are you stupid or what?'

Ruari didn't answer. He wished they were somewhere other than Jack's, anywhere that Jack couldn't shout at him like this. He wanted to remind Jack about the children upstairs but Nora had gone up to read them a story and besides it was a lovely house with thick walls and ceilings so they probably couldn't hear anyway.

'You don't know what it was like leaving here,' he said now.

'It's over,' Jack insisted.

'No, it isn't,' and it was then that Ruari acknowledged for the first time how much Jenna still meant to him and how much he had hoped. 'You know nothing about it and you've never . . .' His voice trailed off there.

'I've never what?' Jack said, still glaring. 'I've never lost the girl I loved? No, I haven't, and do you think you're going to get her back this way?'

'I'm never going to get her back,' Ruari yelled.

'Well, at least you know it. She's married to somebody else, man, she married him because she was having his kid and it's nothing to do with you. She chose him and she stayed with him. When will you ever get over it?'

'Do you think I haven't tried?'

Jack was silent for a few moments and then he said more softly, 'You cannot go on like this, hating Sorrel Maddison. He did what he did for his club. And he was right, wasn't he? In a way he was right, because he knew what he'd lost. It was defeat, Ruari, he hated you in defeat. You got the better of a powerful man like him and he didn't like it but you're still here and you're still bettering him. You won and now you've gone back there and you're battering the shit out of him—'

'He made me go back!'

'Aye, he did, because you're the best and he knows it and you wanted to be the best, nothing less would do. When other people had given up and gone home you practised. Second anything wouldn't do for you and a lot of it was to show him what he had done, what he had lost. Those years you spent at Teeshaven you and I both know those are a footballer's best years.

'You're a North End boy, you should have been there in the place where you were born and where your dad died and where the girl you loved lived but you couldn't. He took it off you and he took it off himself and there's no way back. People will never forget the way that you have played and you did it for another club and he has had to put up with the fact that he did that. But he didn't cause you to lose Jenna.'

'His son did,' Ruari said bitterly.

'No,' Jack said, 'you did it yourself, you even told me. For Christ's sake, admit it just once. You wanted to play football, you wanted everything that comes with it, and you sacrificed the girl that you loved so that you could have it. You know it's true. I think you've always known it and you can't live with the person you are and you go on playing up to him, behaving like a bastard.'

There was silence. It was one of those silences as thick as bricks.

'No.'

'Yes, you did.'

There was another silence during which Ruari would have given anything at all to get out of the room but for some reason he couldn't move and had to listen to the long silence which followed and put up with Jack, saying the things that nobody should say to him.

'I thought I could have everything.'

'Yes, well, you cannot,' Jack said.

'You have.'

'No, I don't. I don't have that talent that destroys everything it touches. You have it and I've seen other people brought down by it, it ruins people, it sends them to drink and to drugs and to people they shouldn't trust and it eats up everything else in their lives until they're obsessed with it, until nothing else matters. And they believe their talent is invincible and unstoppable and that it will carry them through their lives and it doesn't and won't.

'And you know it doesn't and that's really hard. People don't understand what this game is really like and the pressures that we put up with for it, being owned and being spat at by the fans and being vilified in the press week after week and being criticized over and over and the managers standing shrieking abuse when we get something wrong.

'You're not going to go back there and have Jenna and have everything come right, Ruari, it's not going to happen.'

This time the silence was complete and it was only when Ruari could bear it no longer that he said, 'You're wasted as a goalie, Jack, you should've been a vicar.'

'I know. Me mam always said I was too clever for my own good,' Jack said.

That Saturday the pitch was muddy like it was December. In really bad weather in winter the green was nothing but a big patch in the middle and it was reminiscent of it now, black and thick and slippery and hell to play on. The rain never stopped. Ruari didn't mind that, a wet pitch could be an advantage, all that sliding around made it even, it was almost like being an ice-skater.

It was strange to be against the team he had played with for so long. There were vague nods and looks but nobody said anything and within moments of the game starting Ruari had completely forgotten they were anything to do with him. He was not confused at the white strip, he was playing in blue now and he knew which way he was going. The rest was automatic.

He scored in the first five minutes and the crowd went wild. It must be odd, he thought, for the fans who had travelled all the way to watch the footballer who had been theirs score against their team. The rain came down even harder until it was difficult to see the ball but he put another one past Jack before half-time and it was satisfying after Jack had shouted so much at him.

He heard Jack curse as he hit the ground the opposite way that the ball went into the net. When he got up he was covered in mud. He wasn't the only one. They went back into the dressing rooms at half-time pushing the wet dirt from their faces and hands.

'You could have passed that to me,' Pat Smith said.

'It went in the net, didn't it?' Ruari said.

He was undeceived. Nobody said anything else but he knew that the other strikers would resent him if he kept all the glory for himself. He could be a one-man team but they all hated a selfish player. It was not just about scoring goals and he had his way to make here but suddenly he was tired and didn't very much care.

The dressing room was soon steaming from the wet heat of everybody and Philips was down there telling them all the things they had got wrong instead of, Ruari thought, telling them all the things they had got right and he resented it. He ignored everybody and sat by himself as much as he could in such cramped quarters, drinking his tea and not thinking about what Philips was saying.

He thought about the other side. Mr Hodgkin would be in there telling them now how wonderful they were, even though they were two down and how in the second half they could defeat the phenomenon that was Ruari Gallacher because they knew him so well, they knew his moves, the way he played, they could defeat him, he was just one man, he was only one player, he could not win here and he was reminding them of what Ruari would do now, inspiring them, assuring them. Ruari couldn't help smiling at the idea. He knew them equally well and was defeating them almost single-handedly.

They came out for the second half and his former teammates did everything they could except stamp on him and hold him down and still he got past them and put another one into the net. Jack was taking it personally by now and swearing horribly, Ruari could hear even beyond the crowd.

It was nearly over and he was glad, he had not realized until then how difficult that first game was and to have the first game against Teeshaven was anything but what he would have wished, any other team would have been easier but it was almost done and it would never be the same again, from now on everything would get easier. He was almost happy, he had shown both sides and the fans what he could do and the North End fans could not doubt his loyalty. He could hear them shouting and singing his name and he thought it might work out here after all.

He would make friends, he could put up with Paul and Jenna being together, he would be near his mam and he might even sell the little house in Yorkshire and buy something here. He could at least persuade his mother that he could buy her house for her and he would take her out for wonderful meals and buy her holidays in warm places in lavish hotels.

Very soon it would be back to the dressing room for a hot bath, into clean clothes and the joy of the victory and then, and he didn't understand what happened, there was nobody near enough to have caused it – he turned suddenly and the wrong way to intercept the ball. There was an agonizing scream from somebody and to his surprise he went down.

The ground came up all over him like a blanket, the very pitch where he should have been playing during those years as his own covered him in inches of cold mud. It was in his eyes and in his mouth, he could taste the gravel, the grit, the grass. Philips was bellowing at him from a long way off to get on his feet.

He couldn't see, he wasn't sure he could breathe and then he could because he needed to breathe because of the pain. It was him, it was his scream, he relived the whole thing instantly and in amazement, it had sounded so far off like nothing to do with him but the pain was coming at him in increasing waves like a great tide over the beach until he had to hold his breath almost all the time because the waves of pain were going into a long line, there was no let up between them. He couldn't see for the pain, he couldn't think for it, he would have given years of his life for relief of any kind. He couldn't bear it but he had to somehow because it didn't stop.

Then Philips was screaming louder, he was nearer and the game had halted, he could see boots, legs and then Philips was near so near that Ruari could feel his warm chewing-gum-fresh breath.

'You bastard, Gallacher, get up,' and then the voices of his former teammates.

'He isn't pretending,' somebody said.

'Ruari, where does it hurt?'

The trainer came on with his magic sponge while Ruari clutched at his knee, although the pain by then was coming from his whole leg so nothing seemed to make any difference and he couldn't make out what the trainer was saying, it hurt so much and then he could hear Jack's voice close.

And after that Philips's voice screaming in his ear, 'You did this on purpose, Gallacher, you bastard,' and the pain went on and on.

Jack got down beside him. 'Ruari?'

Ruari shook his head. The tears of pain were running down his face.

It didn't get better and he didn't think he could stand it for another second. The trouble was when there was nobody and nothing to better it you didn't have any choice. The game was halted, the rain poured down and after a short eternity a reassuring voice said something into his ear and after that they moved him away from the pitch, beyond the shouting and the noises changed. They put him into an ambulance and put a needle into him and the pain started to ease up a bit.

He had never been so thankful for anything, he remembered afterwards thanking the ambulance man over and over and the way that he began to be able to take breaths so that there was a little space between the pains, they began to even out a little and as he went on they evened out further and further. He had never liked hospitals but oh, he was so glad of it now, grateful to be lifted down and taken inside and through the long corridor and then eventually for the doctors to put him beyond pain and into a hospital bed. He was so glad he could have cried.

It felt so comfortable, smelled so clean. He had thrown up with the pain and was covered in mud and vomit but he was cleaned up and put into bed and filled full of whatever dulled the pain and he went thankfully into oblivion.

The first thing Jenna wanted to do was dash off to the hospital but she couldn't because Paul came home to tell her about what had happened and it would have been too much for him to stand.

'Is it serious?' she asked Paul when she heard him clash the front door and she ran into the hall. Paul didn't look at her.

'For God's sake, tell me!'

'He twisted his knee somehow or other.'

'It doesn't sound bad.'

Paul grimaced.

'People have done less and not been able to play. It's an accumulation of injuries with them, every time they get on to the bloody pitch . . . Do you realize how much he cost? He could be out all season. I think the bastard did it on purpose.'

'Why would he do that?'

'To get even with Dad and me because of you.'

'That's ridiculous,' Jenna said. 'He loves his football, he loves it more than anything. Why don't you still understand how these things work?'

'He might.'

'And how could he, anyway?'

'I don't know.'

'Oh, Paul, I don't think he would.'

Paul brushed her off because he obviously didn't want to discuss it. She followed him through into the sitting room while he stood in the middle of the floor, shaking his head as though he couldn't believe this had happened. Finally he looked across the room at her.

'You think he's still the kid from the back lane, don't you? Your little friend has changed quite a lot.'

She was about to say, 'I don't think he has,' and then she remembered that Paul couldn't bear this and anyway he was right and she had flashes of guilt because she felt that she had caused all of this, it was a strange feeling, she had upset so many things, set so many events in motion just by betraying Ruari that once with Paul. All these things had started then and all the hatred and resentment was because of her. She wanted to try and make it better but she didn't know how, she thought of what she might say and came up with, 'Surely he wants to play. That's what footballers do.' And as she said the words she knew it wasn't so, she wasn't sure that Ruari cared any more and then she began to doubt him. She wanted to see him so badly, to see herself whether he was going to recover quickly. He must, this was his whole life.

There were varying reports on the news and in the papers which she scanned but she could do nothing but wait and fret. She didn't sleep she was so anxious and when finally Paul went out the following day which was the first opportunity she had she drove to the hospital.

There was nobody about, it was not visiting hours, but he was in a private room in a private wing and she thought any of his friends could go in at any time. She didn't ask anybody, she dodged people in case she shouldn't be there and made her way past reporters inside and outside the building by taking another route and then slipped quietly into his room. Nobody was expecting her so she wore a hat and pushed her hair up inside it and looked as though she was confidently going to visit somebody else and finally she reached him.

The dark September day had already given itself up and rain

besieged the window. In here all was quiet and a single light burned near the bed. He was still, he was asleep but as she sat down he murmured, 'Mam?'

'No, it's me.' She spoke softly. He looked exhausted, white, with great dark shadows on his face. He didn't answer so she said, 'Ruari, it's me, Jenna.'

'Oh.' He opened his eyes. They were full of pain, Jenna thought, but lightened a little when he saw who it was. 'She was here a minute ago, I think she went to get a cup of tea.'

'How do you feel?'

'Oh . . . you know. Won't be playing much football for a while. They had to operate to try and put it right.' He put out a hand to her and Jenna moved nearer and clasped his cold fingers in hers.

He went to sleep and then the door opened and his mother stood there, her face white, her lips thin when she saw who was there.

'It was good of you to come,' she said stiffly as though he was her private property, Jenna thought, hurt, and then remembered she had no rights here.

'What did they say?'

'Nobody tells you anything.'

They sat by the bed for a while but Jenna was uncomfortable now that his mother was there. She had to stop herself from apologizing. His mam knew exactly what had happened. She didn't say anything more, she didn't even look at Jenna, she just watched Ruari, afraid no doubt for what the future would hold. His mother had seen things go wrong before, perhaps even expected them to all the time. Was that what being middle-aged taught you?

'He only twisted it,' was all she could think to say.

'Apparently there have been other injuries, they all have them, and this was the final kind of straw.'

'What do you mean?' Jenna said, stopping and remembering what Paul had said.

'He might not play again. Wait until Sorrel Maddison finds that out.'

'Not play?' Jenna couldn't imagine a world where Ruari wouldn't be able to play football, it was his whole life, he had given up everything for it and even though he was bitter now she knew that when he was on the pitch it was the only thing which mattered to him. 'Have they said that?' she asked, trying to make things better.

His mother looked as though she was about to cry.

'Not yet but they haven't said anything positive either. I wish it didn't matter so much. I can't imagine what he would be like if he couldn't play. What on earth would he do and . . . his whole life would change? How would he . . . make a living? It's not as though he's good at anything else, when did he ever give himself a chance to be?'

Mrs Robson seemed agitated, which was hardly surprising, Jenna thought.

'You must be tired,' Jenna said, 'why don't you go home for a little while? I'll stay with him.'

'He keeps asking for me. I don't like to leave him and besides I would only worry more there, I don't have to go to work, they've been ever so good, that was one thing, they covered it for me. They know who Ruari is, everybody at work is so proud of him.'

Jenna didn't want to leave him either but she made herself go home when his mother would not be moved and he went on sleeping. The anaesthetic did that for you, she thought, put you into an easier, more comfortable place.

The photographers had another go at her when she left the hospital but she no longer cared. She kept her head down and didn't give anybody a decent picture and although they threw questions at her, some of them very rude she thought, she didn't answer. At least she had learned that much though she knew that now she had been to the hospital the speculation, the columns and the photographs would be all over the place by evening and even more so by the next day.

Paul came home late, Jenna was in bed.

'So,' he said, flicking on the bedside light at his side, 'you went to see Wonderboy.' He sounded exasperated.

Jenna wanted to ask who had told him but she didn't. Paul smelled heavily of drink, so much so that when he got into bed she wanted to turn away.

'Gallacher may not be much of a prospect any more,' Paul said, 'six months from now nobody will remember him. Except Dad, of course. He'll never bloody well forget.'

'Aren't you getting a bit ahead of yourself?'

'I managed to get the doctor to speak to me. We aren't talking about something which will be better in six weeks. It might not be better in six months.'

'Have you told your father?'

'No, I thought I'd leave it to the doctor,' Paul said calmly. 'He was at the hospital with me. I came out and left him to it.'

'Does Ruari know?'

'I think he does,' Paul said. 'Did you not think about the tabloids? Did you have to go? Did you not think about me or my family or yours?'

The truth was that she had not and she was not about to get into a discussion about it so she just turned the other way and pretended to go to sleep. She had the feeling that Paul did exactly the same. He turned over a lot during the night and even got up a couple of times and was gone from the bed for a long time.

'I won't play again, is that what you're telling me?' Ruari stared at the doctor. The sun was pouring into the window of his private room. He was coming to hate that room, the silence of the night and the uncertainty of the days, it felt like months since he had last been on the pitch but the trouble was when he thought about playing now he associated it with pain and that was something you didn't forget.

'I'm not saying that,' the doctor said. They didn't deal in definite things, Ruari had come to realize, they would put off saying anything for as long as they could. Medicine was an inexact science and the trouble was that people needed it to be exact, needed to be assured that things would get better, that they would recover, that they would always be here to greet the sun tomorrow, that the world could be patched up and made well, even perfect.

'Then what are you saying?' Ruari tried to insist though he wasn't feeling strong enough either physically or mentally and he was afraid that once they told him he couldn't play that the most awful thing in the world would happen and he would never play, he would never get better, he would have the future to face without football and it was not a thought to be borne.

'I'm saying it's very unlikely that you will play in the immediate future. It will certainly take a very long time to heal.'

'I thought weeks.'

'Think months or . . . even longer.'

'You don't know, in other words.'

The doctor didn't comment. He was not going to fall into a hole of saying he didn't know. He left and Ruari lay there, frustrated, afraid for the immediate future and a lot more afraid for what might happen after that. It was like looking into a black hole.

It must be bad because his mother had walked into his hospital room some time later so she must have been talking to them and he could see that she had been crying though she was doing her best not to now. He thought he had never been as glad to see anybody.

'Don't worry,' she said, 'as soon as we can we're going to get you home. You'll be better there.'

'I can't just do that.'

'Ruari, you can't walk,' his mother pointed out. 'You aren't going to be much good to Mr Maddison like this.'

'But . . .' She couldn't want him there but he could see that she did, she expected him to go back with her and he couldn't tell her that the very last thing he wanted was to go to the little house in the back lane where he had started, in case he should finish there, that his career would really be ended and he would have nothing left but the back lane full of puddles and his dreams dashed and over. Whatever would he do? It made him panic, the big beating wings of uncertainty flapped around inside him and his hands shook. He tried to hide all this from his mother but she knew him too well, she was not deceived.

'They said what?' Harry stared at Sorrel. They were in Sorrel's office at the club. 'We've just bought the little bastard. He has to play.'

Sorrel shook his head. 'He can hardly stand. He did it on purpose.' Sorrel thought his head would explode he was so angry.

'You cannot do summat like that on purpose, Mr Maddison. I saw him go down. He's torn all his leg up—'

'I saw it, I was bloody there, you know.'

'Didn't it look real to you?'

'I know what it looked like, it looked like money down the drain,' Sorrel said and came to rest and sat down in his chair and sighed.

'He's finished,' Harry said. 'If he was a horse they'd shoot him.'

Sorrel could not believe the Almighty would treat him as badly as this. He had paid more for Ruari Gallacher than he had ever paid for a player, he had wondered at the time whether any footballer was worth that much but if Ruari couldn't play then he couldn't be sold, he was a liability. He had cost a fortune. Sorrel sat there for a very long time while he tried to take in the enormity of what had happened. Eventually of course they wouldn't have to pay him but every penny now was money wasted, money he could have used to buy other players, and worst of all he didn't think the team could get to the top without its star player so it was not just the money, it was prestige and excitement and the club's future over the next two or three years because he wouldn't be able to buy anybody else for a long while.

He retained a faint hope that Ruari would play again but in the meanwhile he would be stuck at home and the team would be doing badly and Sorrel would have to sit through it all and there was nothing he could do. He was not used to feeling helpless, it made him angry. There was only one thing which would help. He would go to the club and see Joanna and he would drink some whisky and take her to bed and try to forget his troubles for a while.

It was odd to go back to his mother's house, it made Ruari feel like a child again, as though he had fallen in the back lane as he did often when he was a little boy and bloodied his knees. It was one place he had thought he would never go again except as a visitor and when the front door shut behind him it was like a prison closing.

Coming in the front way was something else he wasn't used to. His mother twittered on about leaving his expensive car outside the house as they must move it from the hotel so that Ruari telephoned Jack and asked him to come and collect it and keep it for the time being. Jack had plenty of space at his house.

'Maybe somebody might buy it,' Ruari said.

'I think you should hang on to it.'

'Why? I'm going to need the money and it isn't as if I'll be able to drive for a while.' He didn't say if at all, he couldn't face that idea and indeed it was a very black way of looking at things but coming back to the little terraced house which he had left so hopefully brought his mood almost to despair.

His mother had got from somewhere a put-up bed so that he could sleep in the front room. He was only glad the bathroom was downstairs, it had been put on some time ago as an addition to the house beyond the kitchen, there having been no bathroom since the house had been built in the early part of the century when coal was the most important thing and workers were needed. Lots of the houses around did the same.

He wanted to suggest to his mother that they should go to live in his cottage for now but he couldn't do that, she had her work, her friends and her own life and though he knew she would go with him if he asked he couldn't ask her to leave here so he put up with it.

From the beginning it was difficult. The people he had hoped to make friends with were no longer interested in him, none of the other North End players even came to see him and he heard nothing from the management. Jack was busy as the football season was now at its height and he had his family to consider so although he rang Ruari told him there was no need to come up, everything was fine and he was feeling better by the day.

He told his mother that she must not alter her life for him, he would manage, but she ended up doing so much that he felt guilty and would try to get up and help. It was difficult in such a small space with crutches and often his efforts to assist were worse than if he had sat down and let her manage by herself.

She worked every day, she still cleaned at the school and she also did offices so she was at home during the day after her early shift and went out each evening. The evenings went on forever and there was nothing to do but read or watch television. He did manage better on his crutches after a few weeks but there was no more progress.

One dark November evening when it had begun raining in the early afternoon and his mother had been gone for about three hours Ruari got so far down in mood that he thought he would never come back up again.

He breathed carefully, tried to think positively about anything at all and when nothing presented itself he ended up imagining that he would be stuck here like this for the rest of his life and then there was a noise in the back yard, in the rain. He gazed through the back window and saw the person come to the door and lift the sneck and then he heard Jenna's voice say, 'It's only me.'

Paul had told her not to go to Ruari, had made her promise she would not see him.

'Why should I not?'

'Because I'm asking you not to. He's caused enough problems. My father has had to try and find another player to replace him and we can't afford it, do you realize how difficult this is making things?'

Jenna did know. It seemed to her that Sorrel blamed her, he wasn't at home much but he rarely spoke to her when he was, though perhaps he just didn't notice, he had so many business problems on his mind.

Faye went to the cottage even in the bad weather. Jenna wished she would not. She hated being in the house by herself all the time and even tentatively suggested one time when Faye was at home that she might visit.

'Oh, you would hate it, there's nothing to do.'

'There's nothing to do here either,' Jenna pointed out.

'Paul's here.'

'He's never in.'

'You should go out and make friends, take on charity work, play badminton, join clubs.'

'Is that what you did?' Jenna said and then wished she hadn't. Faye looked at her.

'That's exactly what I did. I was like you, I wanted to have children and after we lost the second and Paul went to school there were hours and hours of leisure.

'Sorrel made so much money we bought this place and could afford cleaners and . . . and he changed the place to suit him and I didn't care for any of it so I no longer wanted to be involved. I like the cottage now, I build up the fire, read, drink whisky and thank God I'm not here waiting for that bastard to come home.'

Jenna was astonished at her mother-in-law's frankness but she didn't think it was much of a fate. Besides, Paul did come back. He arranged for them to go dancing with his friends the first weekend after Ruari's accident and they went to a very exclusive club, not one of their own, that would have been like being at work, he said.

In the ladies' room there was another rich young woman, who had a diamond in each ear and one around her neck and an expensive silver dress and high heels. Jenna was looking in the mirror putting on more lipstick, when Kate said,

'And how is Wonderboy now? What a comedown for him and by implication of course for you.'

'What do you mean?' Jenna stopped applying lipstick and looked at her.

Kate laughed. 'Oh, don't tell me you weren't having an affair. Paul must be relieved even if his father is upset.'

Jenna was about to deny this hotly but realized that that was what most people were thinking and denying it would not change that. Kate was looking enviously at her too as though Ruari was some kind of superior animal who had had his uses and didn't any more.

She put the lipstick back into her bag and walked calmly into the darkness of the club where Paul was waiting for her. He was already drunk. He had come home and had several whiskies before they left, had assumed that she would drive.

When he got to the club he went on drinking and stumbled when they danced so that she insisted on sitting down. The music was too loud for conversation and then he suggested to the men they were with that they should go downstairs and play roulette so she was stuck with Kate and Kate's friends, none of whom seemed to have anything to say to her, though perhaps she should have been glad of that.

One girl, Susan, came and sat down with her.

'I'm glad to get rid of Gary, honestly, I wish they wouldn't drink quite so much,' she said. 'How's Ruari?'

'I haven't seen him.'

Susan looked at her.

'There was a picture in our paper of you coming out of the hospital.'

'Oh, yes, well, his mother was there,' Jenna said as though that explained everything. 'We were children together, lived next door.'

'Were you? I didn't know that. I thought the romance was something new.'

'It's not a romance, Susan.'

'Isn't it? I gained the impression you were very thick and certainly at Paul's birthday party Ruari looked as though he was happy dancing with you. Paul didn't seem very happy about it but then men are all alike, aren't they, they always want what they think they can't have.'

'Do they? I don't know.'

'You don't know much, do you?' Susan said. 'Well, I'm going to the bar, it doesn't look like any of the men are here to buy me another drink. Can I get you anything?'

'No, thanks.'

'New boyfriend maybe? There are certainly lots of good-looking types there, I might see if I can get one for myself,' and off she went.

The evening was endless. At one o'clock in the morning Paul still didn't want to go home and when they left at two he sang for the first part of the journey, snored the rest and had to be helped up the stairs to bed but when they got into bed he reached for her.

'No, you smell of whisky.'

'You wouldn't say that if I was Gallacher, though, would you? Tell me, Jenna, why do you never do for me the things you did for him?'

'I don't know what you mean.' She pushed him off but Paul got hold of her. He didn't exactly force her, Jenna thought afterwards because she gave in, because he was drunk and wouldn't listen to anything she said and because it was going to be a big struggle and then maybe he would shout and swear but he made her very unhappy because he didn't seem to care that she didn't want him or was it just that he was too drunk to understand any protestation short of physical defence?

She let him have her. She didn't cry either then or afterwards, it was brief and Paul was too drunk to be violent. He went straight to sleep after that and she thought it was probably no worse than what thousands of men did to thousands of women on Saturday nights when they had been to the pub.

She told herself that it wasn't worth getting upset about but she lay awake all through the night and listened to the rain on the window and thought again that if they had had a child it would never have come to this, they would have had more to focus upon than Paul's business. She spent several minutes rerunning her marriage as something perfect with two small children, holidays, Christmases, christenings, Sorrel and Faye would have been involved too and would have been pleased. Sorrel would have come home in the evenings and Faye would not spend all her time at the cottage and . . .

The rain had not stopped even halfway through Sunday morning when Paul awoke and came downstairs into the kitchen.

'Make me some breakfast, eh?' he said, slumping down at the table.

Jenna tried to move away when he touched her shoulder and he got hold of her and pushed her up against the cupboard and said, 'Don't do that.'

'What?'

'Like you can't bear me touching you.'

'You were drunk,' she said.

'It was Saturday night,' Paul said but he didn't meet her eyes and he let go of her in a fashion which suggested to her that he was ashamed of himself. Then he said softly, 'Just tell me one thing.'

'What's that?'

'Whether you slept with Gallacher.'

She said, 'Oh,' impatiently. She was going to try and brush it off as unworthy of an answer and ask him what he wanted to eat but he stood in the middle of the floor and he looked so pathetic somehow that she went on, 'Of course I didn't sleep with him, how could you think that I would?'

Instant relief held his eyes and she remembered uncomfortably how he had been when they had first met, how much he had loved her and how the circumstances had chased the better feelings away.

'You gave the impression that you did.'

'I did nothing of the kind. People jump to conclusions and the newspapers . . . You and I are married. As far as I'm concerned that's it. I would never sleep with anybody else, don't you know that?'

He didn't answer but when neither of them said anything or moved he eventually said in a low voice, 'I didn't hurt you, did I?'

'No,' Jenna said stiffly, 'you didn't hurt me, I just wish you wouldn't get drunk like that. I didn't want you and you didn't care.'

'It's your fault.' His eyes flashed with temper since he knew he had been in the wrong but wasn't about to admit it. She wanted to deny it had been her fault but couldn't because she thought they were both to blame and in the end she just asked him what he wanted for breakfast.

'I would like bacon and egg and some toast and marmalade and some freshly ground coffee and some orange juice and I'd like it in the dining room.'

Sunday was the only day they had no help so she could hardly object, it was his mood she objected to, but at least making the breakfast would get her out of his way. She went into the dining room and laid the table and when she came back into the kitchen he went in there and sat down and read the newspapers. She was eager to have something to do so that she didn't have to put up with him any further.

Ruari was staring at her now as she walked into the little pit house. She was trembling. It wasn't because she was breaking her promise to Paul, it was because she too had thought he would never come back here. In some ways there were too many memories, she could think of being a little girl here and of Ruari's mother having taken them to the beach and as they came in the back door she would take their buckets and spades from them after they had spent all the afternoon building sandcastles on the beach.

They would come back quite late sometimes because they would want to wait for the tide to come in and for the water to fill their castle moats. Jenna always put flowers on her castles and Ruari would search the beach for shells for her. She liked razor shells best and sometimes he would find some which were quite unbroken and bring them proudly to her so that she could put them into the top of the middle of her castle. Her dearest memory was of trying to stop the incoming waves from destroying the castles. She and Ruari would build back furiously the destroyed walls which the tide was reducing to wet sand.

His mother would toast teacakes for them when they got home and sometimes she would buy them ice cream while they were on the beach though they only took sandwiches once because Ruari dropped them. Jenna had thought it very funny how sandy they were after that.

She ventured inside very carefully now, over the back step and down the step from the pantry into the back room and he was sitting at the kitchen table like somebody who had nowhere to go and he looked so unlike the brash young man who had entertained her with champagne in his lavish hotel room that she was aghast. He had lost weight, his eyes were uncertain, but the look turned to pleasure when he saw who it was and said her name and she went over and hugged him as best she could considering he was sitting on a kitchen chair and she was bending down to him.

'Oh, it's so lovely to see you,' she said, 'it's like really coming home, all my best memories are of here.'

He hid his face against her for so long that she was disconcerted.

'My back's aching,' she objected and heard his muffled laughter and when he drew back he said,

'I would ask you into the front room but there's nowhere to sit except my bed.'

She saw now that the sofa was in this room so that it was crowded now that it did for dining room, kitchen and sitting room. She was also surprised at how she felt, she had forgotten how poorly they had all lived, how small the rooms were. There was nowhere to get away from anybody even when there was just two of you.

In the end they sat on the tiny sofa side by side and she half expected to hear Stan come clashing in at the back door as he had done so many times when they were children, she had never been afraid of him because he was such an amiable drunk, smiling at her and waving his arms and staggering up the stairs to bed to sleep off the midday drinking session on Sundays so that he would be fit to go back to the pub when it opened later. How had she and Ruari come to this and lost everything which mattered?

Ruari's house had always contained a certain kind of comfort which her own home had lacked. There was always the smell of paint next door as her mother put layer upon layer to hide whatever she could not bear and she was always too busy to go anywhere or take Jenna anywhere.

It was Ruari's mother who spent time with them even though she went out to work. Jenna could remember the evenings, being alone there with Ruari in the house as they got older and his mother was happy to leave them by themselves but she would come in with gossip and a warm greeting and the fire was always banked up when the weather was cold and she would hug Jenna as though she didn't live next door and see her every day. It was the on-goingness of it which made Jenna ache for the past, that casual way they had always had, the security of not even thinking that things might be any different.

She got hold of Ruari's hand now, tentatively laced her fingers through his and he let her. He didn't say anything but he didn't move from her and Jenna wished she could hold the moment because soon his mother would come back from work and the spell would be broken and she hadn't felt like this in so very long that she couldn't remember the last time she had sat still and comfortable so that the only thing that broke the silence was the sound of the coals shifting a little in the grate.

She didn't want to go now, she felt as though she never wanted to leave, as though Paul would come to collect her and she would cling to the nearest piece of furniture like a child and be dragged, protesting, from the one place where she now felt safe and happy.

She turned to him, waited until he looked at her and she kissed him full on the mouth, her hands deep in his hair and she realized that it was not for him, it was for herself, it was to rid her mind of Paul's possession of her, of his harshness, of the way that he felt threatened and when she kissed Ruari she knew that it was not surprising Paul was worried, there was something to worry about.

It was the best kiss she could remember and in some ways that made everything just that little bit harder and she didn't know how much more she could bear. Guilt held her, remembering Paul's eyes when he had accused her of having an affair with Ruari.

She heard footsteps up the yard and his mother came in. She couldn't hide her surprise either but it was uncomplicated.

'Why, Jenna,' she said, 'how lovely to see you. Has our Ruari let the kettle boil dry again? He'll never learn,' and Jenna thought his mother was enjoying having him at home despite the circumstances.

That was what she was like, used to making the best of a situation however awful it seemed and this was truly awful.

Her eyes were not lit, she felt her son's disappointment, his frustration, his boredom but she would not make him think she was worried. She went through into the pantry and put more water in the kettle and when it boiled she made tea and gave Jenna some sponge cake with raspberry jam in the middle and they sat over the fire while she told them about the people at work and who she had seen and which girl of her acquaintance had just had her first baby.

The kitchen fire, even though it was the only warm room in the house, beat any other kind of heating and they watched the flames until Jenna knew she must go.

'Here, Ruari, see the lass out, it's dark,' his mother said and she protested.

'No, I left my car out the front and walked round. I'll be fine if I go out the front way.'

He got up and limped through into the front room and his mother came and put the lights on and kissed her goodbye and told her not to be long in coming back, it had been so lovely to see her, and Ruari insisted on seeing her to her car though he needed both crutches once he was out of the door. His mother had gone back in. Jenna got hold of him and kissed him again.

'I'll come tomorrow.'

'No, you mustn't.' His voice had taken on a serious note.

'But—'

'It isn't fair to Paul.' He stopped there and then he said, 'It isn't fair to you and me either and if the newspapers see you we'll still make news, in spite of how things are. Don't come back. Please.'

'You don't understand,' she said, 'this is for me.'

'Not even for you,' he said, 'I'm finished, Jenna, I'm done here. When I can I will leave but it won't be like before.'

'What makes you think I want it like before?'

'No, well, you know what I mean. I don't think I'll ever play again. I'm not being downhearted,' he said as she tried to interrupt, 'I'm just trying to be realistic. I don't know what I'm going to do or where I'm going to go when I can but . . .'

'Have you somewhere to go?'

'Aye, I have a cottage.'

'Have you really? Where?'

'Yorkshire moors.'

'I didn't know you had a house.'

'It's just little,' he said, 'in a village and when I'm well enough I'll go there.'

'Wouldn't you like to go there for a visit?'

'Above everything, but—'

'I'll take you,' she said.

She wouldn't be talked out of it, Paul's bullying was at the front of her mind and she was determined not to think about it any more, she insisted that she would come over on the first fine day, provided she could, and they would go over and they would have lunch at a pub or she could bring a picnic and they could eat at the cottage. He said it would be too cold to go, much too cold to eat there but Jenna didn't listen. She waved and left and it was only when she had driven away that she began to cry.

She had done all the wrong things, she shouldn't have gone there, she shouldn't have kissed him, he was right, it wasn't fair, it wouldn't do, it would only make things worse.

She should not have said that she would see him again, that she would take him to the cottage, that they would spend time together and then she thought back to how he had looked when she had first opened the door and it was despair, loneliness, she could see it. She couldn't leave him to his fate, she just couldn't do it.

Ruari stood there in the cold darkness long after she had left, alone on the front street, wishing he could go after her, wishing everything different, until his mother came out and said, 'You'll catch your death, on top of everything else, come in,' and he followed her inside. He did so, closed the front door and went from the chilly front room which was his bedroom into the kitchen and closed that door to keep in the heat because the stairs went up from the kitchen and warmed the upstairs and his mother said, in quite a different tone than she had used when Jenna was there, 'What on earth is that lass doing here?'

He didn't answer. She was right and he had been right to try and persuade Jenna not to come back. Not that he realized it had done any good or she had taken any notice.

His mother let the silence increase for a few minutes so that he could feel her gaze and her agitation but when he said nothing she said, 'No good will come of it, Ruari. She's married and they're a rich and powerful family and you have no right encouraging her.'

'I didn't.'

'You must have done. I knew it was a mistake when you came back here.'

'It wasn't my mistake.'

'No, well. That Sorrel Maddison, he's nothing but a troublemaker,' his mother said as though Sorrel was still in the schoolyard.

'Will you stop worrying?' Ruari said.

His mother said nothing and from her saying nothing he realized how upset she was and finally she said, 'You should have been married, I always thought so.'

'Aye, I always thought so too.'

'I don't understand why things never work out.'

He heard the quiver in her voice and went to her where she was laying the table for breakfast as she always did mid-evening and she turned and smiled at him and then she kissed him on the cheek and he knew they would talk no more about it.

The following day there was a letter for him and when he opened it it was from the *Northern Echo*, the newspaper based in Darlington, asking him if he would write an article for them on the state of the football league. Ruari had never thought of such a thing but since they were offering to pay him and he had nothing else to do he sat down and spent the day trying to and when it was done his mother asked Cissie next door if her daughter might type it out for him as she was a clerk at one of the local factories. This done it was sent off and that weekend was published.

It had not occurred to Ruari that he could manage to do such a thing but lots of people wrote letters to the newspaper that week enthusing about it so the newspaper asked him if he would do another and when that was done if he would do one every week and he was so enthusiastic at having something to do that it made the days shorter and less grey.

Just after that he heard from a national newspaper and they too wanted him to write for them and he had now to keep up with football for a good reason and not just as something he was not part of any more. It brought a whole new dimension to his days, gave him something to look forward to, a new angle, and he liked the writing, he liked the precision of it. He even bought a typewriter and taught himself the basics so that he didn't have to rely on anybody else.

It was about this time that Jenna began to feel different about everything. She had thought was it Ruari, the gladness of seeing him,

but after a week or so when the feeling did not go away she realized that it was physical, she felt almost like a different person. She
began to wonder whether there was something wrong, she was so
very tired, so moody. It couldn't be Paul, he had not touched her
since the night he had got drunk, as though he was trying to make
up for everything.

She felt like crying so very often, it was ridiculous. She thought
that it was the time of year, the lead-up to Christmas when every
day was dark. She had promised Ruari that they would go to the
cottage but the trouble was there was no fine day, the rain and sometimes sleet poured down day after day until she barely wanted to
go over the doorstep.

She went to the doctor in the end, telling him that she thought
she was depressed. He looked severely at her.

'Depressed?'

'People do get depressed. I feel awful, tired, like I don't want to
get out of bed and like I can't take an interest in anything.'

He asked if he could take a look at her and when she lay down
on the bed tested her breathing and felt her stomach and generally
made her feel as though she wished she hadn't gone there. When she
had put her clothes on and sat down again he said, 'You're pregnant.'

Jenna stared at him.

'What? Are you sure?'

'Well, I would say so. Tiredness, no periods, feeling very different—'
Her bleeding had stopped some weeks since but she had just thought
that she was down and nothing was going right and her body was
responding accordingly.

'You're been trying for a baby for a long time. You must be
pleased,' he said.

Jenna was stunned. She didn't go home. She sat in the car outside
the surgery for a long time and tried to take in what the doctor
had said. The sleet was turning to snow and what light there had
been was already gone and it was only mid-afternoon. Slowly she
made her way back and spent the rest of the afternoon sitting over
a log fire with a book on her knee trying to take in the idea.

Ruari didn't like to say anything to his mother but he wanted to
leave and one night when she had fussed more than usual trying to
do everything he said abruptly, 'I'm thinking about going and living
at my house, I'm managing my crutches much better now and I've
got lots more energy.'

They were sitting at the table, drinking tea, having just finished eating and she was about to protest, he could see, and then she looked down and she said, 'Yes, I think you should.'

He was so relieved and he realized then that his mother found it difficult having her house turned upside down by somebody moody and difficult and needing looking after.

'You've been grand,' he said.

'I'm your mother, Ruari, that's what mothers are supposed to be. I think you'd be better in your own home and away from here. I think the timing is right and in a lot of ways it would be better for both of us. You need to move on and if you can get sufficient newspaper work it'll be a big help.'

She didn't say, 'And away from Jenna,' though she might just as well have done. Jenna had not come back and he had not seen her but he thought about her every day and had no doubt that his mother was right.

'I shall miss you very much,' she said.

'You can come and visit,' he said but he knew she wouldn't. She hated being away from home and having never lived in the country she felt like it was a different world.


The following day was a change at last, the sun came out and although she wasn't sure she wanted to go Jenna remembered her promise to Ruari. Although he denied it, it was obvious that he had been hoping she would remember and he put up objections only because he felt guilty about dragging her all the way to Yorkshire.

It was not really a long drive but it felt like one. She had never driven with Ruari and was expecting that he would be like Paul who criticized her driving to such an extent that she tried never to drive with him in the car, but Ruari looked around him with increasing interest as they left County Durham and into North Yorkshire and the scenery was lovely, the up and down of cliffs on the coast, the industrial bits interspersed with neat little market towns and small farms.

She followed the coast and then cut across to where the little villages were all stone cottages and had narrow streets and he directed her to the place that he had chosen to live. It was not a big village but it had a stream running through the middle of it and a stone arched bridge at either end. There were three pubs and a village shop and post office and the terraces were short. One of these was his. She parked outside. It had a little front garden and a white front door and small white windows.

Ruari went first and opened the door and he let Jenna inside. It was so cold that you could see your breath. The door opened straight into the sitting room where there was a wood-burning stove in a neat fireplace, baskets of logs at either side, a sofa and two armchairs and further over a table and chairs.

The walls were thick and the room was square. Across the tiny hall was a kitchen, quite new, and a downstairs cloakroom. Jenna ran upstairs and there were two good-size bedrooms and a bath-room and the back windows looked out over a neat garden.

'It's beautiful,' she said.

'It's absolutely bloody freezing,' he said, 'let's go to the pub.'

'Certainly not. I've brought a picnic.'

When she came back he had lit the woodstove. The room began to warm up straight away and Jenna, interested in his tiny kitchen like she had never been interested in a kitchen before, went in there and put the kettle on and made tea. She liked that she had brought tea and milk, she felt so organized and domestic as she didn't need to be at home. She had made beef sandwiches with horseradish and there were bags of crisps and a fruit cake so as the house warmed they sat by the wood-burner with the doors open and had their picnic and several cups of hot tea.

'I've got a job,' he said. 'Writing about football.'

'I didn't know you could do things like that.'

'Neither did I until a newspaper asked if I would write a column for them. I've done it a few times now and I've had other offers so I must be getting something right. The thing is . . .'

She looked at him. She didn't want to because she hated the direction in which the conversation was going but she felt that she had to even though there was a sick feeling inside her which was nothing to do with the baby.

'I'm getting better, I mean I can get about with crutches quite well now and . . .'

Ruari didn't look at her.

'I'm going to move down here. I can manage and I think it's time I did.'

Jenna didn't say anything. She leaned over and put another log on the fire and closed the doors.

'It's almost an hour and a half away.'

He didn't say anything to that.

'It's a long way for me to come and visit.'

'I didn't think you would,' he said.

'You don't want me to?'

'No. No, I don't want you to.'

He said it slowly and with emphasis as though he was not quite sure, as though he didn't want to believe it, and he watched the flames flickering through the little square glass doors instead of looking at her. There seemed nothing more to say somehow, she felt panicked, as though everything was finished, as though she was going to lose him again for the second time and that this time it might be for good and maybe he had another reason for moving.

'Do you have somebody here?'

'Of course I don't.' He turned his face to her then, in surprise she thought with joy and so quickly that Jenna looked carefully at him.

'You did have a lot of girlfriends,' she said.

'I never wanted anybody but you,' he said and kept his voice steady.

It was the thing she most liked hearing and in some ways the worst. Jenna thought about the baby. She thought of how she had cheated Paul of his first child. She hadn't loved him, she hadn't wanted him, and in spite of all that he had taken her and married her because of the child and he had loved her in spite of it all and then she had lost the baby and the whole reason for their marriage was gone and that was why it had failed, she knew.

'And it isn't right,' he said, 'going on like this when Paul doesn't know and doesn't like me. You're married and as far as I'm concerned that's all there is to it. So, I wanted to see you and I wanted to show you this place and . . .'

'It seems stupid that you should be here by yourself and I should be there like that.'

'It's the right thing to do, though, isn't it?'

She wanted to say, 'Why should we do the right thing?' but she understood what he meant. It wasn't fair to Paul now that she was pregnant to spend time with Ruari, she knew that it wasn't, that none of it could ever work if she betrayed him now, especially when she had such good news. She had never belonged more to Paul than she did now so she didn't argue with him, she washed up and put the cutlery and crockery into the right places and then she packed up the remnants of the picnic and then she came through and said, 'When will you move here?'

'For Christmas, I think. Jack and his family would come over and it would be nice to settle in then. I don't know whether my mam would come, I'll have to try and talk her into it.'

It seemed such a long drive back somehow and nobody spoke as she hurled the little car forward through the darkness. It was stupid, she thought, and so typical that she should be pregnant now. She imagined her marriage getting better because of it, she thought of what Christmas would be like with a baby and how pleased Paul would be and how Sorrel and Faye would become involved.

Things would get so much better, the whole house, all their lives would be altered by this child but she also acknowledged to herself that if she had not been pregnant she would have begged Ruari to take her with him. It was like a replay of what had happened the first time and so unfair that she could not believe it was happening again. It was as though the gods did not choose to let her be with Ruari, as though the time never would be right.

She dropped Ruari off at his door. He said he could manage perfectly well, thanked her for the day, and neither of them even hugged or offered another word. It was a frosty night and once she had seen him in at his front door without slipping she set off again.

She had to go through the town to get back to the manor house. She was not looking forward to it. Paul would not be home until two or three at least, it was one of his late nights and there would probably be nobody at home at all. The place would be in darkness.

She half wished that Ruari had asked her in but it was so awkward between them that she didn't think it would have helped. She was glad that he was trying to do something with his life, to change things, she was glad he had such a lovely little place to live and she thought of him sitting there by the fire with his mother on Christmas Day.

She pulled up at the traffic lights on the edge of the town because they were on red and she had to wait and as she did so she saw Paul's car. He still had the red Ferrari his father had bought for him the night that she had lost the baby. It was sitting outside the fish-and-chip shop and it stuck out like a sore thumb she thought, nobody else had a red Ferrari. She could see into the fish-and-chip shop and Paul was standing at the front of the queue next to a young blonde girl.

It seemed strange that he should be having fish and chips, had his father had a sudden craving for such a thing? She didn't think so, Sorrel was too conscious of his waistline to eat things like that on impulse and in the evenings he was too busy to eat most of the time.

At clubs or in meetings she didn't think he would have done such a thing. Paul was probably just hungry, it was not surprising, she thought in sudden affection, because his father never stopped and Paul had probably had nothing to eat all day and was on the way to one of the clubs and had smelled the salt and vinegar and frying chips on the wind.

She imagined stopping the car and going into the shop and getting him to buy fish and chips for her, the smell was so good, and then she would tell him about the baby and then she thought she should wait until he came home because doubtless he wouldn't have time now for such things and his having to go back to work would ruin her surprise. How pleased he would be, how very glad. Maybe her Christmas would be good too.

Paul, his fish and chips wrapped now, came out of the shop and the lights turned green and Jenna didn't go. She just sat there. The blonde girl was coming out with him. It must be one of Sorrel's beautiful secretaries, Jenna thought, there were so many of them. She had to go before people started pipping but a small worm of doubt troubled her almost immediately and she turned off and waited. Within a few moments the Ferrari had turned down the same street as she had somehow known it would so she set off and followed it.

He was making for the coast road where the old Edwardian houses were on the edge of the town. She had sometimes thought, when she was a little girl, that she would love to live there. They had always looked so glamorous with their three storeys, their gardens which fell away at the back and from the front looked out across the sea. It was where the rich people had lived in olden times, she thought. Now they were flats, some of them really nice from what she could observe from the outside.

Paul's car pulled up here. She was surprised when he stopped. She had to go on of course though she doubted he would have noticed anyway. It was dark and there were various cars about. She pulled up again further along, conscious of her heart beating though still not quite sure why she was here. Was he giving somebody a lift home?

She turned around. His car was very handily parked under a street lamp and she could see now that he was leaning over. Was he going to let her out, opening the door for her, a compromise between getting out and opening the door which would have been ludicrous and letting her get out by herself which might have seemed to him rude?

And then Jenna stared. He was kissing the girl, and there was nothing polite about that, she was getting nearer and had both arms around his neck and the kiss went on and on. Finally they drew apart and then they got out of the car and tripped away into the house and Jenna was left, numb. She should have driven away, she should have gone home, but she sat there, telling herself that she had not seen what she had seen.

The car became cold and she was just reaching that temperature when it seemed too much of an effort to start the car up, to get warm again, and then she thought of the baby and then she thought of Paul kissing the other girl but she started the car up then and drove back to the house. It was in darkness and suddenly she was driving away again, she was driving through the town and towards her mother's house.

She parked outside and hammered on the front door. There were lights in the back room. She had to bang harder and when she did so she still had to wait a long time. Even here, she thought, people did not come to the front door and eventually she heard her mother's voice and saw the curtains twitch and said impatiently, 'It's me, Jenna.'

'Who?'

'Jenna.'

She heard the bolts go back in the front door and then her mother cautiously opened the door.

'What on earth are you doing here at this time of night?' she said as though it was two in the morning.

'Can I come in?'

It was not much warmer inside and her mother closed the door quickly and ushered her through, shutting the sitting-room door firmly.

'Is there something the matter?'

There would have to be, Jenna thought grimly, her mother might be pleased she had married Paul but they hardly ever saw one another. There was the smell of paint in the hall, her mother must have been decorating the stairs.

Jenna didn't know what to say. She couldn't tell her mother about Paul. She couldn't tell her mother about the baby. In fact she wasn't sure why she had come here just that she could not think where else to go.

'Where's Dad?'

'He's at a darts match. Is everything all right?' Her mother's face was concerned and not sympathetic, she didn't want her evening interrupted, Jenna thought, she didn't want bad news. I always bring bad news with me, no wonder she looks so worried.

'No, I . . . I just wondered how you were.'

'We're fine. I mean your dad's sciatica's playing him up a bit and my knees aren't too good but . . . You look peaky.'

Jenna longed for her mother to be the sort of person you could confide in, somebody who would care. No, that was not right, her mother did care she just wished things to go well and there was nothing wrong with that.

'Shall I make you a cup of tea?' her mother offered, getting up.

'No. No, really. I have to go.'

'But you've just got here. Is there really nothing the matter?'

'No, it's all fine, it was just that . . . it was just that we wondered what you were doing for Christmas and I thought I'd come and ask you. Maybe you'd like to come to us.'

Her mother looked well pleased, she loved the few invitations she ever received to the Maddison household.

'Well, we did plan to stop here but I'm sure your dad wouldn't mind.'

Her father always liked his own fireside best, Jenna thought with affection. He was not prepared to give it up for the grand setting of the manor house but her mother would persuade him, he would do anything for her mother.

'That's good. That was all it was. We're having goose stuffed with apricots.'

'That'll be lovely,' her mother said, knowing that her father insisted on turkey.

The house had become insufferably hot somehow, she hated the constant smell of paint and in her condition it was making her feel sick. It was just like the last time, she thought, she trying to tell her mother, only this time she couldn't and not telling her father and having to face up to things she didn't want to face up to.

She had always hated this house, the little castle which her mother loved so much and lavished all her time and affection on. It never looked any different, it never looked any better, Jenna thought savagely, and suddenly she couldn't bear being there any more, so far away from everything she cared about and even as her mother protested that she had just got there she left, slamming her way into the little car.

Once she was away she tried not to drive too fast, she didn't want to have an accident, not the way she was. Did she really want Paul's baby? She wished and wished it could have been Ruari's. Were things never going to go right for her? She almost gave up caring.

She almost thought if she could crash into a tree or a lamppost and finish the whole thing how much would it really matter to anybody but somehow the little car found its way home to Back Church Street and she managed to get out of it and found herself hammering once again on the front door. She had to wait, the wind was screaming past her now and the hail was sideways.

'For God's sake,' she implored, 'open the bloody door,' and when he did, and it was Ruari, she had been afraid it was his mother, she cast herself on him even as she saw his astonished face and then she broke down in tears.

He gathered her into the house and his mother was there by then.

'Why, lass,' she said, drawing her away from Ruari and inside, 'what is it? Come in, come by the fire.'

In the back room, which she realized now she had left such a short time ago, they sat her down and he held her hands and she tried to stop crying and his mam said, 'It cannot be as bad as that,' and she said,

'Oh, yes it can. It's just as bad as last time and I've got nowhere to go and I don't know what to do.'

Mrs Robson gave her tea and though she didn't drink it somehow the warmth of the cup in her hands and the warmth from the fire and how safe she began to feel made the situation easier and then she remembered quite how awful it was.

'What is it, Jen?'

He hadn't called her Jen in years and his soft reassuring voice made her want to tell him but if he found out she was pregnant he would urge her to go back and she couldn't do that.

'Can I stay? I don't want to go back there, I don't ever want to.'

'Nobody's going to make you go anywhere,' Ruari said as his mother nodded.

They didn't question her any further. Mrs Robson ushered her into a freezing bedroom and gave her a thick full-length nightdress with long sleeves. Jenna hadn't been in a cold bedroom for so long that she was amazed at how awful it was but when she had undressed and climbed into the bed there was the joy of an electric blanket and she was so exhausted that she curled up into a ball, glad of the warmth and the darkness where nobody and nothing could reach her, and she went to sleep, she couldn't manage any more.

Paul got home as he usually did at about three in the morning to discover his bed empty. He thought that Jenna had a cold or some such and had gone into the other room but when he ventured in she wasn't there either. He went back downstairs and searched in the sitting room, perhaps she couldn't sleep – and then in the kitchen. Maybe she had got up to make some tea, he thought, but she was nowhere to be found and he began to worry and when he put on a coat and went outside her car had gone.

He ran quickly back into the house and up the stairs and banged hard on his parents' bedroom door. There was a short wait and then his father appeared, wearing a pair of expensive blue pyjamas. He peered into the light of the hall, looking bewildered.

'Where's Jenna?' Paul said.

Sorrel looked blankly at him.

'She's missing. She isn't here,' Paul explained carefully.

'Missing?'

'Was she here when you came in?'

'I was late,' his father said as though he should have known and Paul could hear his mother's voice and she came to the door, tying a dressing gown around her.

'What is it?' she said.

'Was Jenna here when you went to bed?'

'I don't know. I presume so. I'd been out playing bridge. I thought she'd gone to bed early.'

'Well, she hasn't; she's not here.'

'She probably went to see her mother and stayed. Is there a note?'

They searched the whole house, all the lights on.

'She probably knew you'd be back late and stayed there,' his father said impatiently.

'She never stays with them. She doesn't get on with her mother,' Paul said. 'I'll have to go and see.'

'You can't go there at this time of night,' his mother protested but he was already halfway down the stairs and collecting his car keys from the hall table.

It was snowing by now. He slipped as he stepped out of the front door and cursed his expensive shoes which were not meant for such things. He tried to go carefully to the garage and then backed the car out, turned it around and drove across the town to where Jenna's parents lived in the little terraced house which he had hardly ever been in and hated, it was tiny and claustrophobic and Jenna's mother was always fussing with bloody wallpaper and paste that stank. He didn't know how her father stood it but then her father was a pathetic little man who wouldn't say boo to a goose.

Paul tore down the roads in spite of the thickening snowflakes so that the windscreen wipers would barely take it and pulled up with a jerk outside their front door. The street was dark and silent as it would be now that it was half-past four. He got out and brayed hell out of their door. He seemed to wait for ages, the snowflakes falling on to his hair and his coat and he cursed under his breath, trying not to panic. She could not have gone far but why had she left the house at all, what was going on?

After he had done knocking hell out of the door twice more, after a short forever lights came on above and so he did it again and after a very long cold period when he became covered in snow the downstairs lights came on and the door was unlocked and Mr Duncan peered out. He wore striped pyjamas and a grey woollen dressing gown and he looked surprised. Paul didn't blame him.

'I need to speak to Jenna.'

Mr Duncan looked at him.

'Jenna?'

'I'm worried about her. She didn't leave a note. She is all right?'

'Isn't she with you?' Mr Duncan said with all the vagueness of somebody who had been sound asleep ten minutes ago.

'She's here. I want to speak to her.'

'She's not here,' and the idea suddenly seemed to hit her father.

He let Paul into the house, or rather he stood back as Paul, tired of being cold, outside and confused, pushed his way inside. By then Mrs Duncan was hovering in the background and when Mr Duncan explained Paul could see the concern on her face. She began to cry. Paul was very embarrassed, he wasn't used to tears. His mother never cried and Jenna had shed few tears except when she lost the baby. Thinking about that time made him feel very uncomfortable.

'She came here earlier,' her mother said.

'When was this?'

'Oh, in the middle of the evening. About nine or something like that. You weren't back from the pub then,' she said to her husband. 'I didn't know there was anything the matter, though she didn't look well. I thought maybe you'd had words or something.'

'Did she say anything?' Paul's patience was almost at an end.

'She invited us to your house for Christmas. I asked her what was wrong, and she didn't look well but she wouldn't stop.'

'So where is she?' Paul said and then he knew and he was angry and hurt and confused. He could see that her parents had no idea where she had gone so he didn't say anything to them. He tried to be reassuring.

He made his apologies, he told them he would let them know when he found her. Mr Duncan offered to help, Paul said brusquely that he didn't need any help and then he urged the car forward through the snow the few streets until he got to Back Church Street and yes, there it was, her car parked so obviously outside Ruari Gallacher's door. He cursed her as he pulled up behind it.

What the bloody hell was she playing at and as for that bastard Gallacher . . . He wrenched on the handbrake, got out and slammed the door and then again began hammering on the wood of the front door. At least the snow had stopped. It gave everything such a strange and almost eerie look. Total silence except for his efforts which seemed huge, big enough to reverberate off the houses opposite.

Here again he had to wait but eventually the door opened and there stood Gallacher, propped by crutches but not looking very surprised.

'Hello, Paul,' he said.

Paul pushed past him, it wasn't difficult, when a man's on crutches he doesn't take a lot of getting past. He saw the small put-up bed and then he looked back at Ruari and he said, 'Where's my wife?'

'She's in bed upstairs.'

'You didn't think to let me know?'

'My mother doesn't have a telephone.'

Paul couldn't believe it. Everybody had telephones. He was about to say there was a public call box on the corner and then he stopped himself. It was ridiculous. Gallacher had had no intention of letting him know his wife was there, didn't care enough to put anybody at their ease, least of all somebody of his family.

'What's going on?' he said.

'I don't know,' Ruari said so convincingly that Paul believed him. 'She was upset when she got here and it was late and she was tired and she wouldn't go home so my mother made up the bed in the other room.'

'I'd like to see her.'

'Maybe you should wait until the morning.'

'I don't think you're in any position to tell me what to do,' Paul said, indicating the crutches.

'Possibly not, but—'

Ruari stopped as both Jenna and his mother appeared behind Paul, who was standing with his back to the room. He turned around. His wife was wearing the most unbecoming nightclothes he had ever seen. They were undoubtedly Gallacher's mother's, long and washed-out looking and she was washed-out looking too. He could not help comparing her to the lovely armful he had left, Trudie in black and cream satin, warm and willing.

Jenna's blonde hair was lank and her eyes were dark and empty and she clutched the front of the shapeless garment she had been offered for warmth, her hands were thin and her face was pale and she stared. And yet he thought she had never looked more beautiful, more appealing, and he had never loved her more. He could have shrieked with frustration. He could see now that what he felt for Trudie would never equal the love he had had for Jenna and went on having in spite of everything that had happened. Trudie was like having one glass of cheap brandy when what you really wanted was two good measures of Rémy Martin.

'What are you doing here?' Paul said. He noticed how his voice was soft with relief but rough with anger. He was glad to find her but hated that she was here in Gallacher's mother's bloody awful little house.

'Ruari,' his mother said, 'I think these people need some space.'

Ruari hobbled off into the kitchen and his mother went with him and closed the door behind her. In some stupid way Paul wished they wouldn't go. Whatever reason Jenna had for coming here he had the feeling he wasn't going to like it and he wanted to put it off for as long as possible.

He also wished he could just whisk her away back to the manor house where he thought she was safe and his and waiting for him, no matter what he had done, he needed her there for him to come back to, he felt it was the only real thing he had left somehow. He tried to keep his voice low so that she would not run off into the other room. At least she and Gallacher were not sleeping in the same bed, it was respectable, his mother was there, he had had the horrible feeling, which he had kept to the back of his mind, that Jenna and Ruari had run away together, though run was perhaps a little generous, considering Gallacher could barely walk.

'I got home and you weren't there,' he said slightly accusing. 'I've searched everywhere, I've even been to your mother's. Are you all right?'

Jenna seemed to take a breath and then she sat down. She didn't say anything for so long that Paul wanted to prompt her but he knew it wouldn't help, he just had to sit there and give her time. Jenna was not the kind of woman who didn't answer questions, she had been brought up to respond no matter how difficult things were, he knew. Eventually she shifted her weight about and then she said honestly and with a sigh, in a way he had always loved, 'No, I'm not all right. Nothing's right in my life at all.'

It was what he was expecting in some ways. He knew nothing was right, he just didn't know any longer how to make it right, because he had tried and tried for so long to make things up to her that he had long since given up and not known how to go on. Muddling along, wasn't that what most people did?

'You could have told me.'

'I think you knew,' she said.

'What did I know?' He sat down on the awful little bed which creaked under his weight so that he thought it might tip up and land them both on the floor.

'How unhappy I was.'

'I didn't know you were unhappy.'

'I've been unhappy for a long time now and I think you have too otherwise why would you have somebody else?'

So that was it, that was what she was doing here. At first he could only be pleased that it was something so unimportant, at least to him, but then she had run to Gallacher. He thought of the awful house which her parents had. She had run there first but had not had any help. Maybe she had had nowhere but here to go. Paul didn't know what to say, she seemed so sure.

'I saw you,' she said, 'tonight, with her. I saw you come out of the fish shop and I saw you kissing her in the car and I saw you go into the pretty Edwardian house.'

Paul didn't know what to say doubly now. He thought about explaining it away but it seemed so pointless. He imagined how it looked to her, how tawdry, how stupid, him acting like a teenager, like he had no wife, no commitment, no comfort. And then he thought that really that had been the problem, there was no comfort with Jenna. That was what Trudie provided. How odd.

He had thought it was the sex, the sexy underwear, the illicitness of it all, the badness, something he thought that most men wanted, for excitement in their lives, when in fact it had been stupid things like the fish and chips, the way that he had been able to go home to Trudie as he had never been able to go home to Jenna.

He had got it wrong, he should have given her her own home, he should have been able to come home to her, and to their child, rather than staying with his parents in a house which he thought, honest now with himself, he had never liked. It was nothing to do with them and the failure of his parents' marriage was so evident in the way that his mother ran to the cottage and his father to that awful club and the young woman he bedded because he wasn't getting any at home. It was no way to live, Paul thought, and yet he had accepted it as inevitable somehow. It was apparently the best they could do, but it shouldn't be.

'And you blame me?' he said.

'I don't blame anybody any more,' she said and there was a weary note in her voice.

He got up. He didn't think the bed would take his weight for much longer.

'Has it been going on for long?' she said.

'Yes, quite a while.' Paul walked about the room, he couldn't sit still or stand still and he didn't know what to say. He could not explain it away because it was his own doing. 'God, it's cold in here. How do people live like this and what made you come here?'

'I tried going to my parents but . . . you know what my mother's like. Do you love her?'

'No.' He felt like a traitor at both sides now. 'I like her a lot, she's fun and she . . . gives me things you don't and . . .' Paul laughed shortly. 'I didn't think I'd turn into my father quite this quickly. I wanted us to be a family but after we lost the baby and in such a way everything seemed to fall apart. I'm sorry, Jenna.'

In the kitchen Ruari's mother brought the fire back to life. He loved how she could do that, she raked the still warm ashes and put on a few sticks and within seconds they burst into flames. He should have been reassured by it, it was what she had been doing for years, and he sat there while she fussed because there was nothing else for either of them to do and he tried not to listen to the conversation which was going on next door. It wasn't easy. The houses had been thrown up by the pit owners years ago, they were not well built and you could hear everything in every room, there was no escape.

The voices were low and even and Ruari thought he didn't know Paul well, was he the kind of man who shouted and threatened or was he more like Sorrel would be, devious and cunning? Jenna hardly spoke at all and his voice was thankfully, most of the time just a low even sound which became more difficult to discern as the fire crackled and burned and his mother put on coal and the flames licked around the blackness of it.

'I knew it wasn't right her coming here in the first place,' his mother said. 'Once people are married everything's different.'

'Not these days, Mam. People get divorced.'

'Divorced women have a very bad time in places like this. They get called names and people think less of them. If she doesn't want to go back with him what will we do then?'

Ruari didn't know what to say. Jenna was all wrong here now. Even in his mother's old nightwear she looked so appealing, like an orphan from a Dickens story, she should have had a house of her own and . . . He thought of her at the cottage and how at home she had looked there but it wasn't right when she was another man's wife.

In the living room Paul said, 'Come back home and we'll sort this out. You can't want to stay here, it's awful.'

Jenna didn't know what to say, what to do. She was half inclined to tell Paul about the baby but she thought, We've been here before and look what happened to us. She hadn't been invited to stay here, Ruari and his mother had just taken her in because they could think of no alternative, she could see, she didn't belong, hadn't belonged here for a very long time. She only wished her parents had been the kind of people who would look after her for a few days until she worked out what to do. And as they sat there the front door went. Paul got up and opened it and there stood her dad.

'I worked it out,' he said, 'it wasn't too difficult,' and he stepped past Paul and into the living room. There he hugged Jenna as she got to her feet. 'I don't know what's going on but I think you should come home with me for a day or two,' he said.

Paul tried to protest but for once Mr Duncan wasn't having any of it.

'No, Paul,' he said so that Jenna was proud of him and he looked Paul in the face and he said, 'This needs sorting out but I don't think it'll be done here. The place for Jenna is back in her own home for the moment.'

'Our house is her home,' Paul protested but even as he said it it sounded all wrong.

Mrs Robson came through and even while Paul was still trying to argue she said, 'Come upstairs, Jenna, and collect your things. I think your dad's right, you need your family now,' so Jenna went into the back room, nodded at Ruari who smiled reassuringly at her and then she went upstairs and changed into her own clothes and picked up her handbag and thanked his mam for her help and then she followed her father's car back to Wesley Road.

It didn't smell of paint any more, either it had dried or she just didn't feel the same about it. Her mam was sitting up in her big blue candlewick dressing gown and she looked so white and worried.

'I've made the bed up for you in your old room and I've put a hot-water bottle in,' she said and Jenna thanked her briefly and for the second time that night got into a bed other than the one she shared with Paul. She had thought she was too upset to rest but she was exhausted. Once again she undressed and this time got into one of her mother's flannelette nighties which wrapped itself comfortingly around her and the moment she cuddled the hot-water bottle to her she closed her eyes on the sweet-smelling pillow and fell asleep.

Paul couldn't believe that the situation had been taken away from him. He wanted to shout and bluster and make a difference like his father would have done but short of violence which had no place here there was nothing he could do as other people did things around him. He wanted Jenna back very badly indeed, wanted to shout that he would give up Trudie, that everything would be like before, and then he remembered what things had been like before and knew that there was nothing he could offer Jenna that she would even consider.

He wanted to blame Gallacher and shout at him and maybe even knock him down but he couldn't do that either, he could only stand by while Mrs Robson fussed and put an arm around her shoulders and talked softly to her like he wished somebody would do to him, anybody to make it feel better and then wait while she went off upstairs.

Her father stood there like a terrier, glaring at him from time to time in a way that Paul had never expected, as though Paul was about to insist she went back to the manor house, as though he could insist on anything any more.

She came back, dressed in clothes he recognized, looking more like herself so that there was a part of him that did not believe she was going to her parents' house, that she would turn around and change her mind and go with him and tell him that she had forgiven him and everything would be all right.

She didn't even look at him, she went off without a word to either Gallacher or himself and once her car had driven off down the road there was nothing left for Paul but to go home. He stepped out into the street and watched the brake lights as she took the corner and then the road was empty and Gallacher had shut the front door of his house, turned the key and put in the bolts and even turned off the lights, he was obviously not taking any risks in that direction in case Paul decided to go back in, though what point there would have been in it Paul could not think. Now he wanted to go home, it was all that was left.

His father and mother were drinking tea in the kitchen. He assured them that Jenna was fine and that she would be back in a day or two, she had gone to her parents. He didn't say anything about Gallacher or his mother.

He thought his parents would accept what he said but they looked at one another and, still sitting at the kitchen table, his mother said baldly, 'Is she leaving you?'

'No, of course not. Whatever gave you that impression?' How on earth had his mother got that far?

'I didn't think it was much of a match right from the beginning,' his mother said. 'I thought you could have done a lot better but there was no point in saying anything. It was never right for you, marrying her like that . . .'

She didn't call Jenna names though she sounded as if she would have liked to and felt such words appropriate, Paul thought.

'Was she at her parents'?'

Trust his father to ask the difficult question. He evaded it.

'She's staying there for a few days, I said. We just need to sort things out, it'll be all right.'

Neither of his parents looked as though they believed him but they got up to go back to bed as though they thought they had done everything they could whereas in fact they had done nothing. His mother put the tea cups in the sink, his father didn't even speak and Paul didn't trust himself to say anything more to him because he had the impression that his father knew exactly what was going on but didn't think it would help to talk about it any more.

Paul escaped to bed but he wished he could have gone to Trudie. He wasn't ever alone in bed, he wasn't used to it and he didn't like it. He was so used to having Jenna there, breathing evenly beside him. He was no good on his own, he panicked by himself, there was too much space in which to think and it was the last thing he wanted to do.

Ruari's mother sat over the newly burning-up fire with him for a while and she said, 'You never did get over that lass. I dare say you never will.'

'Maybe not.'

'It was good her dad came for her, they didn't do enough, at least he managed that.' She got up with a sigh. 'It's just as well you're going,' she said and then she went to bed.

Ruari didn't want to go back into the freezing front room. He lay down on the sofa with a thick blanket over him and a pillow which his mother had brought in, having already read his mind. He thanked her and he didn't even try to sleep. He couldn't help but imagine what it would have been like if he and Jenna could have gone to live in his lovely little cottage. He wouldn't have been lonely then. He thought of them buying a Christmas tree, maybe hanging decorations, sitting over the fire and even going to bed together, something they had never done. Why could he not accept that things like that didn't happen?

She would go back to Paul, he was her husband, why should she not? He wished he could have heard their conversation properly. He still didn't know why she had left, though she must have had a very good reason. He wished she had been able to tell him what was going on, why she was so very upset. Paul seemed equally as upset. Could it be that they had just quarrelled and she had taken it badly and run away and he had got frightened as to what had happened?

Ruari tried not to think about it. He tried to think about the future. His leg was getting better. He thought he could just about manage with a stick. He needed to be more confident, he had got so used to crutches but with a stick he would be able to get about much more easily, he would be able to manage by himself at the cottage.

He would be so glad to go. He could hire a taxi to take him there. He would even be able to go to the shops in the village and if they delivered the groceries for him he thought he would be able to manage the rest. He couldn't wait to leave. He would have his writing to do.

The following morning while he and his mother were having breakfast the post arrived and she went through into the front and picked up the letters and there was one for him. When he opened it at the kitchen table it was a letter from a publisher. They wanted him to write his autobiography. His mother laughed.

'At your age?' she said.

'It's about football, Mam.'

'Well, I never,' she said, 'and do you think you can do it?'

'I don't see why I shouldn't.'

'And are they going to pay you to do it?'

'They are.'

'Well, that's wonderful,' his mother said and she sat down and buttered her second piece of toast.

Jenna awoke in the back room at her mother's house. It brought back all the memories of being there when Ruari had left and she had been pregnant and Paul had agreed to marry her. Now she had another problem to sort out. She was not prepared for Paul to turn up just after nine.

She wished her father had still been there but he had gone off to work. Her mother was no defence. To her Paul was still the white knight who had rescued Jenna from Ruari, he was the best thing that had happened to her and if she couldn't keep it together it was most likely her own fault though she had been relieved to see Jenna back under her roof. She greeted Paul like he was the cavalry, Jenna could hear her ushering him into the front room where Jenna sat over the fire. It was a banana colour these days in there, it was hideous, she thought.

'I've come to take you back with me,' he said when her mother had ostentatiously left them as though they were lovers about to be reconciled.

He was wearing the same clothes he had had on the day before, which was not like him, Jenna thought. He looked dishevelled, as though he didn't care about such things, as though he had not slept, and he kept avoiding her eyes.

'I think I might stay here for a day or two, Paul, if it's all the same to you.'

'It isn't all the same to me. My parents are worried about you and you belong with us.'

He was still trying to bully her, she couldn't believe it. Jenna wanted to say not as long as you have somebody else but she had started thinking about this and she realized that it was not the point. She was having Paul's child. She didn't imagine that somebody would wave a magic wand and he would give up the blonde girl for her and even if he was to do that she thought that in time he would probably do the same thing again.

She had no illusions about babies bringing people together when their marriages were rocky. She had the feeling that another person taking up her time and needing her attention so very much would make Paul feel so insecure that he would not stay with her any more than he had to but it was his child. She didn't want to go back, her instincts were to run away once again to Back Church Street, but she knew it was not fair on Ruari or his mother and especially it was not fair to go to Ruari when she was carrying Paul's child.

Her father came back. She was astonished. She thought he had gone to work but maybe he had known what would happen and that if he wasn't there worse would follow. He didn't give Paul a chance to say anything, he just came into the room.

'Jenna isn't going back today, Paul,' he said. 'She needs a rest from all that.'

Paul was not, Jenna thought with dry humour, about to enquire what 'all that' was but her father for once was not giving in and he didn't even go out of the room so that they could talk by themselves so Paul had no alternative. He could hardly insist and look like he was forcing her.

'I was so bothered last night, Jenna,' her father confided when he had gone. 'I wish I'd been here when you came and hadn't let you go. I wish you'd told me what the problem was. I'm not saying I could have done anything but I would have listened.'

Jenna didn't say anything.

'Is it that lad? You went there. How could you do that? Are you doing something you shouldn't?'

'No, I'm not,' Jenna said.

She was so pleased when her dad came back again at tea time and that it was Sunday the following day and he would not be going to work. It was a fine bright day and cold and he took her for a walk on the beach and she put her hand through his arm. Her mother made a Sunday dinner and she quite enjoyed that day, sitting over the fire when the darkness fell in the late afternoon, but come the following morning when he went to work and she was left with her mother she didn't want to be there any more and she thanked her mother for having her and left. She didn't go home, she went to Ruari's.

When he opened the door he was using only a stick and she was so pleased that they didn't talk about anything else. His mother had gone shopping and Jenna was only pleased to have him to herself.

'I wanted to talk to you,' she said as he showed her into the back room.

'I was hoping you would come. Can you tell me what's going on or would you rather not?'

She told him about what she had seen after she had left his house, about Paul and the blonde girl and that he had had someone else for some time and then she said, 'I don't want to stay with him. If I have to I'll find a little flat and get a job, I'll manage something. I'm not going back to my parents, my mother doesn't really want me there and I couldn't bear it but I'm not staying with Paul now. I can't go and live there knowing that he has somebody else.'

'Wouldn't he give her up?'

'He might but the reason he has her is because we have such an awful marriage. There are no two ways about it, it's horrible,' she said. 'The thing is . . .' She wanted to say it but couldn't. 'The thing is . . .'

'Jenna, look,' he said and then he stopped and then he said, 'Will you come with me? I haven't got much to offer any more but I've always loved you. It might be very difficult and Paul might kick up a bad fuss but if you want to you can come to Yorkshire. I've got the cottage and I can change the car for something more sensible, I don't think I could drive it anyway like this, I don't feel as if I could but I got a good offer from a publisher to write a book about the football I've played and I think I might get more work in journalism so it could turn out to be all right. What do you think?'

It was such a long speech on his part that Jenna could only stare. She didn't know whether she could afford to be honest with him and then she knew that if she was going with him that she had to be.

'I'm having a baby,' she said.

Ruari stared for so long that she wished she hadn't said it, yet what else could she do?

'Does Paul know?'

Jenna shook her head. 'I was ready to tell him. After that lovely day we had at your cottage I wished I didn't have to but I thought I might be able to have some kind of a life without you if only we had a child but I don't think it would matter, that it would make the difference. What's spoiled our marriage is that I never loved him like I love you, I couldn't do it and though I tried it didn't work out. In some ways I shouldn't blame him for going to another girl. I should never have married him. He did the right thing but then . . . he cared for me and I think he hoped in time that I would care for him but after the baby died . . .'

'You don't think it might happen now?'

'I want you,' she said.

'I want you too but . . . his kid.'

'You wouldn't want it?'

'Of course I would want it, didn't I say that I would have taken the first?'

'Well, then.'

'But for him not to know.'

'If I tell him we'll never get out of here,' Jenna said.

'It doesn't seem right.'

'It's the only way.'

'So what are you going to tell him?'

Jenna looked Ruari straight in the eyes.

'I'm going to tell him you and I have been having an affair ever since you got here and it's yours.'

'That doesn't seem right either.'

'I know but again, I've thought a lot about it over the last couple of days and I think it's the only way we'll ever have any peace. I don't want him and his family to have rights over our baby and it'll be ours if we bring it up. The Maddisons have never bothered with me, I was always in the way.

'If Paul and I divorce at least he would have the chance to marry somebody they might like or at least approve of. I was never good enough for them. I don't want them connected to us or Paul having rights to the baby while he's been out sleeping with somebody else all this while.

'I'm not going to put up with it so if you don't want to be part of this, Ruari, just say so because I will leave anyway and I will manage. I'm not stopping here to have the Maddisons run my life any more. Do you want me to come with you or not?

'Make up your mind because that's what I'm going to tell him, regardless of whether you let me come with you. You can deny it of course but I'll blame you and nobody will believe anything else by the time I'm finished. I'll make sure the papers get it.'

She thought Ruari looked astonished but that he could see she meant it. She waited and finally he said, 'I want you. I've always wanted you.'

She came to him and put her arms around him and then she kissed him.

'I'm going back there for my stuff, just the little that's mine, and when your mam comes back you can tell her and we could go to the cottage today because I can look after you.'

Jenna got into her car and drove back to the manor house. Only Paul's mother was at home. Jenna didn't bother with her, she just took her suitcases, opened them on the bed and began putting her clothes and make-up and toiletries into them. After a while she noticed Faye standing in the doorway.

'You are going, then?'

'I am, yes. You must be glad.'

'Well, I have to say that I was never very happy about it.'

'I'm taking nothing that isn't mine,' Jenna pointed out.

'Take what you want,' Faye said. 'Is it Gallacher?'

'Yes.'

'He's nice,' Faye said. 'I hope you find what you're looking for,' and she turned around and walked out.

Jenna didn't even say goodbye and Faye didn't offer to help. She was so obviously glad to be rid of Jenna, no doubt thinking that her son would find somebody else soon, men like him always did and that possibly she would have grandchildren. It was quite ironic in some ways, Jenna thought. She carried two suitcases downstairs and put them into the car. She considered whether to tell her mother and then she thought she wouldn't bother. She would ring so that they wouldn't worry but she didn't want to see them, she didn't want anybody trying to talk her out of this when her mind was made up.

She was just about to leave when the red Ferrari pulled up in the driveway. The sickness that Jenna felt was nothing to do with the baby but then she thought, I couldn't really have gone without telling him, it would have been cowardly, so she stood there.

Paul got slowly out of the car, his gaze fixed on this evidence of her leaving.

'You're back early. I was going to come to the office and tell you,' she said.

'Jenna, I can make it different, honestly I can. I'll give up Trudie and we'll start again, we'll buy a house of our own and—'

'I don't want to live like this any more,' Jenna said.

'It won't be like this—'

'I'm having Ruari Gallacher's baby,' Jenna said.

She held her breath to see whether he would accept this but she thought that in the trashy world where the Maddisons lived this was what people did, how they behaved, perhaps even expected it. They betrayed one another without thought, what mattered to them most was money and power and football, not the decent things of life like giving time and effort to the people they said they loved.

Paul stared at her but she could see that he was ready to think she had done exactly what he had done only worse and she didn't care. She thought of all the evenings when he had left her, the nights she had been alone, the days when he hadn't even bothered to ask her what she was doing or where she was going or whether she was lonely. Paul had been taught by selfish self-indulgent people in a selfish self-indulgent world such as football was and it had taught him to be ruthless and self-seeking. She had never managed to be part of it and in some ways neither had Ruari.

'We've been having an affair ever since he got back.' She looked Paul straight in the eyes when she said this and there was a small sense of satisfaction in it somehow even though she knew it was cruel.

'Couldn't it be mine?' It was the one thing she had known he would ask but she had not counted on the hungry look in his eyes when he said it and her insides twisted when she went on watching him and she told him the lie.

'It's Ruari's,' she said and she knew immediately that he believed it, they had had sex so very infrequently.

That was when he lost his temper and shouted and called Ruari names and called her names as though he had done nothing wrong himself and she thought back to the night she had lost her first baby. All she could remember was that he hadn't been there and that was the point somehow. Paul was not and never had been there for her, he wanted her waiting at home so that he could not come back to her like she was a prisoner, like the girl in the tower who let down her hair. Well, she had finally let down her hair and escaped. It was through a lie and it would never be right but she thought just this once she would do what she wanted to do or she would never have any real say over herself.

He tried to stop her from leaving, he got hold of her when she was about to get into the car but his father had turned up by then, maybe his mother had telephoned, Jenna didn't know, just that Sorrel's car came screaming up the drive in a shower of gravel and he got out and got hold of his son and he said, 'Let her go. Let her go, Paul.'

Paul turned around, suddenly realizing that his father had hold of him, and for the first time that Jenna could remember he turned with sudden resignation into his father's arms and to Jenna's horror he began to cry, huge agonizing sobs. She stood, rooted. She now had nothing to stop her but she couldn't move.

Over his son's head Sorrel looked at her, nodded towards the car. He didn't say anything and somehow Jenna got her feet to move, slammed shut the boot, got into the driver's seat and very slowly forced herself, trying to remember how the car worked and telling herself that if she didn't go now she would be sentencing herself to a lifetime of the Maddisons. Once she had stayed and told Paul the baby was his she would never escape. She managed to get the car into gear and it began to move slowly away down the drive. She got to the gates and turned into the road and a little feeling of relief and freedom began to edge its way into her mind.

When she walked into the little house in Back Church Street, Ruari's mother hugged her.

'Oh, Jenna,' she said, 'I wish it didn't have to be like this but there isn't any other way and I do want my Ruari to be happy.'

'I think I might promise you that,' Jenna said.

She stood there shaking while Ruari came to her. She couldn't quite meet his eyes but he loaded suitcases into the back of her car without speaking as though somehow the decision between them was so tenuous that conversation would not hold it. Nobody said anything and though it could only have taken a few minutes for Jenna it was a lifetime during which she somehow expected everything to go wrong as it had gone wrong so often, as though she never would get to spend the rest of her life with the man she should have been with always but nobody screamed around the corner in a car, nobody shouted, nobody suddenly appeared calling her a liar. She didn't think she would ever forget how Paul had turned stricken to his father, she would live with it. Her baby would become Ruari's and they would have other children.

He finally looked at her when he had loaded his belongings and then he hugged his mother and she nodded at Jenna and then they got into the car and Jenna ignored her shaking hands and started up the car and began to drive slowly down the road away from Back Church Street, away from the little town which had been her life towards something new. She brought to mind the little cottage and a slow wisp of excitement began to edge its way through her. She would have the little cottage and Ruari and the baby all to herself, nobody could stop her now.

'I just hope that lad Gallacher goes a long way away from me,' Sorrel said that evening when Paul had gone back to work and he and Faye were for once sitting over the fire together. Sorrel had insisted that he should go and sort out the problem at one of the clubs, it would give him something to do, he thought. 'He's caused me more bloody trouble than anybody else I ever met and as for Jenna . . .'

'I'm just glad to see the back of her,' Faye said.

'Maybe if he found somebody else we might get a grandchild out of it,' Sorrel said and he poured himself a large whisky and soda and sat down with the evening papers to read before going to bed.

# Books used for reference and information

The *Football Man* by Arthur Hopcraft, Aurum Press Limited.
*England Managers* by Brian Glanville, Headline.
*England! England! The Complete Who's Who of Players Since 1946* by Dean P. Hayes, Sutton Publishing.
*The Glory Game* by Hunter Davies, Mainstream Publishing Company.
*Blessed* by George Best, Ebury Press.
*Shearer: My Story So Far* by Alan Shearer with Dave Harrison, Hodder & Stoughton.
*A Photographic History of English Football* by Tim Hill, Parragon.
*Fashion Sourcebooks: The 1960s* by John Peacock, Thames and Hudson.
*Fashion Sourcebooks: The 1970s* by John Peacock, Thames and Hudson.
*White Heat* by Dominic Sandbrook, Abacus.
*Sunderland: The Complete Record* by Rob Mason, Breedon Books Publishing.